## Praise for *The Muse of F*

'Expert storytelling, clever plotting and convincing characters make this not only an absorbing and highly entertaining tale, but also a thought-provoking reflection on the truths that art can tell, or hide'
**Hilary Taylor**

'A glorious caper – full of humour, engaging characters and infatuation. A thoroughly enjoyable read'
**Nicky Downes**

'A brilliantly funny and twisting plot, driven by real, eccentric characters. You feel like you're in the room with them, and you wouldn't want to be anywhere else'
**Tim Ewins**

'A witty, well-written novel exploring the world of painting, modelling and art-as-commodity, with an unexpected criminal caper at its heart. An exuberant debut that is both fun and thoughtful'
**Richard Francis**

'Alan Kane Fraser's beautiful work about life the other side of the easel – its impact, its anonymity, the inevitable betrayal – both compels and disturbs. He has that unusual ability of allowing characters to collide whilst not being a devotee of either'
**Jeff Weston**

ALAN KANE FRASER was raised in Handsworth, Birmingham, in the era when that district was famous for its riots. He has been variously a priest, a housing officer and a charity CEO, in which capacity he wrote for a number of publications, including the *Guardian*. He is also the author of an award-winning play, *Random Acts of Malice*.

He still lives in Birmingham, with his wife and a woefully inadequate number of bookshelves.

# THE MUSE OF HOPE FALLS

# THE MUSE OF HOPE FALLS

### ALAN KANE FRASER

Lightning Books

Published in 2023
by Lightning Books
Imprint of Eye Books Ltd
29A Barrow Street
Much Wenlock
Shropshire
TF13 6EN

www.lightning-books.com

Cover design by Nell Wood
Typeset in Dante MT Std and Flood Std

British Library Cataloguing in Publication Data
A catalogue record for this book is available from the British Library.

ISBN: 9781785633744

*For Fiona Walker, ('Tennis Girl')*
*and Elizabeth Siddal,*
*both of whom inspired this story in different ways*

*And in loving memory of Carol Poole*

For the early Coke executive Robert Woodruff, who said that
'Coca-Cola should always be within an arm's reach of desire',
Coke represents the eternally unsatisfied emptiness
we seek to fill with something ungraspable
**A.S. Hamrah,** *The Paris Review*

# PART 1

## SUSANNA & THE ELDERS

### SEPTEMBER 2019, HOPE FALLS, NEW YORK

*It's hard to be a diamond in a rhinestone world*
**Dolly Parton**

# ONE

I first met the wild and impenetrable gaze of Christie McGraw when I saw her one evening, half-naked, at a gallery on Cork Street. It was sixteen years ago, and I'd been sent to cover the opening of an Erik von Holunder retrospective at the Redfern.

'Wow! Who the hell is that, I wonder?' I'd asked rhetorically, while standing in front of 1978's *Bikini-Girl Gunslinger.*

'Judy McGraw,' Suzy said. 'But Von Holunder insisted on calling her Christie. Said she looked more like a Christie than a Judy.'

'I guess I can see that,' I said. The only Judy I could think of was Judy Garland and Christie certainly didn't look like her. There was something about Christie's stare that made demands of you, rather than suggesting that you might make demands of her. It was unnerving but undoubtedly energised the paintings in which she appeared.

'Anyway, that's the name that made her famous, so that's

what she got stuck with.' Suzy turned to look at me. 'Did you not know that?'

I sensed the first trace of disappointment in her voice. This was a sensation with which I was to become wearyingly familiar over the next thirteen years, and perhaps I should've taken it as a warning of what was to come, but that night it was sickeningly new. Suzy's final-year dissertation was something to do with the representation of women as objects of desire in twentieth-century art. Her tutor had suggested that Erik's portrayal of Christie represented an interesting counterpoint to the portrayal of Walburga Neuzil in the paintings of Egon Schiele, so she considered herself a bit of an authority. But back then I knew almost nothing about Von Holunder. After that fateful press night though, in a desperate attempt to win back Suzy's respect, I resolved to become an expert in the life and works of Erik von Holunder, and I like to think I did. Yet as I walked up and knocked on the door of Christie's residential trailer in a long-forgotten corner of New York fifteen years (and one divorce) later, I still felt like I knew nothing definite about his thrilling and captivating muse.

'I was expecting a girl,' she said, eyeing me with suspicion. She was in her late sixties by then, and I had anticipated being welcomed by a white-haired retiree, her face creased with regrets. But to my surprise she retained the statuesque beauty that had first transfixed viewers when she'd stared out defiantly at them from the frame of 1975's *If All the World Was Like Your Smile*.

'I get that a lot, but that would be Gabrielle. I'm Gabriel.' I offered her my hand. 'Gabe Viejo.'

She declined to shake it.

'Have you got some ID?'

I still had an NUJ card, courtesy of my reviews for *The Art Newspaper*, so I offered her that. She took it from me and examined it sceptically at arm's length while I waited outside.

'If you need to get your glasses, that's fine,' I said in an attempt to be helpful. Big mistake.

'I will have you know, young man, there's nothing wrong with my eyes,' she snapped. 'I just need longer arms.'

Despite this, she disappeared back inside her trailer, taking my ID with her.

I turned my head and looked around the rest of the trailer park while I waited. It was called, without apparent irony, Hope Falls.

It was just a few days from the end of September and the weather had begun to turn. A dull drizzle fell wearily from a slate-grey sky, low cloud blanketing the whole of Hope Falls in a gloomy shroud. What could still be seen seemed to have been slowly falling apart for years until now it resembled a Cubist parody of a low-income trailer park. The trailers themselves were patched up like wounded soldiers, their awnings concertinaed like the ruffles on an ugly ante bellum ballgown. Any sense that this place might really be *the low-cost housing choice for the discerning professional*, as the hoarding at the entrance had, rather optimistically, sought to proclaim, had long since disappeared. Now the name felt like a sick joke. Hope had not just fallen; it had died a slow and lingering death here.

'Well, I guess you might as well come in,' Christie said, returning to the doorway and handing me back my card, a pair of half-lune glasses perched on the end of her nose. 'The neighbours'll be talking about me already anyway.' And the way she flicked a wary glance up and down the avenue of trailers gave me the distinct impression that the name of Christie McGraw came up a lot whenever couples in Hope Falls argued.

I took a seat in her living area and a few moments later she placed a pot of lemon tea I hadn't asked for in front of me. It was accompanied by a china cup which may once have been beautiful, but which was now scarred by glazing which had become tessellated over many years of use.

'I didn't run off with the money, if that's what you've come to ask me,' she said in an acerbic Bette Davis drawl, but to be honest, that much was obvious just from looking around me. The foiling on the particleboard worktops was slowly peeling off; the throw on the sofa couldn't quite cover the worn fabric on the seat and arms, and the pattern on the linoleum in the kitchen had faded through wear in two spots. The air freshener that had clearly been liberally applied in anticipation of my arrival could not fully mask the musky aroma of long-term water penetration.

She obviously noticed the look on my face. 'What? You're surprised to see me living like this?'

Her voice sounded like the movies of my childhood: rich and deep, with the smokiness of a good scotch. She dripped it over you teasingly, and I loved it.

'Well, it's just that... Erik was a wealthy man... And you were together for so long...'

She let go a dismissive snort. 'Yeah, well, every love story becomes a tragedy if you wait long enough. Welcome to mine.'

I'd managed to get a commission to write a biography of Von Holunder to mark the centenary of his birth, and, after months of getting nowhere, I'd finally got Christie to agree to meet with me on condition that I flew out to New York.

She hadn't spoken to anyone in the media or the art world for nearly thirty years, not since a brief period of detention for selling a controlled substance. This fact helped me to convince my reluctant publisher to pay for a brief trip on the grounds that the cost could probably be recouped by syndicating the interview. At the same time, he had left me in no doubt as to the consequences for the company – and therefore me – if I failed to deliver a syndicate-able interview. Given the parlous state of my own post-divorce finances, this was not the start that I'd hoped for and I took to fawning over her in a desperate attempt to turn things around.

'Well, I guess I'm interested in the love story, Ms McGraw. In the incredible relationship you clearly had with Erik,' I said, 'and how that inspired him.'

This was meant to be an acknowledgement of her status in the creative process, but Christie looked unconvinced. In all honesty, she appeared unconvinced by most things. Her face seemed to adopt a pose of wry scepticism by default. It was one of the things that had given the paintings such life.

'In my experience he was absolutely the best lover a woman could ever have… Although, obviously, I can't talk for Mimi,' she added, raising her perfectly plucked eyebrow into a sardonic arch.

I blushed at her forthrightness. Christie still wore her sexuality like a ribbon. In the seventies and eighties Erik had portrayed her as symbolising the kind of sexual charisma that men found difficult to resist, but also impossible to control. And the row of Jane Fonda exercise videos bore testimony to the fact that she clearly still took great efforts over her appearance. If she had to fight, then this was her weapon of choice. Mimi had never stood a chance.

I didn't know how to respond, and felt the pause between us lengthening. Eventually she decided to put me out of my misery.

'So, you're from London, Mr Viejo?'

'Gabriel, please. Or Gabe. And yes, I'm from London.'

Her brow furrowed as she examined me. 'You don't *sound* like you're from London.'

'Well, I lived in Buenos Aires until I was twelve. They teach American English at the international school, and I guess my vowels are still stranded somewhere in the mid-Atlantic.'

'Buenos Aires? I wondered about that. So I guess you're related to Joaquín Viejo?'

I got asked this a lot when I met with people from the art world and I wasn't embarrassed to answer. I was proud of my heritage. 'Yes, he was my grandad.'

'I thought so. I knew old Jo – I knew all the dealers back then. He had a big house just by the Parque Las Heras, didn't he? And that beautiful place on Lake Morenito. We spent a weekend there once, me and Erik, on our way back from the Biennale.'

This didn't surprise me. Most people in the art world of the seventies and eighties at least knew *of* Grandpa Jo. He was a big dealer back then – one of the biggest outside of London, Paris and New York – and he loved to entertain.

'He was quite a…character, wasn't he?' she said.

I couldn't tell what she meant by this, but the look in her eye suggested that it was not a straightforward compliment.

We carried on talking for a while; about how she'd met Erik, and how she'd ended up posing for him. I was trying to get a sense of the man behind all the bluster and braggadocio, and of the extent to which she'd contributed to the extraordinarily charged images of which she was the subject. But nothing seemed to flow. She seemed bored by my questions, and I was certainly bored by her answers. Looking back at my notes now, I can see that they're a combination of quotes I could have pulled off the internet and idle tittle tattle about people on the art scene thirty or forty years ago. It was as though she was holding something back while she judged me. I didn't like it, and found that, to my surprise, it really mattered to me whether she liked me or not.

It occurred to me that perhaps what was annoying her was my attempt to establish myself as the world's foremost authority on Erik von Holunder. From her perspective, I guessed that must have seemed like a ridiculous presumption. She was, after all, his mistress for twelve years. I thought it might be worth my acknowledging this.

'Look,' I said, taking a sip of my lemon tea and fidgeting nervously with the cup, 'I know this might sound like a stupid question—'

'There's no such thing as a stupid question, honey,' she interjected. 'Only stupid people. Go ahead. Ask whatever you want. I promise you I won't think it's the question that's stupid.' And she smiled a smile that didn't even manage to convince her own face it was sincere.

I decided to confront her reticence full-on. 'Have I done something to offend you, Ms McGraw?'

'Erik always shaved when he was with me,' she said, finally getting tired of my obtuseness. 'Even when he was in his studio, working – *especially* when he was working. It was a point of professional pride.'

I hadn't shaved – I mean, nobody under forty does now, right? – but it immediately became obvious that I should have. Christie set high standards for herself, and she had a commensurately low tolerance for those who didn't set them for themselves. I could see that she took my stubble as a personal discourtesy. I closed my notebook and placed it carefully on her coffee table.

'Ms McGraw, I owe you an apology. I want you to know that I appreciate that now. Can we push the reset button?'

She smiled a forgiving smile. 'Indeed we can. Come back tomorrow – when you've had time for a shave,' she said. 'And a tie would be nice. A man should never wear an open-neck shirt after 11am unless he's a lumberjack or holidaying in the south of France, and you, young man, are neither.'

I retired to a local coffee house to lick my wounds. As if I wasn't feeling bad enough, no sooner had I sat down than a text came through from Suzy. It was the usual thing she had taken to sending me giving me *one last chance to do the right thing*. One last chance. She'd been giving me one last chance for the past two years and I had determinedly avoided taking any of them. The financial settlement had been signed off by a judge and the decree absolute issued six months previously, so it seemed a bit late to be trying to renegotiate things now. And besides, I'd given her fifty per cent of the house and my other English assets – which was, as I had repeatedly pointed out, the right thing to do. I certainly wasn't going to be giving her a share of Grandpa Jo's stuff as well. It was nothing to do with her and besides, I needed it to help me to get back on my feet after the ruination of my divorce.

I deleted the text without responding and tried to forget about it.

I've thought a lot about that decision since, but even now, I don't know what else I could have done.

# TWO

I didn't expect to see Christie until the following afternoon, but a couple of hours later I got a call on my mobile asking me if I would care to take her out for the evening. 'And don't bother to turn up if you've not had a shave,' she'd added. Something about the way that she said it suggested that she was both setting me a test and helpfully providing me with the answer, just to make sure that I passed. I didn't understand the significance of that at the time and took the mere fact that she'd asked me as a compliment. Looking back, it seems unbelievably arrogant now, but at the time I just assumed that she was lonely and was genuinely interested in spending time in my company.

For my part, I was stuck in a hotel room miles from home with nothing to do, so the chance to spend an evening picking her brains about Erik at my publisher's expense felt like too good an opportunity to miss. At the very least it felt like it was worth having a shave for.

And what a difference it made. The walls of suspicion which I had marched around so frustratingly that afternoon were removed the moment she opened the door and saw my clean-shaven face (and the bunch of flowers I'd brought with me).

It was difficult to tell if Christie had a nose for a good party or whether she attracted action by some kind of inner magnetic force. All I know is she came alive that night – and it was glorious. We left her trailer at 7pm for what I thought would be a quiet evening at the local diner discussing her life with Erik, and six hours later I found myself in a back-street bar downtown wearing a standard issue NYPD police hat, and salsa-dancing on top of a table with Christie and a Latvian acupuncturist called Liga from Riga.

I'd started off being slightly frustrated by Liga's presence, but it soon became clear that she and Christie worked as a team, and I was the chosen audience for their entertainment. I suspected Liga had been chosen as Christie's social partner because she met her exacting standards for personal glamour without quite overshadowing Christie herself. I also began to suspect that Christie was trying to hook me up with her pal. Certainly, when Liga disappeared briefly to powder her nose Christie wasted no time in asking me whether I might be interested. Liga, whose sharp-cut blonde bob set off a wide and innocent face, was undoubtedly an attractive young woman. She'd assured me that she could help people give up smoking, but after an evening of gyrating on tabletops in between her and Christie, interspersed with listening to them talking about the various men they'd dated, frankly I was just about ready to start again. So, in response to Christie's question, I muttered something about the brevity of my stay and not really having the time to mix my business with pleasure. Christie was not impressed.

'Oh *puh-lease!*' she said, rolling her eyes. (Christie was a woman born for italics – and whenever she became animated it felt like the eyeroll had been invented just for her too.) 'I'd slap you in the face and tell you to act like a man if I didn't think it would turn you on!'

It seemed like a minor provocation designed to sow a seed in my mind; inviting me to probe her interest further. Yet no sooner had she said it than Liga returned, and the conversation moved on.

Utterances like that were Christie's hallmark. There was something both alluring and yet disorienting about them so that, despite all the carousing on the tabletops, the thing that struck me most was not how much fun Christie was, but how beguiling. She drew you in, but at the same time kept you out. It felt like a talent.

And I was clearly not alone in my admiration of her: throughout the night there were plenty of guys attempting to start up conversation or join our little trio, and when Christie got up to go to the bathroom her path was marked by a line of turning heads. I don't imagine anyone knew who she was or what she'd been, but you could tell from their looks that they all wished they did.

Liga must have noticed my eyes following Christie across the room because she interrupted my reverie with a question, asked in a tone which hinted at some disappointment with me.

'You like Christie, don't you?'

I got the impression that she was used to asking this question, and was used to being disappointed by the answer, so I wanted to remain non-committal in order to preserve the dignity of both parties.

'I think she's a fascinating woman. And what a story she has to tell.'

'That's good – that you think she's fascinating. She is. That's what I admire about her: she can make men be fascinated by her. I wish I could.'

'Oh, of course you can,' I said in a way that was meant to sound encouraging but which I immediately worried sounded like I was hitting on her. She didn't seem to take it that way though.

'Not like her. She can make men pay attention to her, but on her own terms. She doesn't give in to them, because she knows what'll happen if she does. I'm really bad at that. I try to be like Christie, but I worry too much that they'll lose interest.'

I suspect that my face betrayed my confusion at what she'd said because she then took a swig of her margarita and spoke to me as though explaining something to a small child.

'Men get their power by having sex; women get their power by *not* having sex. And Christie's not had sex with more men than any woman I know.'

I didn't know quite what to say, but I could sense what she meant. Christie didn't discourage anyone's attentions, but neither did she encourage them. Or, to put it another way, her ability to attract men seemed predicated on an equal but opposite ability to hold them at bay.

Perhaps sensing my discomfort, Liga decided to change the subject.

'So, you're divorced.'

I started. 'How did you know?'

Liga smirked. 'Your ring finger. There's a pale stripe on it. I guess there was a ring there once.'

I blushed. 'Yes. There was.'

My divorce was not the only failure of my life, but it was the most public, and it still felt raw. I had somehow come to believe that just by looking at me everyone could see that I was divorced – an insane idea that Liga had just reinforced.

'What went wrong?' she asked, avoiding eye contact and playing with her drink.

I wasn't used to people being so direct. In Britain they tended to skirt around the issue. This tendency was exacerbated in my case by the fact that everyone who knew me knew exactly what had gone wrong and thought it so obvious that it would be rude of them to keep pointing it out to me.

'I come from a family that some people would regard as fairly wealthy – which, just to be clear, doesn't mean that *I'm* wealthy. I'm not. Not at all. And certainly not now. Anyway, my wife had a...she came from a very different background. Not that there's anything wrong with that. It's just that... When we met...I think she had a certain impression of what life with someone like me might be like, and I think the reality was a disappointment to her.'

Liga looked up at me with curiosity. 'The reality?'

'It's not all holidays on the Côte d'Azur and servants to tidy up after you. We both still had to work. I still had to worry about the mortgage. It was probably pretty similar to the life she'd left behind, and I think she was expecting it to be different.'

'So you think she was a gold digger?'

I paused for a moment. This was one open goal I felt it would be unwise for me to score into too enthusiastically. I decided to demur lest I appear ungentlemanly.

'Other people – people who knew us as a couple – they've suggested that to me. Friends warned me about it before we got married. But I hope there was more to it than that. Honestly, I don't think she was a bad person.' I tried to convince myself as I spoke those words that this observation was true about twenty-five per cent of the time. 'I think she genuinely convinced herself that she loved me – at least at the beginning. She just expected me to make her life something that I couldn't make it. Or rather, I think she expected people to treat her differently, and got frustrated with me when they didn't.'

I'd travelled three-and-a-half thousand miles in the hope that for a few brief days I might escape the constant reminders of my ignominy, but here I was talking to a young woman whom Christie had clearly only invited along as a potential romantic interest for me, and even she only seemed interested in my divorce.

I looked up, hoping that Christie might reappear and rescue me, and was relieved to see her returning from the bathroom. As she sauntered back to our table, I caught sight of one of the patrons being told in no uncertain terms by his female companion to avert his gaze.

'If you look over your left shoulder there's a guy being told off for looking at you by a woman young enough to be your daughter,' I joked as she resumed her seat. I thought she would take some pride in this, but it seemed to bore her.

'I don't look, honey. Ever. I'm looked *at*.'

It sounded ridiculous even as she said it – the kind of self-aggrandising narcissism that I found so annoying in Gen Z'ers and certainly didn't expect from a sexagenarian (even one as prone to self-dramatising as Christie). And yet I found myself being pulled into a subtly different orbit. No longer were my thoughts centred on my regrets about Suzy or my hopes for my biography of Von Holunder, but on this extraordinary woman who seemed to stand in wilful defiance of all that society said she could be.

Perhaps it was this ability to shape the universe around her – to organise other people in relation to her by means of her own personal gravitational force – that made me feel as though I was being admitted to a very select club. Whatever it was, it was one of Christie's more unsettling traits that she somehow managed to get you to tell her more than you knew you should. I was supposed to be interviewing her, but by 2am I had still not managed to glean any useful information for my book, while, as the alcohol began to take hold, I found myself verbalising thoughts about my marriage and divorce that I'd never articulated explicitly before, even to myself.

'It was never really an equal partnership – financially, socially, even intellectually. Because of my grandfather, I had a lot of contacts that were quite useful to Suzy. I'd got access to a couple of holiday homes that were in the family too. And I like to think that my name has a certain amount of intellectual heft in the art world. Suzy wanted to leverage all of that, but she didn't have anything she could offer in return. Except her beauty, and that…well, that's not really the same thing.'

'So you think she was a gold digger?' Christie asked.

'That's what I said!' Liga interjected. 'But apparently it's not that simple.'

'I opened lots of doors for her,' I said, 'but, for whatever reason, she never quite managed to walk through them. She never felt she belonged. And she came to blame me for that, I think.'

'But why?' asked Christie. 'I mean, you did your bit.'

'I like to think so – although obviously, you can't help

wondering if you could have done more – given how things worked out. But there's no doubt that, by the end, I came to feel guilty about my relative success – however modest it was in reality – and I came to feel responsible for her sense of failure. And she came to resent me for the first of those things and blame me for the second.'

'Jesus, honey,' Christie said when I'd finally run out of steam, 'it sure doesn't sound like your relationship was much fun.' And she gazed at me sympathetically.

'I don't really think of it as a relationship,' I replied. 'More a kind of character-building experience.'

Something about her look changed. It became deeper, as though examining me. I'd noticed this look in the paintings. There it was arresting, but in person, when she was directing it at you individually, it felt strangely intoxicating.

'Is that why you're doing this? This book?' she asked.

The question took me by surprise.

'I don't understand. I admire Erik and want to bring his legacy to a new generation.'

'But you also need to get your mojo back – put your marriage behind you.'

I shuffled uncomfortably. 'Look, this is a great gig for me. I don't deny it. But that's not what this is about. There'll be lots of interest in the centenary. I want to capitalise on that. Mimi's trying to organise a retrospective.'

She gave me a wry look. 'Really? Even now?'

'I know Erik's been out of fashion for a while, but we're hoping it might lead to a reappraisal.'

I saw her bridle. '"We"? So did Mimi send you?'

'No!' I protested. 'My publisher sent me.'

'But you have spoken to Mimi?'

I considered this issue for a moment before deciding that it was best not to lie. 'Of course. She was his wife, and she's always been happy to talk about Erik to anyone who'll listen. It's an authorised biography because she's authorising it.'

Christie gave a dismissive snort. 'And no doubt she painted him as a saint who was led astray by this dreadful scarlet woman.'

'Not at all.' This was true, although only because Mimi had not once mentioned Christie during our nine hours of interviews. In Mimi's narrative, which she had already set out at length in her 1992 memoir of life with Erik, Von Holunder was simply a great and glorious artist who had been cruelly marginalised by an art world establishment that had inexplicably had its head turned by the twin attractions of novelty and mediocrity. (Like dogs and their owners, I find that the subjects of biographies invariably come to resemble their authors.) This was clearly the narrative that she anticipated my more considered volume would also take, even though it was far from being the whole story. Yet it occurred to me that I could use the antipathy between the two women to my advantage.

'Yes, she's given me the official version of Erik. What I want is your version. After all these years of silence, I think that's what's going to sell my book.' For the first time I consciously met her stare. 'I want to tell your story.'

'That's great. But are you sure you're ready to hear it?'

'Of course.'

'Because my story is filled with broken promises, terrible choices and ugly truths.' She leant forward. 'But I guess that's what makes it interesting.'

And with that she had me hooked.

# THREE

I woke about eleven. After a night of bar light and indiscretion, the sun felt searing on my eyes. My mind was filled with a dull fog and my stomach was struggling to contain the roiling sea of Tequila slammers inside. I took some aspirin and shaved – again – but couldn't yet face the day, so returned to my bed and doom-scrolled on my phone.

Back in England, I could see that the news websites were fixated with the story of an unravelling corruption scandal that was currently playing out in the courts. The primary figure implicated in this was the Greek business tycoon, Constantine Gerou. I vaguely knew Conny because, apart from Mimi, he held probably the largest private collection of Von Holunders in the world, so I'd been in touch with his office when I'd put together Erik's *catalogue raisonné*, and he contacted me sometimes if he wanted someone to vouch for a painting he was being offered. We'd met a couple of times, although I'd mainly dealt with his entourage.

Anyway, it seemed that Conny had recently left Greece rather abruptly after a series of his associates were arrested. The assumption was that he was trying to get to his American home, but in the event he had got no further than London before the Greek government requested his extradition – a request to which the British authorities were legally obliged to accede. But Gerou was not unduly keen to return to his homeland and, accordingly, was currently holed up in one of London's most exclusive hotels while his appeal played out in the courts. It occurred to me, reading the coverage of the trial, that while Conny made great play of the fact that he was a self-made man whose fortune came solely from his business, he had always been studiously vague about what his business actually was. There had been some suggestions that he ran an import/export company, but exactly what he was importing and exporting had never been made clear. The Greek government now seemed to be suggesting it had found out and was not impressed.

I smiled to myself and moved on in the naïve belief that the story was simply about a grifter getting his comeuppance and had nothing to do with me.

By 3pm I still felt dreadful and imagined that Christie would too. Yet when I eventually turned up at her trailer (sporting the tie I'd managed to pick up at JC Penney's on the way) she was sipping grapefruit juice and looked as fresh and lively as a new-born lamb.

'Now, don't you look smart?' she said, as though I was an eleven-year-old on my first day at secondary school. 'You look tired, though – did you not sleep well?'

To my shame, I couldn't bring myself to admit that I'd been outdrunk by a woman old enough to be my mother, so I mumbled something about the hotel beds being uncomfortable.

'Well anyway, come in, young man. I've got something to show you,' she said. 'I hope you'll like it,' she added, with just a hint of nervousness.

At the point at which she grabbed my hand and pulled me into her living quarters, the spectrum of possibilities of what she was about to show me ranged, in my mind, from a homemade blueberry pie to the severed head of Liga from Riga. After seeing Christie in full flow the night before, almost anything between those two extremes would not have caused me to bat an eyelid.

But nothing could have prepared me for what I did see. For there in front of me, propped up against the easy chair that I had been sitting in not twenty-four hours previously, was a five-foot by four-foot oil painting featuring a naked woman bathing in her garden.

I had spent more time than was probably healthy over the previous decade-and-a-half looking at the couple of hundred or so authenticated paintings of Erik von Holunder, and I could see instantly that it bore all the hallmarks of his work. The style, the colour palette, the framing of the scene were all classic examples of late-period Von Holunder. In all those hours of searching through private collections, exhibition catalogues and the archives of some of Europe and America's finest museums, however, I had never seen this painting before. Yet here it was, in a down-at-heel residential trailer park; its glory a secret Christie was sharing only with me.

But what a glory it was.

'He called it *Susanna & the Elders* – like the Rembrandt,' she explained.

I stared at the painting in front of me with a mixture of stunned awe and an excitement I could barely contain. I knew that towards the end of his life Von Holunder had painted a series of eleven reinterpretations of works by the Old Masters. He'd never been entirely happy with them, and most had been dismissed by the critics (including me) as derivative and uninspiring. But what Christie showed me that afternoon was extraordinary. It was a representation of a scene from the biblical Apocrypha, most famously painted by Rembrandt, where the young Susanna is caught bathing in her garden by two lecherous old men. For the most part it was an unremarkable re-imagining of a story that was perhaps over-familiar to students of art. But there, at the heart of the canvas, was Christie – and her presence transformed everything.

Whereas it was traditional for Susanna to be shown as virginal and pure – caught unawares with no idea what she should do – Christie's Susanna knew *exactly* what she was doing. Her face suggested that, far from feeling terrified and powerless, it was the unsuspecting elders who were caught in *her* trap. Blinded by their lust, they didn't seem to realise that the object of their desires was more worldly-wise than they supposed and had anticipated the weaknesses of men and prepared, somewhat ruefully, for them. Her expectations had been proved right, but she took no pleasure in that. In fact, it seemed to fill her with a strange combination of Machiavellian determination and sorrow.

It was, in short, a *Susanna* unlike any I had ever seen. Vignon, Badalocchio, Von Hagelstein, even Reubens and Tintoretto – none of them had captured anything as interesting, as transformative, as the look on Christie's face in that picture. Von Holunder had taken the tired and familiar trope of the passive, victimised woman, and turned it on its head. This was a powerful woman given agency and emotional depth, while the men were rendered impotent by their desires.

I wanted to tell Christie all this, but my mind was racing so far ahead of my mouth I could barely construct a coherent sentence.

'Christie... What...? How...? I mean...this is incredible!' was as much as I could say.

'I know,' she replied, without raising either her voice, or her eyelids.

'But...where – I mean, why haven't we seen this before? Why did Erik not include this in the show? This is better than any of the others. Hell, it's better than anything else he ever produced!'

'That's what I told him. Apparently, he didn't think it did justice to my *bo-sooms!* Difficult to argue with him on that point,' Christie said, with a hint of pride. 'But I guess there's only so much you can do with a paintbrush.'

At that point I remembered something I'd come across in some of Von Holunder's obituaries. There was rumoured to be a twelfth painting in the *Old Masters* series that had never been put on display. In one version of the story, Von Holunder had been so disappointed by it that he'd thrown it out. In another, though – the version that Mimi had mentioned in her book – Von Holunder had liked it so much that he'd kept it for himself, until he'd fallen out with Christie a few months before his death and the painting had been mysteriously lost. Mimi's version had largely been dismissed for lack of supporting evidence but had found some currency among

Von Holunder aficionados on the internet. Yet as I stared in wonder at the painting before me, I felt immediately, with a certainty greater than anything I had ever felt in my career, that this was that work. This was Von Holunder's great, undiscovered masterpiece; the work that his other paintings had hinted he was capable of, but which we had never before seen him produce. I had studied him for years, yet until now he had always remained an enigma. This single work, however, seemed to unlock something in his psyche that meant my subject no longer felt impenetrable.

'Thank you! Thank you for letting me see this. It changes everything.' I was conscious of starting to sound like a gushing schoolboy, but there was something else I wanted to tell her; something I sensed she needed to hear. 'I mean, I know Mimi said some horrible things about you in her book, but this will change how people see your relationship with Erik – it will change the whole story... He loved you, Christie. Even after all this time looking at his paintings, I couldn't quite be sure – you hear so many things. But this...this nails it. The way he's painted you there.' I turned again to look at the painting. 'The way he's worked the paint for your figure – it's different: more tender, more compassionate than anywhere else on the canvas. He's trying to convey something to you there that maybe he couldn't tell you to your face. He loved you, and nobody could look at this painting and not believe that.'

And then something remarkable happened. The veneer of the hard-boiled, sassy American fell away before me, and her eyes glassed with the suggestion of tears.

'Thank you,' she said with genuine tenderness. It was the first thing she said that I'd really believed; the first thing that didn't feel like an act. 'Hearing you say that...well, it helps me to believe that I'm not mad for seeing it too. I've tried to hold onto that for so long, but on the bad days I tell myself that I've been imagining it all these years.' And for the briefest of moments she didn't seem quite so self-possessed.

It didn't last for long.

'So. Do you think you could help me sell it?'

This was not what I had been expecting. 'What? Why?'

'I've done my research, young man. You know more about Erik than anyone else. And you obviously care about his work.'

'No, not "why me?" I mean, why do you want to sell it? You've kept it over thirty years, right? Why now?'

Something about her face changed. It broke, there's no other word for it, and for the first time she looked every one of her sixty-seven years. 'Look around you, kid.'

I looked around. There was a lot of love and a lot of pride in that trailer – everything was clean and there was not a speck of dust anywhere – but that couldn't hide what it was. It was clear that nothing had been replaced since the turn of the millennium. The photos on the walls, the knick-knacks on the sideboard, even the crockery on display in a chipped mahogany cabinet – they all hinted at a great and glorious past, but there was no getting away from the fact that this was a museum to a life that was now just a memory.

I didn't know what to say. Sensing my discomfort, Christie decided to pile on more.

'And you know what the worst of it is? I can't even make the rent on this.'

It was the first admission of any kind of vulnerability that she'd made, and I took it as a gift. But getting me to sell *Susanna & the Elders* on her behalf didn't seem like a sensible strategy.

'Look, Christie. We're paying you for this interview. I can

phone my editor up to see if we can get payment through a bit quicker – just to help tide you over. And I'm sure when the book comes out it'll reignite a lot of interest and bring in some more offers of—'

'Oh, that's not the worst of it. Honestly, if it was just the rent, I could figure something out. I've done it plenty of times before. I'm an attractive woman, Mr Viejo. I've never had a problem with suitors. There are always people keen to help,' and I could see, even as she said it, that there was not a flicker of doubt in her mind that it was true, even then. 'But things are a lot tougher now… I've got bigger problems.'

She slumped down into the sofa, crumpling in on herself like a collapsing soufflé. I couldn't think of anything worse than the prospect of losing your home, even one as ostensibly undesirable as this, but Christie soon disabused me of that.

'I have cancer,' she said, trying to regain her poise. 'There, I've said it. I'm at stage 2. Actually, I'm at stage 2B, if you want to be precise, although I'm not sure what the difference is.'

Her news dragged a silence out of the room which threatened to smother me until I felt compelled to break it. 'Oh, God. I'm sorry… I'm so sorry.' I didn't know what else to say.

'Don't be; it's not your fault. Even at 2B it's still treatable. This doesn't have to be the end. But I don't have insurance, and we don't have your socialist healthcare system over here, so I need money – lots of it. And I need it now. Once we get to stage 3 my prospects look a lot less rosy.'

I had laboured under the delusion that Christie's emergence from her self-imposed silence had been something to do with me; that she'd read my admiring comparison of Von Holunder with Freud in the spring edition of *World Art*, or perhaps even my monograph on his change of style from 1975 onwards, and decided that I was the person she could finally trust to tell her side of the story. But, like most things to do with Christie, it seemed I was naïve. I'd just been lucky enough to write to her requesting an interview at precisely the point she was most desperate for cash.

'So, what d'ya say? Are you gonna help me sell it?'

I sucked in a long breath and played for time by asking for a coffee while I gingerly began to piece my thoughts together. Slowly, an appropriate response began to form in my mind.

'Look, this is a fabulous opportunity and I'm obviously very flattered. But I'm not a dealer. I'm a critic. This is not what I do.'

It was a response that I had carefully calibrated in my mind to avoid causing any offence, but also to try and draw a line under the issue politely. However, subtle English social signalling was not something that Christie seemed to pick up on.

'I know, but I kinda figured you could help me out. For Erik.' Then she looked at me with her big blue eyes and I felt a little tug at my heart.

'I would love to. But I feel I've got to be honest with you here. Erik's work can be tough to sell at the moment. You don't need me: you need an experienced dealer.'

'Yeah, but I don't know who to go to. Most of the people Erik and I used to hang around with are dead now. Or at least, they're not taking my calls. I can't get anyone to speak to me. Not anyone who counts.'

'Look, I know someone who works for Marian Goodman. She specialises in contemporary European art for the American market. I'm pretty certain that Erik gave her some stuff to sell when she first opened in '77. I'm sure my friend would be happy to take a look at this for you. I can put you in touch.'

'Is she under forty?'

'Marian? God, no. She's even older than you!'

'Imagine!' she said, in mock surprise. 'No, I meant your friend.' My chastened silence indicated to Christie that she was. 'Because to be honest with you, if she is, I'm not sure that she'll take my call. No one under forty seems to have even heard of me.' And everything in her weak attempt to muster a smile told me that she had been brutally exposed to the bitter truth of that fact.

It seemed a genuine travesty. Even with the market's rather sniffy recent valuations of Erik's work, a decent Von Holunder could still reach $400,000. *Without You I'm Nothing* had even sold for $500,000 in New York just three or four years previously – still well below the prices that Erik's work was fetching in the late seventies and early eighties, but certainly not to be sniffed at. Yet the woman who had been their subject was stuck in a shitty trailer, penniless, and facing cancer alone. In a world of unfairness, I knew that this was hardly the unfairest thing of all, but it suddenly felt deeply unfair in a way that I'd never noticed before. And it was one unfairness I could actually do something about.

I fixed Christie with a firm stare. 'She'll take your call for this. I promise you.'

'Really?' She sounded like she couldn't quite believe it. 'I mean, a picture of a naked woman – it's not exactly the zeitgeist right now.'

I grew animated. 'But this is different. It's a naked woman who's in control, who's fighting back. It's a naked woman who won't put up with it all any more, who's changing the narrative. That captures the zeitgeist perfectly.'

'Hashtag – MeToo,' said Christie, sarcastically. She fought with all her might with the weapons at her disposal and clearly had no truck with those who wanted to fight another way. It was the one thing that disappointed me about her even then, and I made the mistake of telling her so.

'Oh, don't tell me you're a feminist,' she replied. It seemed to disappoint her in a way that suggested some question of my manhood was at stake.

'How is that a bad thing?'

'Let me tell you something, honey: the guys who call themselves feminists are always the first to put their hand on your ass.'

I could tell immediately from her weary timbre that this was more than just a wisecrack. Something in me wondered for a moment if it wasn't also a warning, but her voice seemed too pregnant with regret for the comment to be aimed directly at me. She was holding on to a disappointment that I decided it was best not to probe.

However, I wanted her to appreciate the potential significance of what she had shown me. I looked her straight in the eye to try and ram the point home.

'Look, you've got something very valuable here, Christie. This is a major work by a significant twentieth-century artist that has never come on the market before. And it has an impeccable provenance.'

Christie's face adopted a demure look, and she glanced at me out of the corner of her eyes. 'Well... I wouldn't say "impeccable".'

I raised a quizzical eyebrow as a frisson of concern shivered down my back. 'You wouldn't?'

'No, I definitely couldn't say that.' She leant forward and put her hand gently on my knee. 'That's kinda why I need you...'

She opened up her deep blue eyes imploringly and invited me to wallow in their oceans.

I used to think I fell in love with Christie, but looking back I wonder if I didn't just fall in love with the idea of Christie. Whichever it was, I do know that it happened in that moment.

And that it was the worst mistake of my life.

# FOUR

I remember reading an interview with Christie – the one she did in the spring of '87 that had so upset Erik – in which she said the only difference between a wife and a mistress was that the mistress got to have all the fun. After Erik's death, however, Christie had learnt just how hollow those words were.

Erik von Holunder had met the young Mimi Crombrugge (always a great name to have tucked up your sleeve if you ever find yourself stuck in a bar-room game of 'Name Three Famous Belgians') in Paris in 1958 when she'd been waiting tables at Fouquet's. They'd married the following year and, as Erik's career began to take off, Mimi had found herself ensconced in an apartment in Paris' eighth arrondissement. But international fame meant international travel, and it became necessary for Erik also to set up homes in London and New York. He'd bought an apartment in Manhattan in 1971 after his first major New York show had been a triumph, and then he'd returned for another show in 1974. It was at the opening of this that he'd met the young Christie McGraw. As part of my research I'd learnt that, actually, Suzy was wrong about the origin of the nickname – Christie had always been called Christie, right from when she was a girl and her exasperated father had threatened to take her to Christie's and auction her off if she didn't behave. By that stage however, it wouldn't have helped negotiations between our lawyers to point out Suzy's error, so I nursed my sense of grievance privately and rested secure in the knowledge that in this matter at least, I was unambiguously right. Christie had moved into Erik's apartment in the Dakota Building in 1975. The apartments in the Dakota were famously large and sprawling and Erik had managed to keep a studio there too, in which he spent his days painting pictures of Christie.

Erik's various domestic arrangements were therefore rigidly demarcated in a tacit agreement between the parties, designed to protect Mimi's dignity and Erik's freedom: Mimi got Paris, while Christie got New York. Christie knew that she could be at Erik's side throughout his various New York sojourns and there was no possibility of her ever having to face an awkward meeting with Mimi. 'When Erik was in New York, he was mine; one hundred per cent!' was how Christie had put it to me the previous night, before the fateful arrival of Liga from Riga. And New York was hers too.

At least that's what she'd thought. The rather messier reality only became apparent after Erik's death. Christie had always known that Mimi would get the Paris apartment and most of Erik's cash. And she would also, of course, become the inheritor of his estate, including his copyright entitlements – any other arrangement would simply have been too embarrassing for

Mimi to have to live with. Christie accepted this as payback for Mimi putting up with Erik's 'little indiscretion', as she called it. Besides, she'd had most of the fun while Erik was alive, so it seemed only fair that his wife got some recompense for that after he died. But Christie had always assumed – in fact she'd been told explicitly by Erik himself – that the apartment at the Dakota was hers.

That was, however, before her interview with *Village Voice* in May 1987. In that interview Christie had made her famous comment about wives and mistresses. Erik had hit the roof. She had made explicit something that had never been made explicit before: Erik was having an affair.

As I sat in her trailer, listening to her trying to explain how she had gone from the Dakota Building to this, I could see she clearly still regarded it as the biggest mistake of her life.

'What can I say? I'd been smoking a joint. Big mistake. Never do an interview stoned – I was higher than a Bee Gees harmony. But hey! It was New York in the eighties.'

She was unusually animated for once, as if it really mattered to her that I understood what had happened.

'But surely everyone knew?' I asked. 'I mean, you were living together when he was in New York – for twelve years.'

'Everyone *knew*, but no one *said*,' explained Christie. 'That was the thing. By saying it – in a magazine where everyone we knew would see it – I was humiliating Mimi publicly. Erik couldn't ignore that. He got on a plane to Paris that night and I never saw him again.'

'And Mimi just took him back? There was no thought he might choose you?' It seemed surprising after the painting I'd just seen. It seemed to show such love.

Christie was rueful. 'Mistresses might have all the fun,

but wives get all the loyalty,' she said. 'Mimi tolerated him because, in the end, she knew he would always come back. And she tolerated me because I didn't rub her nose in it. And Erik appreciated me because I didn't rub Mimi's nose in it. I don't think I understood that until then. I took it for granted that he loved me and didn't love her. But it wasn't about love. Marriage never is, is it?'

That was the thing about Christie: sometimes she could punch you in the gut with an insight, but she'd say it like she was reciting a shopping list.

'I guess not,' was all I could think to say in response.

'Besides, I'd made him look like a schmuck. Somehow, there's something romantic about an artist and his muse. But an old man and his mistress just looks kinda sordid. And that's what we'd become. He felt I'd ruined his reputation somehow. He could never forgive me for that.'

'But you stayed in the Dakota?'

'At that point, yeah. I mean, I didn't know what was happening. This was before mobile phones or social media: I couldn't WhatsApp him or drop him a text. I didn't even have the number of the apartment in Paris. He always called me. Until he didn't. And I just had to put up with it. But I kinda figured he would get over it eventually.'

But when Erik met his untimely death five months later, it transpired that he had not got over it. In fact he had changed his will that week so that Christie no longer inherited the New York apartment. More than thirty years later she was clearly still bruised by the whole experience.

'It was *my* apartment! I'd lived there – twelve months a year – for twelve years! I made a home for us there. Erik was never there for more than four months of the year because of…everything else… But that was our home. And I made it – I chose the carpets, the furniture, the wallpaper, the art on the walls.' She counted them out on her fingers. 'Everything. Hell – I even chose that apartment. If it wasn't for me, he'd still have been living in the Olcott. Jesus! Can you imagine?' Christie was flushing red as the emotion rose within her. 'It was me who said to get something at the Dakota. John and Yoko were in there by then and I could see that the prices were only going to go up. We were the floor down from them. Yoko loved living so close to an artist like Erik. She'd come round to discuss art with him whenever John was being a dick – which, let me tell you, was a helluva lot of the time. And when Erik wasn't about, she'd just talk to me.'

'Really? Wow! What about?

'Just girl stuff, y'know. Let's just say, John and Erik were both difficult dogs to keep on the porch, so we had plenty we could talk about.'

She took a seat on the sofa. She seemed to have blown herself out and I didn't know what to say. I'd asked her why she couldn't vouch for the provenance of *Susanna & The Elders,* and this is what I'd got. It didn't feel like much of an explanation.

'I couldn't believe it when the letter came from the solicitor. Four weeks they gave me. After twelve years, and all the love I'd poured into that apartment, they gave me four weeks to get out. It was Mimi's. And not just the apartment. "The apartment *and all its contents."* That's what the will said. I got to keep my clothes and my make-up and that was it.'

I knew about the apartment going to Mimi, but I hadn't appreciated till then that Christie had been cut out of the picture quite so ruthlessly. For the first time I really felt the injustice of it.

'So after twelve years with Erik, you were left a couple of suitcases of clothes and your make-up bag?'

'I think it was six suitcases, but basically, yeah. That was it. No money, no personal effects. Hell, I didn't even have any health insurance or social security contributions for those twelve years. I was basically starting over with nothing except a few Azzedine Alaïa dresses...' She paused for a moment and looked up at me coyly. 'And that painting.'

'So Erik left that to you?' I said, indicating the painting that sat between us.

'No,' she said, exasperated. 'That's what I've been trying to tell you.' My look must have betrayed my confusion, because she then let out a heavy sigh and took a long swig from her grapefruit juice before placing the glass carefully on the table. 'The painting was in the apartment. But the apartment *and all its contents* had been left to Mimi.'

'So the painting was hers?'

'Technically. Except she didn't know that. No one did. Everyone thought Erik had scrapped it – which he had. But I loved it, so when he went back to Paris in '85 I snuck into his workshop and salvaged it, before he had a chance to paint over it. I put it up over the fireplace. Erik wasn't very happy about that, let me tell you. The *Old Masters* series had just bombed, and he was very depressed. He said it reminded him of his failure. But I said that it shouldn't. It should remind him of his talent. And anyway, I loved it and wanted to keep it, even if he didn't, so he let me keep it. I didn't even think to get it registered. I mean, why would you? We were living together, and everything was going swell, as far as I could see. I never imagined things would end the way they did. But when he died, and I found out that Mimi was getting everything... Well, that was just too much. I wasn't going to let her get her hands on this painting – the other ones we'd got in the apartment I could live with her having – but this one: no way.'

'So you took it?'

'Yep,' said Christie, defiantly. 'And I'm not ashamed to say it. This was my painting. Absolutely. It wouldn't even have still existed if it hadn't been for me.'

'But that's not how the lawyers see it, I guess.'

'Well that's the thing. I don't know how the lawyers see it. I mean, the painting wasn't there when they took possession of the apartment, but nobody came to me to suggest it was missing or asking me where it was. Mimi's never complained. She hasn't accused me of stealing it – and hell, you've read her book; she's accused me of just about everything else.'

I bowed my eyes in embarrassment. 'As far as everyone was concerned it had been destroyed. That's what the obituaries said.'

'Exactly.'

'Which means you get to keep it, and nobody's suspicious.' But my mind was slowly starting to piece together the jigsaw that Christie had thrown down chaotically in front of me. I raised my head and looked her straight in the eye as the realisation struck me.

'However, if you were to place it on the open market then that would alert people to its existence and that could put you in an...awkward position, legally.'

'You got it, kiddo. I mean it's never mattered before, because I've never needed to sell it, but now I've got to find two hundred and fifty grand pronto to keep a roof over my head and fund my treatment. Otherwise the park owners'll be throwing it in a dumpster – along with my corpse – when they come to clear out my things.'

Her bluntness made me flush.

'I get all that, really, I do. And I can see the predicament you're in. But what I can't see is how I can help you.'

'Oh you can help me. You can definitely help me.'

She gathered herself, and the way that she did so suggested she'd been rehearsing this moment in her head for some time.

'You know Conny, right? Conny Gerou.'

'Vaguely. He's a big collector of Erik's stuff.'

'Well, me and Conny go way back, and I'm pretty sure that he's going to want to buy this painting.'

I couldn't quite stop myself emitting a small sigh.

'Well, if you know him, then presumably you'll also know that's he's in a spot of bother at the moment. I'm not sure that buying paintings of doubtful provenance is going to be top of his to-do list right now.'

'Oh, but I think it is. Look,' she said, grabbing a copy of the previous day's *Washington Post*. 'Conny arrived at Heathrow with a whole load of luggage labelled "diplomatic baggage".'

'How did he get himself designated a Greek diplomat?'

'Nobody quite knows how, but somehow he's now officially a trade attaché apparently.' She found the relevant paragraph in the report. '*In recognition of his outstanding contribution to Greek trade.*'

Eyes were duly rolled.

'Anyway,' she continued, swapping over to the *National Enquirer*, 'some of that diplomatic baggage is reported to be full of cash.'

I had seen from my own reading that morning that Conny's luggage was indeed the subject of much speculation, although the BBC reports had not mentioned the possibility of diplomatic baggage being used to smuggle illicit cash out of the country.

'That's the *National Enquirer*, Christie. It's not been confirmed.'

'That's my point. I'd bet my life – hell, I *am* betting my life – that he isn't going to want it to be confirmed. The police in England can't touch it; it's diplomatic baggage. But when he gets sent back to Greece – which he will do – they can do what they like: those pouches are government property.'

'And if they were found to be full of cash rather than confidential diplomatic papers, well...I guess things wouldn't look good.'

'Exactly. So I'm betting that what he needs to do before he gets sent back to Greece – and needs to do pretty desperately – is to find an easy way of getting rid of a large amount of cash very quickly.'

This raised an intriguing opportunity for Christie, which she helpfully spelt out.

'If I can get Conny to buy my painting, then I solve both our problems: I get a decent chunk of cash to clear my debts and fund my treatment, and he turns a hefty chunk of his dirty money into a legitimate asset.'

'Yes, but your problem is that it's *not* legitimate. It's not yours to sell, Christie. How is Conny going to explain how he got it? Unless he can do that, it's as worthless for him as it is for you.'

'Well here's the thing – he actually came round to the apartment at the Dakota in '85. I've got a photo.'

She reached over to an envelope resting on the coffee table between us and took out an old Polaroid. It showed Erik and

Conny together, each holding a glass of cognac, standing in Erik's studio. And there behind them, on the floor, partially obscured by Erik's legs, was *Susanna & the Elders*. You couldn't see Christie's face in the painting, but it was unmistakably the same picture. And immediately I could see who the second of the elders was.

'Is that...?'

'Conny? Yes, it is! Erik never said anything, but I think he picked up that Conny had a bit of a thing for me. He tried not to be jealous – he was hardly in a position to throw stones on that score – but he was very aware of the age gap between us, and Con was much nearer my age. So I think this was his way of making a point.'

'That's a great story.'

'Isn't it just? But isn't it a great explanation too? Of how Conny came to get the painting? He saw it that day in the studio, and when Erik told him he was going to throw it out he offered to take it off his hands. Who wouldn't believe that? We don't have a bill of sale, but we do have the story of the painting, and why there never was a bill of sale – and we even have the photo to back it all up. It's all completely plausible.'

Indeed it was. The fact was that Christie's photo and the well-established story of Erik wanting to throw the painting out made Conny the perfect buyer for it now, because only he could construct a plausible story as to how the painting might have come into his possession legitimately. This would mean that he wasn't simply throwing his money away; it would be a genuine investment. Conny was the only person in the world who could sell *Susanna & the Elders* on to someone else, if he ever needed to, without the threat of legal action from Mimi.

I looked at Christie as she stood before me with a face that seemed as open and honest as any I had come across recently (although working in the contemporary art market, this was not a particularly high threshold to cross). Her smile was warm, her eyes sparkling. In my hungover state it appeared to me as though she really had thought of everything.

There remained, however, one nagging doubt in the back of my mind.

'That's all great, Christie, but – I have to ask – why do you need me? If you know the guy, why not just take the painting over to London yourself and sell it to Conny face-to-face? Surely, given your history, he'd be more likely to buy it off you directly.'

Christie sighed and slumped back down on the sofa. 'Do you think I want to involve you? Sorry, honey, but I need to be blunt: if there was any way I could do this without you, I'd do it. But I got two problems. Firstly, I can't create a link between me and Conny. I mean, Mimi – Jesus! That woman is vindictive. Christ, you've read her book, so you don't need me to tell you that. If she could get her hands on this painting, she'd do it in a heartbeat. And if she could steal it off me in the process, so much the better. If she gets any hint that I might have any financial interest in this painting her lawyers will be all over it. But if Conny turns up with the painting and a plausible provenance, then she's got nothing to go against. And let's be honest – his lawyers are probably more expensive than her lawyers. Me? Well, if I can't make the rent on this then I certainly can't afford a legal fight with Mimi.

I could see that this made sense.

'But my second problem,' she continued, 'is convincing Conny that this painting is a genuine investment. You know how suspicious he can be, so what I need is someone who can reassure him that the rest of the art world is going to believe him when he tells them this is the great lost Von Holunder masterpiece that everyone's been looking for.

'He knows you, and he knows you know more than anyone else about Erik's paintings, so I think it would make more sense for him to hear that from you.'

To be fair to her, this wasn't completely unreasonable. Conny and I weren't friends as such, but I felt confident that if it was me offering him the chance to buy *Susanna & the Elders*, he would at least feel obliged to hear me out.

I tried to think of all the things that could go wrong, but the more I did so, the more I realised Christie was right: I couldn't get into trouble. There was no record of the painting, so there was no way anyone could prove that it was stolen. If push came to shove in negotiations with Conny, therefore, there was no way he could implicate me in a crime. But, more than that, why would he want to? Given his current situation, it was highly likely that he would want as little to do with the police as possible. So even if he didn't want the painting, the likelihood was that he would just politely pass on it.

'You know what, Christie?' I said. 'You've convinced me to change my mind. I'm in.'

So you can see that I agreed to help Christie in her trailer that day before we'd even discussed money. I think it's worth pointing that out because of what was suggested later. At the outset this was simply a humane response from me to a vulnerable woman in desperate need, towards whom I had immediately warmed. I didn't expect anything from her for my trouble and if the whole deal had proceeded as I imagined it would do, then I'd have been quite happy with that; I honestly would have. But obviously, that's not how things unfolded.

# FIVE

Christie decided that we needed to go out to celebrate the cementing of our new business venture. This point felt moot to me, but she was insistent in a way that only Christie could be.

'I'll call Liga – I think she liked you,' she said with a twinkle.

'Me? Oh, I'm not sure about that.' I really wasn't, but Christie dangled the possibility in front of me enticingly like a twenty-dollar bill.

'Are you kidding me? Well, you must be blind then. That woman was so far up your ass last night I thought I was going to have to send out for a snorkel and flippers.'

The compromise position was that before we did anything that might involve alcohol, we'd head midtown and take a leisurely stroll around the newly refurbished and extended Museum of Modern Art. I knew it was open till 9pm over the summer so I thought that would give me enough time to get my constitution back into some sort of shape before the night's endeavours with Christie and Liga. But I also knew that MoMA had got one of Erik's earliest portraits of Christie in their collection, *Juvenile Heart Attack* (1975), and I really wanted to see it with her. It wasn't particularly one of my favourites – they'd only just met when he painted it and it always felt to me as though Von Holunder was more obsessed at that time with how she looked than with who she was – but I thought that seeing it with Christie and hearing her recollections of how it was painted might bring it to life, and perhaps give me an insightful anecdote or two for the biography.

Christie affected nonchalance, as though she was doing this to humour me, but on the train into Manhattan I could tell she was feeling a certain frisson of excitement at the prospect of seeing herself on display.

'Haven't you ever been to MoMA before?' I asked. 'I mean, they've had the painting for nearly forty years.'

'At twenty-five bucks a time? Are you kidding me? I'm only coming now because you're paying...' There was a momentary flash of anxiety in her voice. 'You *are* paying, right? I mean—'

'Don't worry. I'm paying.'

And she relaxed back into her seat. 'Very generous, young man.'

A few moments later, a call came through on my mobile. I looked at the screen and saw the familiar name of Jasper Wong.

'Hi Jasper! Look, I'm on a train in New York at the moment. So if we get cut off—'

I had been expecting the call and was hoping for – although not necessarily expecting – some good news.

'Hi, Gabe. No worries. Look I was just ringing to let you

know, Dad's really appreciative of your offer and everything, but it's not quite enough. He's exploring other options at the moment. I'd really love you to come in on this with me though, so I just wanted to give you a chance to come back with a higher offer. Any chance, mate?'

'I wish there was. But honestly, that's all I've got. Like I told you, Suzy's got the rest.'

'I get it. But I'm not going to lie, you're just not in the frame at the moment.'

'And just as a matter of interest, what would get me in the frame?... Jasper?... Jasper?'

The line had gone dead.

'Business?' asked Christie.

'Kind of. Old friend of mine from school. You won't know him but he runs a gallery with his dad. They've done pretty well for themselves riding the wave in the Chinese market. Anyway, his dad's looking to sell up and retire now and Jasper's looking for a partner to buy into the business with him. I've been trying to see if I could put something together but...this damn divorce.'

Christie looked at me quizzically.

'She really left you with nothing?'

I didn't want to get into the intricate details of my divorce settlement so I just said, 'Pretty much...'

'I would've thought the judge would make sure everyone gets a fair settlement.'

'Well, fair or not, it's not enough to get me a seat at the table. Which is a shame because there's a lot of money to be made in the Chinese market at the moment.'

Christie contemplated me as though appraising a painting, then turned her head and looked out of the window.

My mood had been deflated by Jasper's call. The reality was that life as a freelance art critic was no more secure than life as an artist's muse, and buying into Jasper's gallery was part of a plan to pivot my career towards the far more lucrative business of art dealing. This was what my grandpa always said I should have done rather than wasting my time (and his money) on a master's at the Courtauld. He'd left me the proceeds of the sale of a sketch by Francis Bacon in his will and my intention had been to use that money to finally follow his advice. It felt like an appropriate way to honour him. But now it seemed even the $200,000 I'd made was not going to be enough. The world of art criticism continued to beckon, and with it, continued penury.

The thought of it meant that the rest of the journey proceeded in glum silence.

I hadn't been to MoMA since the much-anticipated opening of the Hines building and was hoping that the major refurbishment of its existing galleries would have restored some dignity to them after the horrors of the Taniguchi renovations. In the event, however, we didn't even get past the entrance hall.

The whole purpose of the extension and renovation work was to increase the amount of gallery space so that more of the museum's collection could be put on display. *Juvenile Heart Attack* had been on display since 1982, when Erik sold it to the museum. Given the pressure on wall space, it was quite an accolade for it to have kept its place for all that time. It hadn't occurred to me therefore, that it wouldn't be on display now, given that there would be an additional four-and-a-half-thousand square metres of gallery space. But when we entered the reception area and Christie buttonholed an official-looking young woman to find out where it was now located, we were met with an anxious stare.

'Uhhhh... I'm sorry, but I don't think that work is on display any more,' came the response eventually, after an embarrassed silence.

This made no sense to me. And it appeared to make no sense to Christie either.

'But why not?'

I'm sure it was meant to be an enquiry rather than an accusation, but the way the woman recoiled I wondered if Christie had asked it rather too forcefully.

'Well, given recent events, we've had to take a long hard look at our collection to ensure that it continues to reflect the values of the MoMA trustees, our sponsors and, of course, our audiences.'

I could see that the young woman – her name badge indicated that she was called Casey – was getting flustered, so I gathered myself for a moment to try and find something suitably emollient to say. Unfortunately, Christie did not feel obliged to observe such courtesies.

'What the actual fuck, young lady?!'

Heads turned, and I decided I needed to intervene. 'I'm sorry. My friend is upset because we've come a long way specifically to see that painting.'

I had wanted to defuse the situation. Christie was having none of it, though.

'That painting has been admired by everyone from Hilton Kramer to Jay Jopling. Its purchase was funded by an endowment precisely *because* it represented the values of MoMA and its audiences – beauty, vitality and a commitment to excellence. Are you telling me that you're not committed to those things any more?'

Casey was stumped. Thankfully, help was at hand. A tall, thin, middle-aged man with an imperious stare and a waxed moustache appeared from out of the crowd.

'Can I help here? Is everything alright, Casey?'

I explained the situation as calmly as I could, while holding Christie's wrist to try and indicate to her that she needed to stop talking before she got us thrown out. Her wrist felt thinner and more fragile than I'd imagined. The skin itself was looser too, so she felt old in that moment in a way that she hadn't felt old before, and I started to sense why she had become so animated, despite the fact that a couple of hours previously she'd been quite happy to head straight to a bar without looking at the painting at all.

'I'm sorry sir, but as my colleague has already explained, that painting is no longer on display. We've had to make some difficult curatorial choices – to reflect on what and who we want to represent as a museum. There are different voices now, more diverse voices, and I think that some of the things that we might have accepted as legitimate artistic choices in the past we're now having to question.'

'What does that even mean?' Christie knew, of course, exactly what it meant, but I could tell from her voice that she wanted to make him say it.

'I just don't think that paintings of young girls in cheerleading outfits are something our visitors would expect to see here, or something we would feel comfortable showing them any more.'

I wanted to say something, to get in first, but there was no stopping Christie.

'Are you kidding me? Erik von Holunder was one of the great figurative artists of the late twentieth century. I can't believe he doesn't deserve a place in what's *supposed* to be,' (more italics, allied with an eyeroll), 'the best modern art museum in the world. People compared him to Lucian Freud for Chrissake!'

This was true, although even I had been forced to admit that when people did so, they invariably concluded that he wasn't quite as good. In the current context however, it didn't seem helpful to back up Christie's observation, because there are few things guaranteed to wind up curatorial staff more than the suggestion that they can't recognise great art when they see it (except, perhaps, the related suggestion that their tastes are in hock to mediocrity) and that is precisely what Christie had done. Sure enough, the ends of the curator's moustache began to twitch with barely suppressed indignation.

'Well, his technique may have had some similarities to Freud, but I think the subject matter was handled more in the manner of Russ Meyer.'

This was perhaps a touch harsh, but it did at least accord with Francis Bacon's views on the subject. When pressed for his opinions on Von Holunder, he had famously dismissed him as 'a Graham Sutherland for the *Carry-On* generation.' But that missed the point. For Christie I could tell that it felt like it was more than just a painting being removed from front of house and placed in the basement. Maybe the curator saw it too, in her face, but he just didn't care. Or maybe he cared but didn't know what to do. Whatever it was, he decided to say something else before Christie had an opportunity to respond.

'I appreciate that Von Holunder had his admirers,' (I couldn't work out if the use of the past tense was a calculated snub or not, yet decided to let it slide in order to try to stop things deteriorating further), 'but I think we've come to see sexually charged images of young girls as...problematic.'

'I will have you know, young man,' (given that he was fifty if he was a day, I was pretty sure this *was* a calculated snub), 'I was twenty-two years old when I posed for that painting! I was not a "young girl", and Erik von Holunder was most certainly not a pervert. He was a great artist who loved beautiful women – *fully-grown women* – like lots of artists before him. If it's "problematic" art you've got to put into storage, then I would have thought that Gauguin should be ahead of Erik in the line. I bet you've still got all those naked Polynesian girls on the walls, haven't you?' There was the briefest of pauses, during which the waxed moustache was angled towards the floor, before Christie continued, her voice rising in anger. 'I'm not saying he was perfect, but Erik was not deviant in any way! He was a great man – and he loved me. You ask this young man here,' she flailed an arm in my direction. 'He'll tell you. He loved me, and he put that love on a canvas. And there's nothing wrong with that. Nothing at all!'

She was quaking with rage, but at the same time seemed to be expending every ounce of her energy on holding herself together with as much poise as she could manage. I wanted to put my arm around her, but suspected that if I did, she would immediately descend into full-throated sobs.

The entrance lobby now was silent, museum patrons frozen in a shared horror at the spectacle that had unfolded before them. To my surprise, it was Casey who broke it.

'You were in that painting?' she asked. 'Oh my God! Do you want to see a counsellor? We have a counsellor available if anyone is triggered while they're here.'

That's when I noticed two security guards hovering on the edge of the scene, not quite sure when or how to intervene but clearly feeling that they should.

'Come on, Christie,' I said. 'Let's go and grab a coffee somewhere.'

And I gently ushered her towards the door.

# SIX

We found a coffee shop a two-minute walk away, on Sixth Avenue. The baristas were all wearing ties, so I thought Christie would appreciate it. In any event, I figured we could at least get an authentic Italian coffee experience while we nursed our wounds.

It was gone six and the whole day seemed tired now. The shop was starting to empty and those who remained looked like people who were de-pressurising after the strains of the day. Laptops had been put away and ties loosened, so it felt like we didn't have to pretend either. It gave us permission to relax into our sadness in a way that New York so rarely did.

I thought that Christie would be her usual, voluble self; that she would want to deconstruct our encounter with the MoMA staff in meticulous detail and at rat-a-tat-tat speed. But instead, she just slowly circulated her spoon around the edge of her Americano while staring into its darkness in silence.

She'd added no sugar or milk, so this action served no obvious purpose, but the metronomic rhythm of the metal gently scraping the ceramic seemed to give a shape to her sorrows. Perhaps it comforted her in a way that I couldn't.

I tried to lift the mood by pointing out that all the baristas were wearing ties, but Christie didn't seem interested. She just grunted and carried on stirring her sadness round and round with her spoon. There were no italics, no eyerolls – and without them Christie somehow seemed less. There was only the silent expressiveness of her face.

You could have swum in the sorrows of that face, in the ocean of tears that lay un-cried behind those eyes.

'I loved that painting,' she said, at last. 'I mean, it wasn't my favourite, but he captured something of what I was like back then that I like to be reminded of.'

'Young?' I ventured.

She snorted. '"Sexually charged." Isn't that what Mr Moustachio said? Well, he was right about that, at least. I was sexually charged – I mean, I guess I still am – but back then I didn't know it. And Erik captured that. The other stuff, the later stuff – well, a lot of that was just acting. But that look, the being-but-not-knowing look… That was me. And that's what made that painting.'

I hadn't seen that in the painting before, but the moment Christie said it, I knew she was right. The difference between *Juvenile Heart Attack* and *Susanna & The Elders* was not in what their subject *was*, but in what she *knew*. So her comment struck me as genuinely insightful in a way that I wasn't expecting. It had never occurred to me that she understood Erik's paintings, only that she was their ('sexually charged') subject. But now I was confronted by the possibility that she understood them better than I did.

'Is this what we've come to?' she asked. 'We can't cope with a pretty young woman being shown as sexual? Have the Puritans taken over now?'

Not for the first time with Christie, I didn't know how to respond. Given the multiplicity of strip joints and massage parlours that plied their lucrative trade within a few miles of where we were sitting, all unworried by the City Fathers, it seemed a bit of a stretch to suggest that America was now a Puritan republic. But something had changed, of that there was no doubt; not within the legislature, but within that most intangible and ungovernable of spheres – society's mores. We viewed art in a different way. The unwritten rules of what made 'good' art were still unwritten, but they were being unwritten by different people with different priorities.

I Googled *Juvenile Heart Attack* and brought up an image on my phone. I hadn't really looked at it for years – not properly. What I saw was an achingly pretty young girl. She was a girl who looked so desperate to be desired but wasn't sure if she was. And that uncertainty gave the viewer a strange kind of power in a situation where they were usually passive. Because what the young girl was asking for was affirmation, and simply by looking at the painting, by allowing yourself to be held in the power of the girl's uncertain stare, you were saying that, yes, she was worth something. So she needed you to stay, and to stare, and to say, 'Yes, you are desirable.' Or at least, she did if you were a straight man. It shifted the balance of power between the viewer and the viewed.

Because what I now realised was that there were other ways of looking at that painting that were altogether less benign. Firstly, she was a girl – despite what Christie said, there was no way she looked twenty-two and it occurred to me that perhaps Von Holunder had painted her that way deliberately. But this suggested another troubling issue.

'You were really twenty-two when this was painted?'

'Sure.'

'So how old was Erik?'

'It was '75 so he'd be fifty-three, fifty-four.'

'And you were sleeping together when he painted this?'

'Well, aren't you the inquisitor?' she said, arching her eyebrow playfully. 'Not when he started it, no. He did my face first and I know we hadn't slept together then, but then he put it to one side for a while and came back to it. We were definitely an item by then.'

'At twenty-two?'

'I was probably twenty-three by then. My birthday's October.'

'And you're OK with that?'

'My birthday being in October? Well I'd have preferred it to be May, like my sister, but what can you do?'

'No, I meant the age gap. It was what? About thirty years?'

'Thirty-one. His birthday was in June.' She looked at me and must have sensed my mounting unease. 'Look, honey, you don't have to worry about me. We were both consenting adults.'

'Oh, I don't doubt it. I just wonder if you were both consenting to the same thing – whether you could, given the age gap.'

'Jeezus! You're worse than that girl at the museum. *Counselling!*' she said, as though it were self-evidently the most ludicrous suggestion in the world. 'I ask you!'

I didn't want to press the issue, given what had happened at

MoMA, but nor did I want her to miss the point I was trying to make.

'Yeah, well let's just think about that girl. How old do you reckon she was?'

'Twenty, twenty-one, I guess.'

'And the guy?'

'I don't know. Early fifties, maybe.'

'And if you found out that he was sleeping with her, you wouldn't have a problem with that?'

Christie threw back her head in a throaty laugh. 'I don't know how to break this to you, honey, but I don't think he sat on "that side of the church", if you know what I'm saying.'

She seemed to be coming back to life, but for once I didn't feel like joining in the joke. 'Maybe not. Probably not. But that's not my point. Imagine if they were.'

This was not a possibility that she seemed willing to entertain. And I could tell from the look on her face that that unsettled her almost as much as it did me. She tried to regroup.

'Look, I was just a young girl' – there was that phrase again – 'from Michigan who loved art and wanted to study where I could meet great artists. So I came to New York. To meet Erik, to become his muse – that was a fantasy for me.' She immediately sensed what I was about to say, so she quickly added, 'And I was a fantasy for him. We were two people who both loved art, locked in a fantasy.'

'Until you weren't.'

'Until we weren't. But let me tell you, for the twelve years that we were, we were tighter than James Brown and the JB's in '71. And he taught me everything I could ever have wanted to know about art and being an artist – more, in fact.'

All of this was new information, and it posed some

questions that I was keen to pursue. 'You came to New York to study art?'

'Sure. I wanted to study at the School of Art, but I didn't have a good enough portfolio, so I decided to come here anyway and hope I could meet lots of other artists and get some great ideas. I got here in '72.'

'But you never actually went to the SoA?'

'Then I met Erik, and I didn't have to.'

She said it as though it were the most obvious thing in the world, but it troubled me.

'But why not? I mean, if you wanted to be an artist, surely you had to study?'

'I *thought* I wanted to be an artist – because I loved art. But what I actually loved was beauty, and being with Erik showed me how ugly the whole business side of art could be.'

It seemed a shame, and I told her so, that she'd come to the city with such big dreams and ended up being someone else's muse. The art world had frightened her off pursuing her own career and had offered her a consolation prize. Yet ultimately even that had been snatched from her grasp.

'Why does it bother you so much that *Juvenile Heart Attack* is on display in the MoMA?' I asked. 'It's not as if it makes you any money.'

She answered without missing a beat, 'Because I want to be seen. And MoMA's where people go to look.'

Among all the lies that followed, it would be easy to forget the truth of that. It was the truest thing she ever said.

# SEVEN

We met up with Liga at a basement club in BoHo that seemed to be doing its best to pretend it wasn't there. But once we got behind the nondescript front door and descended the stairs, it was as if we had innocently removed a rock to discover teeming life beneath. It ticked all the usual boxes for an edgy club – naked masonry, flaunted cabling and indecently exposed ductwork – but despite that, it seemed to have attracted a very distinct subculture that was scuttling about and drinking cocktails while a large guy in a rainbow T-shirt set up the stage.

Liga was already there, dressed to the nines and with what I couldn't help but feel was a distinct twinkle in her eye. Despite the healthy crowd that was beginning to gather, she'd managed to hold a table close to the front. The ease with which she had done so should, perhaps, have given me pause for thought, but my initial reaction was just relief that I wasn't going to have to stand up all night.

The first sign that our good luck was not wholly benign was when the bargirl came to clear our table. 'Are you guys going to be alright sitting at the front? You do know what kind of a show we have on Thursdays, don't you?'

I had no idea at all. Christie had explained nothing, and Liga's text had given us just an address to head to, not even a club name. But Christie seemed pretty relaxed. 'Sure, honey. Don't you worry about us. We're game for anything,' she replied.

It transpired that Thursday night was Drag Show night, the highlight of which was a black Bette Midler tribute act called, with a crushing sense of inevitability, Bette Noir. (Bette didn't specify pronouns but the MC introduced all the Queens as 'she' so that's what I'm using here.)

Bette put on quite a show and audience participation was a key part. The moment she called out, 'Is there anyone out there who wants to help me with my next song?' the reason why the audience was gathered, like loyal Anglicans, largely at the back of the club became clear.

I was fully intending to keep my head down in the hope that someone else might volunteer, but, to my horror, both Liga and Christie began calling out, 'Over here!' and pointing wildly in my direction so that before I could do anything about it, I found myself being hauled up on stage. From thirty feet away Bette had looked a million dollars; from two feet away, however, she looked like she was designed to be seen from thirty feet away. At least.

I will spare you the details of what unfolded next in order to preserve what little dignity I have left, but suffice to say, it involved shaving cream, a generously proportioned sex toy, and a version of 'My One True Friend' that I don't think anyone who witnessed it will forget in a hurry. When Bette announced that she was going to follow it up with 'Hello In There' I was genuinely worried about where things were heading, but thankfully, once the audience laughter had died down, she ushered me back to the safety of my seat.

Christie and Liga were whooping and hollering with delight, and I even got a kiss on the cheek from Liga, but I immediately sensed that any possibility there might have been of the two of us getting together was now very much gone. There is, I've learnt, a point at which a woman's interest in a man moves from being motivated by intrigue to being motivated by pity, and once that shift takes place the possibility of a romantic relationship disappears for ever. Liga's eyes betrayed that that point had just been definitively passed.

Not that I was worried, particularly. I'd come to New York for Christie, and she was proving herself to be more than I could possibly ever have imagined.

Twenty minutes later, as the final bars of 'Wind Beneath My Wings' faded into the distance and the Divine Mx M took her leave, Christie turned to me and said. 'I'll have a Martini, please; and I want it so dry it can quote Oscar Wilde. Thanks very much.'

There was something in her tone that gave me pause, as if she wanted me to get her a drink beforehand just in case what she was about to say might cause me to think again about helping her sell her painting. The truth was, I'd bought most of Christie's drinks that night and the one before, and I was far from convinced that my publisher was going to permit me to count them all as allowable expenses. But I knew that she was going through tough times, and she was great company, so it seemed like good value for money even if I ended up footing the bill myself. And now that we had 'our arrangement', as Christie insisted on calling it, I'd allowed myself to imagine that there might be a genuine opportunity for me to get a modest commission from helping her to sell *Susanna & the Elders*, so I considered the bar bill as an astute investment.

By the time I returned with our drinks Liga had disappeared. Christie told me she was queuing up to get her boob signed by someone who looked suspiciously like RuPaul (although, to be frank, a lot of the club's clientele looked like RuPaul, and a significant proportion of the rest looked like Grayson Perry.) 'That means that you and I can have a good chat, Mr Viejo.'

The look in her eye suggested to me that this wasn't going to involve any anecdotes for my book.

'It occurs to me, young man, that we haven't discussed how all of this is going to work.'

I was confused. 'All of what?'

'Selling the painting. I mean, I can't just let you have it, can I?'

'Uh…I suppose not.'

Truth to tell, I hadn't given the details a huge amount of thought but, thinking about it, I realised that that's pretty much what I had assumed would happen: I would take the painting to London, sell it to Conny and then, after taking whatever she might agree to as my commission, I'd send the balance on to Christie. But all of a sudden, the flaws in this plan began to become blindingly apparent.

'You see, honey, I think this painting is worth, what? About $400,000? I mean, I know there's some issues around provenance, but I think it's still pretty good.'

'Absolutely. Four hundred grand isn't unreasonable.'

'But whatever we get for it, my point is, this is a highly

valuable painting. It's also the only thing I have that might keep me alive with a roof over my head. So, much as I like you, you've gotta understand I can't just let you walk out of my home with my painting under your arm without some kind of guarantee. I mean, you seem like a nice enough guy, but after barely twenty-four hours I can hardly be expected to trust you with something so valuable. I need to know that I'm not going to be left with nothing. Like I was before,' she added pointedly. 'So here's what I propose.'

She took a purposeful swig from her drink, took a deep breath in and pushed her chest out toward me.

'I don't want to be greedy. I gotta pay for my treatment and clear my debts. That's gonna take two hundred and fifty grand so that's what I want to make sure I get. But I recognise that you're taking a risk too, so anything you can get above that, you can keep.'

Given what I thought the painting was worth, I couldn't quite believe what I was hearing.

'Are you serious?' I asked.

Even if she'd agreed to a commission of ten or fifteen percent – which I had not anticipated at all – I was looking at being paid $40-60,000 at most. But if Conny really could be convinced to part with $400,000, then under Christie's proposal I could be walking away with a cool one hundred and fifty grand.

'Unless we get above $500,000. Then we split everything fifty-fifty.'

I laughed. 'That seems fair,' I said. It actually seemed absurdly generous of her, but also a touch naïve: no painting of Erik's had sold for more than $500,000 for years.

I thought that was an end to the matter, but then I noticed

her eyes drop from my face and become fixated with the cocktail in front of her. She slowly and deliberately began stirring her Martini with the olive skewer.

'But I need my money up front.' She stopped stirring and looked at me uncertainly, her breathing deepening. 'All of it.'

I'd sensed she'd been building up to a 'but', but her suggestion still took the wind out of me.

'What? You need me to give you $250,000 in cash? Just like that? Christie, I don't have that kind of money lying around.'

She was unmoved. 'Those are my terms,' she said, taking a sip of her drink and swallowing it with a nervous gulp. 'Take them or leave them.' Then, almost as an afterthought, she stuck her chin out defiantly.

I was frustrated. If she'd asked me to do this for her as a favour, I'd have done it. This wasn't wholly altruistic: after the disappointment of Jasper's rebuff, I'd allowed myself to see this deal as an opportunity to dabble in dealing without having to find a large cash sum up front.

But introducing money into our arrangement changed everything. Having dangled the prospect of a lucrative payday tantalisingly in front me, Christie had whipped it away again almost immediately through the imposition of a condition that I couldn't possibly meet. It was perhaps this that made me do something that I had never done before with Christie and would never do again: I snapped.

'Do you actually know anything about how real people have to live, Christie?'

I knew the moment I'd said it that it was a mistake. Her mouth clamped shut and her eyes widened in anger. She pushed her top lip out and I thought for a moment that she might be about to cry. But instead, after a moment's pause, she exploded.

'As a matter of fact, Mr Viejo, I do. I live in a two-bit trailer in a trashy trailer park where I'm just about the only person not outta my head on drugs or alcohol. This,' she said, waving her arm airily around the room to indicate the cornucopia of extravagance and glamour that surrounded her, 'isn't real. These aren't real people. Come back into Manhattan tomorrow and you'll see these people without their make-up, pushing patients around hospital wards, greeting visitors at reception desks, and serving you your coffee in Starbucks. This is just what they do in between times when they need to forget about their real lives.'

I was about to interject to apologise, but she wasn't finished. 'Oh, they *want* this to be real; they really do. But it sure-as-hell ain't any more real than that plastic dick they were threatening to shove up your ass half an hour ago.'

I opened my mouth again only to have it firmly shut by her raising of a single index finger. There was a pause while she gathered herself. She lowered her finger and leant forward, fixing me intently with those steely-blue eyes.

'You know what?' she said. 'I'm fed up with reality. I'm tired of having to live a real life. I want what I'm owed. I want my dues – and I want someone else to pay them for once.'

I was still trying to work out exactly what Christie meant by this, when she helpfully spelt it out for me, emphasising each point with her index finger on the table. 'Two hundred and fifty grand. In cash. Up front.'

'But Christie, look.' I brought up the banking app on my mobile phone. 'That's the balance on my current account. There's the balance on my savings. I've got a stocks and shares ISA that's tanking in value at the moment. I'm telling you

Christie, even if you add all of that together you don't get to anywhere near two hundred and fifty grand. My ex-wife took half of everything – even my pension.'

'Half of *everything*? Really?'

'She cleaned me out, I'm telling you.'

'Your grandpa was Joaquín Viejo, and let me tell you, I can't believe a man with that much money left his family penniless. So don't tell me you haven't got the money. What about that money you were going to pay your friend with?'

This was not something that I wanted to discuss.

'If you want this deal,' she continued, 'if you *really* want it, you can make it happen. You know you can.'

She leant back and dispatched the rest of her drink in a single slug.

'I think there's still time for you to get me another. I'll have a Margarita this time, thank you very much. As cold and dry as your ex-wife's heart.'

And with that she planted her empty glass down in front of me, like a full stop at the end of a sentence. Negotiations, such as they were, had been concluded.

I wanted to argue back, but the fact was that Christie had touched on a sensitive issue: the money I'd inherited from the sale of Grandpa Jo's Bacon sketch.

My basic premise was, and always had been, to keep it safe and use it to buy into Jasper's gallery. The pathway to that dream appeared to have been crushed. Now, however, Christie's demand had suggested a way in which it could potentially be revived.

If I could get Christie to compromise on the amount she was demanding up front, and if we could get Conny to pay $400,000 for *Susanna & the Elders,* then I would add $150,000 to my capital virtually overnight. This was the kind of level at which Jasper's dad might start to think about offering me a share of the gallery, and my aspiration to actually make some money out of art (rather than simply writing about how much money everyone else was making out of art) would start to become plausible.

But I didn't want to risk the full $200,000 I had at my disposal. I figured that if Christie got everything she needed up front she had no incentive to make sure the deal happened. She could just take the money and make her exit, leaving me holding a painting for which I almost certainly wouldn't be able to find another buyer if Conny wasn't interested.

Yet the hard facts were that Conny was the most obvious purchaser of the painting and, if he really did need to launder some dirty cash quickly, as everyone seemed to suppose, then there was every reason to believe he wouldn't balk at our asking price. So using at least some of my inheritance money to give me a stake in the deal – and to make sure that it actually happened – could be seen as a wise investment rather than as an act of charity to Christie. This was the kind of 'mindset shift' that Grandpa Jo always said a good dealer needed to make.

It was a mad plan, even in that moment I understood that, but as I returned from my trip to the bar with a couple of margaritas inside of me and two more in my hands, I managed to convince myself that it might just work.

'OK, Christie,' I said, retaking my seat and handing over her drink. 'I said I would help you and I will. But I don't have two hundred and fifty grand to give you – and even if I did, I wouldn't, because I think that leaves too much of the risk with me. So here's what I propose: I'll give you half what you want up front – one hundred and twenty-five grand. That shares the risk between us. But we split the proceeds straight down the middle.'

'But if we sell the painting for $400,000 – which is what we think we can get – I'll only get two hundred grand. That's not enough. I need my two fifty.'

'OK. How about if you take the first hundred and twenty-five thousand of any sale price? That way, with the money I give you, you'll have all the money you need. But I get the next two fifty. We can split anything else fifty-fifty?'

She thought about this for a moment. 'That'll work. As long as you pay for me to accompany you and the painting to London. I can't let you wander off with my painting when I'm still a hundred and twenty-five grand short. Deal?' She reached her hand across the table.

This was not quite as lucrative an arrangement for me as it had appeared to be ten minutes previously, but I was still looking at adding over a hundred grand to my money for a couple of days of work.

'Deal,' I said, inserting my hand in hers and shaking.

'Great!' said Christie. 'You won't regret this, I promise you.'

She actually said that. I mean, obviously she didn't know then exactly how things were going to work out – how could she? – but she knew enough.

# EIGHT

When I got back to my hotel room a couple of hours later, I logged on to the Argentinian bank account Grandpa Jo had set up for me and saw that I was actually slightly better off than I'd anticipated. Interest and investment gains had added nearly $10,000 to my initial sum in the time since the money had been deposited. I made the mistake of mentioning this to Christie over the phone the following morning.

'Great! That means you'll have no problem paying for me to come over!' she said.

I laughed. 'I should hope not, Christie – even at short notice I think I can pick up a return flight for you for less than two grand.'

There was a pause at the other end of the line before she replied, with utter seriousness, 'Young man, I *never* fly coach.'

Given what she'd told me about her finances this seemed, at best, debatable – and certainly a wholly unnecessary extravagance in the context of our arrangement. But it soon became clear that this wasn't really about our arrangement; it was about something else entirely. Before that fateful interview in 1987, first-class flights to the Biennale or a weekend by Lake Morenito were an integral part of her life with Erik. It wasn't extravagant, it was just how one lived if one was the muse of one of the world's most popular artists. To Christie, it wasn't those twelve years that she was with Erik that were the anomaly, it was the other fifty-five years of her life when she had been forced to live like everyone else.

I eventually managed to get her to compromise: she would fly business rather than first class, and would take a suite at the Dorchester for two nights rather than a penthouse for three. But this still left me nursing a bill of over $7,000. Transit and packaging costs to have the painting safely despatched to London took up more than $2,500. By the time I'd settled Christie's bar bill I was pretty convinced I'd be flat broke. But, heading back to her trailer with my laptop under my arm, I was not deflated. Because it was clear that if this deal came off then I could reasonably expect my $135,000 investment to be more than doubled.

As I arrived at Hope Falls, a burst of late summer sun seemed to have bleached out the full extent of its awfulness, perhaps assisted by my own distraction. The clouds had been torn apart to reveal a deep blue sky, and sunshine spilt out over everything, including Christie. She wore the sunlight in her hair, igniting a halo of light around her. As before, it was as though the previous night was but a distant memory. Even in the trailer she somehow looked golden, her skin shining under a loose-fitting summer dress that couldn't quite contain her lustre. Fingers of light flicked across her as she hurriedly cleared a space for my laptop on her breakfast bar, until even the blonde hairs on her arm seemed to sparkle. She took a swig of her grapefruit juice, looked up at me and smiled a smile that was as bright and sunny as the weather outside. She was pure class; there was no doubt about it. It was something I always admired about her – the fact that, no matter what life threw at her, she could rise above her circumstances like an eagle and just glow.

'Well, of course, young man,' she replied when I mentioned this to her. 'Attitude is the one thing in your life you *can* control.'

I couldn't help but wonder how she did it, although it did occur to me that it might be something to do with the \$125,000 she was about to have transferred into her bank account.

'You can set everything up here,' she said, briskly moving the last of the coffee mugs into the sink. 'I'll just go and get Liga.'

'Liga?' This is not what I had expected. Liga had not been party to any of the discussions about our arrangement, and suddenly introducing her into the equation now caught me off guard.

'Yes, Liga. I want her here. To witness stuff.' She caught the look in my eye. 'Is there a problem?'

'No, no, of course not... It's just that...'

'What? It's Liga for Chrissake – not my lawyer!'

'I get that. It's just that...well, I wasn't expecting it.'

She paused for a moment to gather herself. 'Look. I just want someone to witness what we're doing here. You're transferring the first part of the money and I'm giving you the painting. I think someone needs to see that, just in case...' She left the sentence dangling, unwilling, it seemed, to make her point explicitly.

'Just in case what?'

She sighed. 'Just in case one of us attempts to suggest later on that either of those things didn't happen.'

I was incensed. 'You think I'm trying defraud you? You think I'd take this painting and then try and deny that I owe you any more money?'

'I didn't say that!'

'Oh I think you did!'

'Look, this is to protect *both* of us. If I try and deny that I ever received the money from you, you'll have a neutral witness who'll be able to back you up.'

'Liga? A neutral witness? Are you kidding me?'

'I'm sorry, but she's the best I can do at short notice. If you've got someone better to suggest, then I'm happy to go with them. But I was kinda guessing that we didn't really want some random person knowing what we're trying to pull here.'

'What the fuck?' said a voice from behind the bedroom door, and then Liga's tousled head emerged. 'I was sleeping in there.'

She walked on into the kitchen area. If there was any doubt in my mind as to whether the burning candle which Christie had insisted Liga held for me was still alight, it was dismissed there and then. In contrast to the previous evenings, she entered now without make-up and in an oversized T-shirt and a pair of briefs. Yet she viewed my presence in the room as no more deserving of self-consciousness than if I was her older brother. In complete contrast to the sophisticated young woman whose stylishness had been so carefully curated the previous evening, that lunchtime she gave her appearance not a second thought. It seemed, from how she looked at least, that the revelry which I had abandoned at midnight had continued, and perhaps even intensified, for some time afterwards.

'I'm sorry we woke you up, honey. But that thing we talked about on the way home last night? Well, I need you to do it now.'

'What? That was for real? I thought you were joking.'

'Wait a minute,' I interjected. 'You've told her about all of this? She knows?'

'Of course! I could hardly ask her to come back and spend the night with me here if I wasn't going to explain why. The poor girl would think I was a lesbian or something.'

I decided to bite my tongue and let this last comment slide. I was trying to fight a battle on a very specific point and the last thing I needed to do was open up another flank.

'Aren't you worried?' I asked.

'That people might think I'm a lesbian? Listen honey, when you've been single in New York for as long as I have, being asked if you're straight or gay is a bit like someone stranded in the Gobi Desert being asked if they'd prefer still or sparkling water.'

'No, I meant about Liga knowing.'

'I am here, you know. I can hear you,' Liga interjected.

'She knows. It's too late to worry about it. And besides, I trust her.' She paused for a moment and then, sensing the rejoinder I was about to make, added, 'And you can trust her too.'

We argued round the whole thing for a few minutes more, but I knew that I'd lost. Christie was right: whatever we decided, Liga knew now anyway, so we couldn't put that particular genie back in its bottle. The only option was to try and make the best of it.

I logged into my bank account on the laptop and then got Christie to go and fetch *Susanna & the Elders* from the bedroom.

'OK. So are we all good to go?' I asked, after she had returned with the painting.

'There's just one thing,' said Liga, stifling a yawn. I couldn't quite stop a sigh coming out. 'What if it isn't genuine?'

'What?' Her question floored me.

'What if it's a fake?'

Christie became flustered. 'Liga! It's not a fake. I've had this painting since Erik painted it – Hell, I *watched* him paint it!'

'So you say. But Gabriel doesn't know that for sure. He only has your word.'

Christie was indignant. 'I thought you were supposed to be on my side!'

'Actually, *I* thought she was supposed to be impartial,' I said.

'Indeed. I am being impartial.'

Liga had made a good point – one that I should have considered myself. The fact that Christie had seen Erik paint it with her own eyes would count for nothing if other people didn't believe that this was true. But, for understandable legal reasons, Christie had to be circumspect about the precise details of the picture's history, so she couldn't rely on that to prove that this was genuinely one of Erik's paintings. Ironically, the one thing that would help to establish its bona fides as a genuine Von Holunder was also the one thing that would make it worthless to Christie.

Liga's suggestion sent Christie into a meltdown. 'Are you suggesting that I'm trying to con this young man? Look at it,' Christie exploded. 'It's incredible! It's an incredible work of art. Look at the brushwork. Look at the way he's captured my face. It's more touching, more moving than any of his other paintings.'

'That's my point. If it really is so much better than his other works then won't that make people suspicious?'

This was an astute observation and it caused me to revisit my assessment of Liga. What I had not factored into my considerations was the irony of the fact that *Susanna & the Elders* looking like a better painting than any of Erik's other works might actually count against it. An unauthenticated work – even one with the undoubted power and beauty of *Susanna & the Elders* – was worth less than a mediocre but authenticated piece by one of the greats.

'OK, everyone. Let's just calm down here,' I said, as much to myself as to Christie and Liga.

We all sat down and calmly chatted: Liga asked questions about how the art market worked, which Christie and I tried to answer to her satisfaction. She was a surprisingly forensic inquisitor, and I found myself regretting the tray of Tequila slammers I'd ordered before leaving the previous evening.

I tried to explain to her that, in the world of art dealers, questions of attribution ultimately boil down to three sources of verification: the paperwork, testimony from friends or relatives, and the collective view of experts. In an ideal world the painting would have been registered and would have an uninterrupted history of bills of sale. If you had that, then you didn't need the other two.

But there were lots of reasons why that might not always be possible. The Bacon sketch that my grandfather had left me was a case in point. The subject of the sketch was Muriel Belcher, owner of the private drinking club, The Colony Room, where Bacon was a member. Belcher, who rarely left her seat at the Colony Room's bar, was an occasional model for Bacon. So it was natural that, after a disastrous night at the tables with Jeffrey Bernard and Daniel Farson, Bacon had hurriedly sketched Belcher to settle his debt to Farson.

Grandpa Jo managed to procure the drawing from Farson years later. Belcher was dead by then, but Grandpa spoke to Bernard, who wrote a brief note confirming that he believed Grandpa Jo's sketch was the one he'd seen Bacon draw and then give to Farson that night at The Colony Room. Grandpa also got Martin Harrison, (the pre-eminent authority on Bacon and editor of his *catalogue raisonné*) to confirm that the style and subject matter of the sketch bore all the hallmarks of an authentic work by Bacon. So the question of whether it actually was a genuine Bacon or not ceased to be relevant: people *believed* it to be a genuine Bacon and that was sufficient for it to be valued accordingly. The fact that he'd been half-cut when he'd drawn it, and that it wasn't actually particularly good, was only relevant to the extent that it made it a less valuable Bacon. But a less valuable Bacon was still worth more than even a brilliantly drafted sketch by Belcher herself.

The point I wanted to make to Liga was that the lack of a bill of sale needn't be an insuperable problem if you had reliable testimony from contemporary sources and recognised experts. Fortunately, in our situation, Christie had seen Erik paint *Susanna & the Elders* and there was photographic proof that Conny had seen it in Erik's studio. Both could reasonably claim, therefore, to know whether this was the same painting or not. There was a great story to back up their assertion, but in order to be convinced that this really was a genuine Von Holunder, an auction house or buyer would ideally want the world's pre-eminent authority on the artist to pronounce definitively on the subject, just as Grandpa Jo had got Martin

Harrison to pronounce definitively on the authenticity of the Bacon sketch. And, by happy coincidence, the world's foremost authority on the work of Erik von Holunder – his official biographer and associate editor of his *catalogue raisonné*, no less – was none other than me.

I therefore spent the next half hour drafting a brief report detailing the painting's known history and my study of it, and why I believed – based on the subject matter, style and painting technique – it was a genuine Von Holunder, and not just any Von Holunder, but the great 'lost' Von Holunder whose existence had long been mooted.

Christie provided her own statement confirming that this painting was the one that she had seen Erik paint, so there was no reason for Conny to doubt its authenticity, even if he couldn't remember seeing the original. She then added a sentence saying that she recalled Erik discussing giving the painting to Conny rather than throwing it away, as he had planned to do. Alongside the photo from Christie, Conny would have enough evidence to strongly suggest: first, that the painting was a genuine Von Holunder; and second, that it had come into his possession entirely lawfully, well before Erik had died.

'So there's really no need for you to be suspicious, Liga,' I reassured her.

'If you say so,' she said. But there was a different timbre in her voice now. The eagerness to please had gone and I found myself surprised at how much that unsettled me.

It was fairly simple to set up the payment from there, and Liga was soon able to confirm that the money had arrived in Christie's account.

'Great! Well I had better get packing!' Christie said. And

with that, she flounced out of the living area and into her bedroom.

Liga needed more coffee and headed toward the percolator where a large pot was still on the go. Her eyes flicked towards the bedroom door as though checking that Christie was going to remain out of earshot. Then she turned and stared at me for a moment, not in any way romantically, but as though there was an answer inside me that she needed to extract.

'Do you believe her?' she asked. There was a coyness in her voice which hinted at a concern that I might not.

'Of course I do.'

Her shoulders seemed to relax at the confirmation. 'That's good,' she said. 'And this money you're paying her with – is it really money you've been hiding offshore?'

There was a horrible moment when it seemed clear to me that I had not been as sober as I'd thought the previous night, because I didn't remember going into quite that level of detail about my finances. But nevertheless, I was determined that, even if indiscretion had got the better of me the previous night, Liga should get her facts straight.

'I don't think "hiding" is the right word,' I said. 'It's my money. It was left to me by my grandfather. There's no reason why anyone else needs to know about it.'

'Because if they did, they might try and claim that it was theirs?'

I wasn't sure where she was heading with this line of questioning, but it made me uncomfortable. 'We seem to live in a culture where everyone assumes that if you're given something, rather than having worked for it, then you've somehow gained it unfairly and you should be forced to share it with them. And sadly, sometimes the law takes their side, even if they've done nothing to earn it either.'

'So you just want to prevent someone from being tempted to think they might be entitled to a share of your money?'

'Exactly.'

'Because you can't be sure that the courts would agree with you.'

'Sadly not. Like Christie and this painting: what's legal and what's right are not always the same thing.'

She seemed reassured by this. 'That's OK then. I just wanted to check.'

Then she gave me the most peculiar smile. It seemed intended to be friendly, but some other emotion was hijacking it, warping it into something altogether different, something almost pitying. It was the last time I saw Liga, but that smile has haunted me ever since.

# NINE

I left Christie in Hope Falls and returned to Manhattan to make arrangements for our trip. Because of Conny's profile and new-found diplomatic status, the English news websites were counting down to the day of his extradition flight. From this we learnt that his plane was due to leave the runway at Heathrow in less than four days. This should have been plenty of time for us to get over to London and execute our plan, but inevitably there were problems. Given what was at stake for Christie, we needed to make absolutely sure that *Susanna & the Elders* got to London safely, and the only way to do that was to have the painting professionally packaged and dispatched. Despite phoning round every company I could think of to get that done as quickly as possible, no one was prepared to commit to having *Susanna & the Elders* in London before midday the day after next. It seemed unrealistic to expect Conny to agree to buy a painting that he hadn't seen, and which we couldn't prove Christie owned, so the sobering reality was that by the time we had the painting to show Conny we'd have less than forty-eight hours left in which to conclude the deal. This felt like a nerve-shreddingly tight timescale, but an afternoon of phone calls and internet searches confirmed that there was nothing we could do to give ourselves more time.

I couldn't get Christie a seat in business class until the end of the following day anyway, so she suggested I put my flight back so we could travel together. I found myself not wanting to leave her company, so enthusiastically agreed. As I was committed to another night in New York I took the liberty of upgrading myself to the Ritz-Carlton, as the cheap place my publisher had booked me in didn't have any availability beyond my original check-out date. These were both additional expenses that put yet more pressure on my credit card, but Christie had convinced me – or maybe I'd convinced myself; I forget – that the deal with Conny was going to leave me with a healthy profit, so I felt entitled to the extravagance. Somehow the Best Western felt beneath me now.

Having done all that and then raced over to the Hanover Square Gallery to have them professionally package and dispatch the painting, I was exhausted. Yet as the afternoon tired and the shadows of the day began to lengthen, I felt I'd done enough to escape for an early evening visit to MoMA, to which I was able to stroll from the Ritz-Carlton under a spectacular bloodied sunset.

As Christie had predicted, the Gauguins were still on display, although now with what I took to be a brief note of apology. Much to my relief I managed to get round the new galleries without coming across Casey or her imperious boss, but decided not to risk staying for dinner at The Modern.

Instead, I walked round the corner to Le Bernardin – another extravagance that edged me ever nearer to my credit limit – and took a table in their Lounge restaurant.

Single male diners were not quite Le Bernardin's target demographic, and it was as busy as its reputation suggested it would be. Thus, even though I'd got the staff at the Ritz-Carlton to book ahead, I was stuck on a table in a dark corner at the back of the Lounge. Christie and I had agreed to meet at the airport the next day and had made no plans to meet again before then. A few minutes later however, I was staring in agony at the menu, trying to choose between Le Bernardin's signature salmon rillette and the seafood causa, when I became aware of an altercation by the front desk that was starting to escalate. I tried to pay it no heed, but suddenly found myself jolted into a mild panic when I heard an instantly recognisable voice explode above the restaurant's gentle hubbub.

'Nothing available? Are you kidding me? I will have you know, young man, that I was personally invited to the opening of this restaurant by Gilbert le Coze himself! Go and ask him if you don't believe me.'

As Le Bernardin had moved from Paris to New York in 1986, and was just a mile from the Dakota, Christie's claim was entirely plausible. Given that Gilbert le Coze had died in 1994 however, her suggestion to the maître d' was not, but I decided it was probably best that I intervene before the hapless man made the mistake of pointing this out. So I reluctantly rose from my table and called out self-consciously across the restaurant floor.

'It's OK, garçon, she's with me.'

The maître d' turned and looked at me with what I took to be withering pity. I could tell he didn't really want to let Christie in at all, but now that she was officially the guest of one of the diners whom they clearly *could* accommodate, declining her entrance risked creating two irate customers rather than one. He therefore showed her to my table and deposited her there with a look which said in no uncertain terms, *She's your responsibility now.*

'Well, fancy meeting you here,' she said, apparently as surprised as I was.

Despite the glorious weather it was still autumn, and Christie was protected from the chill by a bright red trench coat that I took to be a new addition to her wardrobe. Several other bags suggested that this had not been a singular purchase.

'Been shopping today by any chance?' I asked.

'Well of course I have! I've been living in stuff from Walmart and the goodwill store for the past thirty years. I think I can treat myself to an afternoon at Bergdorf Goodman's now that I can finally afford it again.' She struck a coquettish pose. 'It's Vivienne Westwood. Do you like it?'

The truth was, I did – and not just the coat. She'd had her hair done too, so that it now shone a lustrous gold. And her make-up was a work of art in itself, subtle, yet clearly precision-engineered by a professional to make her face glow. It took ten years off her.

'You look great,' I said weakly, as my heart ached with the pain of all the things I found myself wanting to say – but knew I couldn't.

'If you think this looks good, just wait till you see what I've got on underneath,' she said, widening her eyes enticingly. With that she suddenly and theatrically flipped the top half of the coat back over her shoulders before letting it slide slowly off her arms and onto the chair behind her.

What she revealed took my breath away. She was wearing a strikingly dramatic strapless gown, comprising two red panels with black lace detailing, which joined together under her bust before pulling apart as they fell to floor. In the gap that was left, a single panel in black lace hung down between her legs. The three panels were held together by a translucent lace skirt which made her waxed and bronzed legs shimmer like golden sand in the early morning sun.

She should have looked ridiculous. In fact, she *did* look ridiculous – if you judged her outfit solely by the scathing looks it received from the female diners present. If, however, you looked past these and focused instead on the reactions of their male companions… Well, let's just say that Christie's sartorial choices could be judged rather more favourably.

'What d'ya think? It's a Reem Acra. Halle Berry wore the same thing to the NAACP Awards, and she's got fifteen years on me,' she said proudly. 'Although obviously, they've had to let the bust out a little on mine,' she added with a self-satisfied smile.

I didn't know how to respond. I was speechless – with shock, with admiration, and with a few other emotions I didn't want to explore too deeply.

Or rather, I *should* have been speechless. Instead, I found myself involuntarily blurting out in astonishment, 'Fuck me, Christie!'

'Was that an exclamation or a request, honey?' she replied without missing a beat. I was embarrassed to admit it, even to myself, but actually, her question prompted in me the realisation that it was both. My body was now telling me in ways that my mind had been reluctant to let me acknowledge, that my attraction to Christie was not motivated purely by an academic and professional interest in her and her story.

I think she might have sensed that because I could see her mouth give the tiniest upturn at the corners.

We took our seats and ordered the second most expensive wine on the wine list ('Hell, we ought to show at least *some* restraint!'). I was happy that Christie was there, but there was something else in the back of my mind troubling me and I couldn't stop that thought from showing itself on my face.

'Look, I know what you're thinking,' she said, after a slowly expanding pause developed in our conversation, 'and it's OK. The first thing I did after you left was go straight to the park administrator and pay off my rent. I even got myself six months ahead, so don't worry. I'm not a total dufus.'

My look clearly betrayed that I wasn't convinced.

'It's one afternoon of shopping, a makeover, and a nice meal. Oh, and a suite at the Four Seasons for the night,' she added as an afterthought. 'Plus a Louis Vuitton luggage set for the trip tomorrow. But I've not spent more than ten or twelve grand on all of it, I promise you.' She quickly did the maths in her head. 'Probably.'

'But what about your treatment, Christie? This money that I'm giving you was supposed to be for your treatment – your *life-saving* treatment. Remember that?'

'The money that you're giving me is an investment that's going to make us both a healthy profit. As long as you get your cut, what I do with my share is my business.'

She said this in a manner which suggested that, as far as she was concerned, the discussion was over.

Maybe the look on my face betrayed a sense of suspicion, although I honestly don't recall feeling that at the time. But whatever it was, her lips pursed in a way that seemed to indicate some anxiety on her part. Then she blurted out: 'Look, I spoke to my oncologist yesterday. He's in Florida Keys for another week, but we've agreed a price and I've even paid him for the first round of chemo. How organised is that?'

'OK, I admit it. That's pretty organised. Well done... But you're going to need more than that, presumably. Are you sure you're going to have enough left to pay for all the other rounds?'

'As long as you get me my two-fifty, it'll be fine,' she replied. 'I'll have more than enough for the operation and the other three rounds.' Then she leant forward and looked at me pleadingly. 'So just let me blow off a bit of steam for once. I haven't been able to live like this for years. I just want to taste that life again – just for a couple of weeks until my treatment starts. Then I'll go back to being a good girl, I promise.' And she drew a large cross, theatrically over her heart.

Much to my surprise, she ordered a salad. It seemed an odd choice when you were dining at one of New York's finest restaurants.

'The world is pretty unforgiving of women who let themselves go,' she explained when I raised this with her. 'I like food, I like drink; of course I do. And let's just say I had a lot of fun in my twenties and thirties. But there comes a point, generally around forty, when you realise that fun is like life insurance: the older you get, the more it costs you, so you need to start thinking about whether you're prepared to pay the price. I decided I wasn't.'

I had assumed that her figure was some kind of biological anomaly, but actually, that night I saw that it was the product of hard work and a degree of self-denial. While she was always surrounded by alcohol, her own drinking only took place at certain times and in prescribed quantities; food was eaten only at mealtimes and in moderation. Her bacchanalian instincts were moderated by some markedly puritanical tendencies.

In contrast I became very aware of my stomach straining against the waistband of my trousers in a way that it hadn't been when I was sitting in the departure lounge at Heathrow just a few days previously. My fortieth birthday, a little more than fifteen months away, had never loomed larger.

'I need to lose some weight,' I said.

'Yes, but you're interesting and intelligent and know a lot about art, so I'm sure there are plenty of women who'll be prepared to make allowances.'

I didn't experience this as the compliment she clearly intended it to be.

'And anyway, honey, it's different for guys.'

'Is it? How?

'Men don't judge each other by how they look. They judge women by how we look – and, sure, it'd be easier if they didn't – but women are exactly the same, so we can hardly blame it all on you. And besides, we sure as hell don't judge guys by how they look. So you eat up, honey; we're not bothered about a bit of puppy fat on a guy. We expect it.'

She resumed eating her salad as though the point had been clarified sufficiently, and I couldn't think of anything to say in response, so I finished the food on my plate. I joined Christie however, in declining the offer of dessert. I also made a mental note to hit the gym when I arrived back in London.

The rest of the dinner was a blur, although largely because the waiter insisted on topping up my wine glass without prompting, so that I was soon too incapacitated to stop Christie from ordering even more. But only for me. After a single glass of Domaine aux Moines Savennières, she stuck to sparkling water and appeared to have no difficulty in deflecting the waiter from her wine glass.

It was at this point that she began to ask me about Grandpa Jo: how long he'd kept working; how the business had been going; when he'd died, and whether he'd left much of the wealth that she remembered him having for the family. I was pleasantly drunk so answered the questions as honestly as I could. I thought it might stand me in good stead with her. She pushed me a bit further than I was comfortable with on the matter of my own inheritance from him, but I deflected those questions and she didn't press me further.

When I attempted to stand at the end of the evening I realised to my horror that I'd polished off the best part of two bottles of wine. Even the short walk along Sixth Avenue back to the Ritz-Carlton felt beyond me and I was bundled into a cab by the maître d' to get me home. I don't think I entirely imagined the look that he gave me as he did so, which I interpreted as saying *I told you so* pretty unsympathetically.

As I walked through the hotel foyer, I was still trying to process my unexpected feelings towards Christie when one of the receptionists called out to me.

'Excuse me, Mr Viejo!' I stopped and turned to look at him while focusing all my efforts on remaining upright. 'Did the lady catch up with you?'

'I'm sorry?'

'The lady – an older lady – she didn't leave her name. She came by just after you'd left, asking if you were in. I hope you don't mind sir, but I took the liberty of telling her that we'd booked a table for you at Le Bernardin. We're not really supposed to, but she seemed to know you very well. She was pretty insistent too,' he said by way of justification, before adding, with a blush, 'and quite…persuasive.'

He was a young man, no more than twenty-one, at a guess. He looked bright and eager to please, which are great qualities for a hotel receptionist. But at the same time – and I felt cruel, even as I reached this judgement in my mind – he also looked untutored in the ways of the world. Which is not a fault in itself, particularly in one so young, but it occurred to me that it could be perceived as a weakness when having to deal with Christie. And it would no doubt have been one that she would have been happy to exploit.

I remember feeling, for the briefest of moments, a slight sense of superiority; as though I was older and wiser and thereby somehow impervious to such manipulation. But then I remembered the size of the bill from Le Bernardin and realised that I had agreed – no, I had *insisted* – on paying all of it.

'Oh, she's persuasive, alright,' I said, ruefully, as I stumbled off towards the lift to try and sleep off the inevitable hangover.

# TEN

The following day was one of those glorious, end-of-summer days in which the oaks, elms, sugar maples and flowering dogwoods of Central Park all conspired to daub the view from my hotel window with a rolling sea of ochres, golds and deep reds like a vast pointillist masterpiece. The autumnal murk that had greeted my arrival at Hope Falls only a few days previously now felt like something from another, less hopeful age. I wanted to spend the morning in bed recovering, but by eleven I could resist the view no more and convinced myself that a bracing walk through the splendours of Central Park might serve me better than the endless supply of espressos on offer from my room's coffee machine. And so it proved.

As our hotels were so close together, I sent Christie a text suggesting that we revisit our previous arrangement and share a ride to JFK. By the time her cab arrived to pick me up after lunch, just the thought of seeing her again left me feeling brighter. Christie offered to pay (although I felt it would look more courteous of me to insist we go Dutch). Predictably she had significantly over-packed, with her two over-sized Louis Vuitton suitcases, matching vanity case, and generous keep-all *bandoulière* taking up the whole of the boot. The result was that my single weekender bag and small backpack had to sit, precariously, between me and Christie on the back seat.

She was as excited as a six year-old on her first school trip, and was clearly determined to make the journey as much a part of the whole experience as the time spent in London itself.

'Are you looking forward to getting back to London?' she asked.

To be honest, I hadn't really thought about it. I was still trying to log into an app on my smartphone that I had been promised would enable me to track *Susanna & the Elders'* whereabouts. Rather like when I went out and forgot to take my phone with me, I felt a strange vulnerability, almost a nakedness, not having the painting to hand. While I had no reason to doubt the fastidiousness of the Hanover Square Gallery's team, I couldn't help reminding myself how much was riding on the safe transit of *Susanna & the Elders,* and being acutely conscious of how far it was all out of my hands.

'I can't wait to see it,' she said. 'I've never been there before. Can you believe that?'

'All that time with Erik and he never took you there?'

Her eyes betrayed something that looked like regret. 'No, never... It was just the way it had to be. There were people there he couldn't risk me meeting.'

Like the English weather, the mood had changed quickly and I didn't know how to respond. Christie eventually filled the void that had grown between us with a question.

'Don't you ever worry about your paths crossing again? With your ex-wife, I mean. After everything that's gone between you, have you thought about how you'd react if you bumped into her?'

'London's a city of nine million people. I think the likelihood of us bumping into each other again by accident is pretty small.'

'Yeah, but you're both art people. There is a chance.'

I balked at the suggestion. 'We are not both art people. I am an art person. Suzy's just someone who would like to be an art person.'

'But you know what I'm saying. You move in the same circles.'

'We certainly don't. The only reason Suzy got anywhere near the same circles as me was because she was with me. She was from a council estate in Birmingham. Her mum was a nurse and her dad – well, the less said about him the better. But suffice to say neither of them knew anything about art.'

'Yeah, but they aren't Suzy. She's her own person. I don't get your point.'

'My point is she had absolutely no art-world connections of her own. Every door she walked through in the art world, I opened for her.'

Christie lifted her chin up and furrowed her brow as though ruminating on something. 'Oh, kinda like me and Erik then.'

'No, no, not like you and Erik at all. I mean you and Erik met at an opening. When I met Suzy, she was cleaning hotel rooms part-time to fund her degree.'

Christie left a brief pause.

'When I met Erik, I was serving him his canapés.' She left another pause as I felt the colour rise in my cheeks. 'When you've got no connections, you rely on other people to open the doors for you. I didn't know anyone when I came to New York. I knew I had to meet some people if I was going to get anywhere. I saw the posters for his show and assumed they'd be looking for waiting staff. I worked that night for two bucks an hour to make sure that I got the gig. Had to buy myself a blouse and skirt, so it ended up costing me money to work.'

She looked at me directly. 'You do what you have to do. Don't ever blame someone for that just because you don't have to do what they do.'

I considered myself duly chastened. I wanted to argue back though; to point out that Suzy and Christie were different people from different generations, whose opportunities and life choices had also been completely different. But the truth was, I was tired trying to justify myself to people who didn't know us. To people who did know us, to the people who were there at the Courtauld when we got together, the truth was obvious. Suzy might not have acknowledged it at the outset – to be honest, I think we both deceived ourselves about the dynamic that was going on – but I think she came to realise it as time wore on.

And if she'd been honest enough to say 'I genuinely thought that I loved you, but actually I've come to see that what I really loved was what I thought you represented for me,' then I could have accepted it. We were both human beings who got swept up in something that felt good and we both ignored all the warning signs. It happens to the best of us (and Suzy and I were far from that).

What I couldn't accept however, was the anger she directed at me, as though somehow I had betrayed her. The reality was, I had shared my life and my connections with Suzy completely openly. If she didn't end up where she wanted to be, if people didn't warm to her as she would have liked, or welcome her into the art world with the open arms she expected, then that was not my doing. I did my bit – and more. The rest was down to her, just as Grandpa Jo's connections could only get me so far and the rest was down to me. That's how it had to be.

But looking at Christie's face, it didn't appear as though she would be receptive to these observations so I decided to keep my own counsel, and contented myself with the knowledge that my friends and I knew the truth.

Christie was not quite finished with the subject, however.

'Do you even know what happened to her? After the two of you split up.'

'The last I'd heard she was freelancing as an occasional gallery assistant for Alison Jacques.'

'Really? That was the last you heard.' For some reason Christie didn't seem to believe me.

'Well, that was the last I heard for definite. On her D81 declaration she claimed she was back working in the hotels, but you're never entirely sure how honestly people fill these things in.'

'Oh, aren't you?' Christie replied with a roll of her eyes.

I felt myself blush and decided it was best to drop the subject.

We arrived at JFK with three hours to spare. The first hour was spent with Christie arguing with an unfortunate check-in assistant about an upgrade to business class for me. Clearly well-trained in spotting an opportunist, the young woman started off gently deflecting Christie's demands, but Christie held her ground and the poor woman eventually had to call her supervisor over. The difference in price between a $500 ticket and a $5,000 ticket was sufficient for me to be embarrassed by Christie's efforts on my behalf, and in an attempt to disassociate myself from them I found I was backing away from the check-in incrementally as Christie's volume increased. By the time the supervisor came over I was fully thirty feet away and hopeful that no one would link me with the unfolding drama.

I couldn't hear the details of the argument, and to be honest I didn't really want to, but even from a distance I could tell that it wasn't going well. I noticed two security guards on routine patrol stop and make eye contact with the supervisor, then gradually move into positions from which they could swiftly intervene if necessary.

But then, from the heart of the small crowd that had built up behind Christie, I heard a young woman's voice rise above the hubbub and ask the question, 'Hey! Is that the lady from that show on CBS?'

No answer was given to this that I could hear, and I'm not even sure if Christie heard it, but at once the conversation at the counter began to change. Rather than trying to remain polite but uncooperative, the supervisor suddenly appeared apologetic. I was too far away by now to hear exactly what was being said, but this distance also gave me a different perspective on Christie to the one I'd gained at our first meeting.

Then her outfit had been contemporary but functional, and she had been surrounded by many of the hallmarks of urban poverty. Today she was wearing a tailored, white trouser suit with tie-neck plunge blouse ('Stella McCartney, if you must know' as she'd told me in the cab). Despite being inside, she insisted on still wearing her newly bought Alain Mikli sunglasses ('encrusted with 270 Swarovski crystals. Can you believe it?'). With the matching Louis Vuitton luggage set she looked like an admittedly-aging-but-nevertheless-stellar Hollywood star entirely used to getting her own way. In a city built on dreams of fame, celebrity was the one thing that always had currency. So it didn't matter that the two women didn't recognise Christie; what mattered was that Christie gave the impression that they *ought* to have recognised her. This gave her a strange power over them. They seemed to want to help her now, in the hope that some of Christie's stardust might rub off on them.

Two minutes later Christie walked over from the desk toward me and slapped my reprinted ticket against my chest. 'Well, isn't this your lucky day? You'd better put on a tie, young man – you're in business with me.' And she gave me a broad smile.

Even behind those impenetrable shades I could see something on Christie's face that I'd not seen up until that point: a look of real accomplishment. She was back in the game.

# PART 2

## SATURN DEVOURING HIS YOUNG

OCTOBER 2019,
HOLBORN, LONDON

*Love is an irresistible desire
to be irresistibly desired*
**Robert Frost**

# ELEVEN

We flew overnight and arrived back in London early in the morning. I had meant to start exercising some kind of financial discipline from the moment we touched down, but the idea of fighting for the privilege of spending an hour on a tube back to my flat in Wood Green was more than I could stomach, and I paid £55 for an Uber instead.

The London that welcomed me back was different to the one I had left. It had surrendered itself to the autumn in a way that New York seemed reluctant to do. A gun-metal sky hung over the whole place like a dire warning. It sucked the colour out of everything and made the city far less impressive than I remembered, although it occurred to me that this might have been because I was experiencing it again for the first time since meeting Christie. Compared to her full-blooded colour, London seemed like a sepia photograph, and I couldn't help but wonder what she was making of it.

She had travelled on to the Dorchester alone, but somehow I found myself imagining her reaction – all the various different ways she would find to say that London was too small and too grey. And yet I also had high hopes that she would illuminate it in the way she had New York.

In this and a thousand other subtle ways I noticed that I was not quite the same person who had left London either. I was orbiting round a different star.

Christie had done some research and somehow confirmed that Constantine Gerou was staying at the Walled Garden Hotel, conveniently located just round the corner from the High Court. The crush that I felt myself developing on her meant I was quite happy to take at face value her assurances that a quick Google search was all that had been required.

Arriving back at my flat, I felt shattered, but couldn't sleep, so got up and spent the morning unpacking and watching the news. There was a brief item on Gerou's eleventh-hour appeal hearing, from which I gleaned that things were not going well for him. The British government was still insisting he would be flown back to Greece in forty-eight hours' time.

When I arrived outside the Walled Garden a couple of hours later, I could see that he was certainly not slumming it with his choice of hotels. It stood proudly on the road, its Classical façade addressing the streetscape with an imposing demeanour. Large, liveried doormen in top hats monitored the door, and those emerging from the hotel paraded an assortment of Hermes birkins, Rolex watches and Chanel shopping bags.

We hadn't discussed a dress code, but it occurred to me as I waited over the road that, with my brushed cotton shirt, chinos and Caterpillar work boots, I might not be allowed in.

I was thankful for once that my desire to impress Christie had prompted me to shave and put on a tie and sports jacket.

Christie had agreed to go to the court to try and find out about the timings for the day, to see if we could get some picture of Conny's likely movements. She arrived at the Walled Garden for our agreed meet-up fifteen minutes late, emerging from a black cab with a regal swoop.

Despite the dull and overcast day, she had kept her sunglasses on, as if without them she was certain to be recognised. She barely stopped to take in my presence and strode towards the entrance as though she were the hotel's owner returning home after a tiresome business trip. As I scurried from the shadows to catch up with her, I couldn't help but feel she should have had a small Pekinese in a diamanté collar under her arm. Maybe she'd tried to get one and that's why she was late.

In any event, I had reason to be grateful that she was wearing a classic above-the-knee pencil skirt suit with peplum decoration. Even in London's autumnal murk she somehow glittered joyously, and once I made it obvious that I was with her, the doormen parted in front of us to allow us to enter. I couldn't help but notice one of them following her in with his eyes, apparently bewitched by the slender line of her stocking seam.

The hotel itself looked exclusive without being showy. There was an understated English style to the contemporary furnishings, which sought to reassure you that you'd made the right choice without trying too hard to impress you. It was a difficult balancing act to pull off, but they seemed to have an impressive taste in contemporary art too, with a couple of Jim Dines and an Etel Adnan adorning the walls, so I felt that they had just about managed it.

We took our seats in the lounge area and Christie ordered a couple of espressos before updating me on her investigations.

'The court's sitting until four this afternoon, then they'll finish for the day. Apparently, he usually comes straight back to the hotel after that.'

'And what? We just collar him as he comes through the door?'

'That's not going to work, honey. According to the receptionist, he never uses the front entrance. They don't know exactly where he does come in and out, but he's got some kind of arrangement with the management to enter and leave in a way that's not obvious, so he isn't swamped by press. And he's also brought a whole goddam entourage with him to keep people at bay – minders, lawyers, the works – so there's no way we can just walk up to him anyway. They won't let us.'

'But surely for you…?'

Her eyes dipped towards her coffee cup. 'I already told you – I've got to stay out of this.'

There was something in her voice that didn't convince me.

'But why?' I asked.

For once, however, Christie seemed determined to keep her inner thoughts to herself. 'I've provided the painting; it's your job to sell it,' she said aggressively. 'You think I'm letting you take two hundred and fifty grand outta the sale price just for showing up? Quit trying to get me to do your job for you.' She was still avoiding my eye. 'Even if that were possible, I don't think it would be a good idea.'

I wanted to ask her why not but something in the look she flashed at me told me she wasn't in the mood to answer such questions. What I understood though, was that I would need to find a way of circumventing Conny's entourage and getting a meeting with him myself. I was still chewing over how I might engineer a meeting with someone who apparently did not want to be met, when, out of the corner of my eye, I saw something that immediately changed the focus of my thoughts. At first, I dismissed it as a figment of an overactive imagination – perhaps one caught in a netherworld of guilt between my recent divorce and my crush on Christie. But as my head turned and the figure moved from the periphery of my vision to its very centre, it became clear that this was no trick of the light. This was Suzy. It was actually, unmistakably, my ex-wife.

# TWELVE

I hadn't been in the same room as Suzy for two years, during which time she'd assumed in my mind the appearance and dimensions of a monster. But there she was, in what appeared to be the corporate livery of the Walled Garden's front-of-house staff, smiling graciously at an ageing businessman who was fixing her with a reptilian grin.

'Oh my God,' I said. 'It's Suzy.'

Christie seemed thrown. 'What?... Your ex-wife? Where?'

She turned and followed my eyes. '*She's* your ex-wife? Wow. She's quite a beauty. Not what I was expecting at all.'

I felt myself wince.

'There's no need to sound so surprised,' I said, but even I could hear the defensiveness in my voice.

Sadly, Christie's observation was typical of the kind of comment I was used to hearing when people who knew me first met Suzy, and even when I didn't hear it I would often see it lurking in the way they would look at her. And the fact was, it was true: I had, as Jasper had rather cruelly noted once, been *'batting above my average'* with Suzy. Her razor-sharp cheekbones, deep brown eyes and smooth, glowing skin were a happy fusion of her parents' Irish and Jamaican genes. My own genetic blend of English rose and Buenos Aires polo-playing set ought perhaps to have blessed me more than it had.

However, this was not the moment for me to nurse that particular grievance. I was more concerned about the scene unfolding in front of me.

There was something just a little too tactile about the way the businessman engaged with her that the Suzy I knew would have been unable to resist bridling at. But this version of my ex-wife maintained a professional and benevolent demeanour throughout, despite the provocations.

I could see it though; that strained look which would sometimes appear on her face when someone made a comment about single-parent families, or ethnic minorities, or children from council estates *'stealing'* their child's university place. In those moments her smile would seem to belong to a different face from the sadness and frustration hidden in her eyes. It was the look she reserved for people she needed to be liked by, people whom she couldn't afford to offend if she was going to get on in the world so, if nothing else, the fact that she was using it here seemed to confirm that she was actually working at the Walled Garden and not a customer. Otherwise, I'm sure she'd have slapped the businessman: it was, she had always assured me, what her (single) mother had taught her to do.

But something about that look awakened in me long-suppressed memories of the woman I'd fallen in love with all those years ago, before the love had been drowned out by the arguing. She was still petite and toned, her muscularity pushing against the constrictions of her grey trouser suit. But now her hair – the tight curls I always recalled springing out joyously from her head in an uncontrollable explosion of delight – was primped and held in good order by an array of pins and clips.

Up to this point the businessman had contented himself with gentle touches of Suzy's elbow. But, having not been chastised for his over-familiarity, he then decided to raise the stakes and put his hand in the small of Suzy's back. Despite everything that had passed between us, there was something about the scenario that made me feel deeply uncomfortable. I still felt protective of her, so seeing her forced by company protocol to put up with such behaviour without complaint, I found myself standing up in protest.

The movement must have caught Suzy's eye because I noticed her head turn towards me. The ageing businessman, until then the centre of her professional attentions, was dismissed peremptorily with a raised hand and she began striding towards me, her jaw clenched. Something happened to her face as she strode across the hotel lobby. It hardened into something colder, more mean-spirited, and more easily recognisable as the Suzy of my more recent experience.

She arrived at our seats and stood there, arms folded, hip pushed out, her eyes inviting me to provide an explanation for my presence. I, however, was stunned into silence at seeing her working here.

'Looks like she wasn't lying on that financial declaration,' Christie whispered in my ear.

I was still speechless. It seemed like quite a step down from Alison Jacques. Yet the Walled Garden was also a considerable step up from the Travelodge she'd been working at part-time when we'd met as students.

Eventually Suzy grew fed up with waiting for me to speak. She savoured her hatred for me like it was a vintage wine, rolling it around on her tongue for a moment before dispensing it contemptuously.

'Well? What the hell are you doin' here?' she said, faint traces of her Birmingham accent slipping out from behind her anger.

'I might ask you the same question.'

She sought to reassert the more neutral tones that had become her studied practice since her time at the Courtauld.

'This is where I work now – as I think I made clear on my financial declaration! Although, to be fair, I wasn't a manager then.'

She flashed me her staff pass, from which I saw that she had taken to styling herself 'Suzy Viejo-Pinnock'. Given the effort she'd made to trash my reputation during the divorce proceedings, it felt ironic that she was still trying to trade on the Viejo name. Rather like the Rumi quote she'd had tattooed up the inside of her arm – *I am not this hair. I am not this skin. I am the soul that lives within* – Suzy seemed to think this would indicate to people that she belonged among the cultured elite, whereas actually, to those already in the cultured elite, it indicated the exact opposite.

Going back to working in hotels, even one as luxurious and exclusive as the Walled Garden, had definitely not been in her career plan. I was trying to enjoy this all-too-rare moment of schadenfreude when she added a rider to her initial observation.

'I'm a duty manager now. In case you hadn't realised, that

means I can have you thrown out.'

And with that, she grabbed the walkie-talkie from her belt and called over to security.

I had noticed, even in my relatively short time in her company, that Christie attracted security guards in the same way that cows attracted flies: it didn't appear that she set out to do it, and she seemed largely oblivious to their presence, but wherever she went they were generally buzzing around her. So far, this strange magnetic power had been mildly amusing to witness, but now I was acutely aware that our plan required that Christie and I didn't get ourselves thrown out of the Walled Garden. As I'd done throughout my relationship with Suzy therefore, I decided that the most effective course of action would be to bite my tongue and try and move the conversation along.

'Suzy, this is Christie. And Christie, this is my ex-wife, Suzy.'

'Pleased to meet you, Suzy. Gabriel's told me *all* about you.'

Christie inserted an eyeroll at this point in a way that suggested to me she was trying to be friendly but might have implied to Suzy that she was being sarcastic. In any event, when Christie proffered her hand, Suzy declined to shake it.

'Bit old for you, isn't she, Gabe?'

I decided to ignore this last remark, even though it wounded me more than it probably should have.

'Christie McGraw,' I clarified.

I couldn't quite hold back a smirk.

Suzy immediately appeared floored by what I'd just said.

'What? Wait – you're Christie McGraw? *The* Christie McGraw?'

'Well I'm the only one that I know,' Christie answered with a slight swagger in her voice. Being recognised suited her.

'Oh my God! I can't believe it. Did Gabriel mention that my final year dissertation—'

'Was on me and Wally Neuzil? Yes, he did.'

'I mean, I don't think Von Holunder really understood women – not as rounded human beings who exist independently of men's perception of them – but I really admire what you did in those paintings. It was you who brought them to life.'

Suzy had a tendency to show off when she met someone who impressed her. I noticed this had provoked the odd arched eyebrow behind her back in the past, but Christie didn't seem to mind. And she positively revelled in Suzy's fawning.

'Why thank you, young lady,' Christie said, almost blushing with pride. 'Gabriel here was telling me that it was me that brought you together.'

'Yes, but I'll try not to hold that against you.'

Two serious-looking men in suits emerged from the office behind reception and began making their way over. One was a short, squat guy perhaps in his early fifties with a pudgy face and thinning black hair. His name badge advised that he was called Mohammed. From his manner he looked like the one who was in charge. His colleague, identified by his badge as Daniel, was younger, taller, and more muscular, with chiselled features and mid-length dreadlocks that were tied back in a tight ponytail. Neither looked as though they were looking to join in our conversation. I decided I needed to move fast before Suzy had me removed.

'Look, Suzy, I didn't come here looking for trouble, I swear—'

'Yeah, well too bad, because trouble's what you've got. I can't have you clarting about in here.' ('Clarting' was what my mother used to call 'a Suzy word'). The security guards stepped forward. 'Mo, can you and Daniel show the gentleman out, please? Let the lady stay though.'

'But I'm *with* the lady. You can't throw me out,' I protested.

'Oh, can't I? See the sign as you came in? *"The management reserves the right to refuse admission"*? Well, I'm the duty manager and I'm refusing you admission.' She motioned to Mohammed with her head. 'Thanks, Mo.'

At this point Christie intervened and, for once, her intervention was designed to calm the situation rather than inflame it.

'I really do need him to be with me, honey.'

'Yes, well I'm sorry, but as far as I'm concerned, this man is a crook,' Suzy said. 'And I'm not going to have him being crooked in my hotel. So I suggest that you get someone else to help you.'

'I'm not being crooked in your hotel,' I protested (although I realised even at the time that this point was debatable). 'I'm helping Ms McGraw with some very important business – some life-saving business. It's just my shitty luck that the person we have to do business with is staying here.'

Suzy paused and looked at me askance. 'It's not Mr Gerou, is it?'

'Damn right it is,' said Christie. 'How did you know?'

Suzy gave us a world-weary look. 'Let's just say it was a lucky hunch.'

'Really? So what do you think's going on up there?' Christie asked.

This was not a subject I felt bore discussion with Suzy, but even as I opened my mouth to divert the conversation onto more helpful areas, Suzy cut me off.

'Well, I'm not sure, but let's just say they don't seem to want anyone to know about it, whatever it is. And if my ex-husband is involved, then that just confirms that it's probably not very ethical. I'm sorry, but I really am going to have to ask you to leave, Gabe. It's more than my job's worth.'

'Look, I appreciate that the two of you have history,' said Christie, 'but if I could just explain.'

Given the ambiguous legal status of our proposed transaction with Conny (and Suzy's potential interest in my own financial involvement in the deal), this did not feel like a good idea to me.

'Christie, I don't think it's necessarily very wise to extend the circle of people who know about what we're doing beyond those who really need—'

'The thing is, Gabe,' Suzy said, interrupting me, 'you're in my hotel and I can have you thrown out if I want to. So if you want to stay here then you need to convince me that whatever you're trying to pull with Mr Gerou isn't going to get me or this hotel into trouble. That means I really do need an explanation.'

She took such pleasure in patronising me that I didn't want to give her any more by showing her how much it needled me.

'Relax, kiddo,' said Christie, briefly touching my arm. 'I understand where you're coming from.' She gave me a quick glance which I think she meant to be reassuring, yet which set my teeth on edge. 'But I also understand where this lovely young woman is coming from too.' She turned and gave Suzy an oleaginous look.

Even as I attempted to interrupt her, Christie proceeded to explain to Suzy those elements of our story that emphasised her need to complete a sale to Conny – her cancer, her utter destitution and consequent lack of health insurance – while deftly skirting those other issues (such as the fact that she didn't legally own the painting she was trying to sell) that might have caused Suzy some concern. Helped by a few judicious interjections on my part to steer the conversation into safer territory, Christie discreetly avoided any mention of my financial involvement in the deal, and instead focused on my position as the foremost authority on Von Holunder's work to explain to Suzy why it was me, specifically, that she needed to assist her. But in response to my gentle promptings, Christie also explained why she needed Suzy's help. In my experience, pandering to Suzy's ego was generally an essential (but not necessarily sufficient) precondition of getting her to do anything for you, and I couldn't help but wonder, as I listened to Christie, if my inability to do so convincingly had been a contributory factor in our divorce. Thankfully, Christie was able to lay it on pretty thick.

'So, you see, honey, I really need you to come through for me here. If you throw Mr Viejo out of this hotel, then he can't get to meet Conny, and if he doesn't meet with Conny...'

She left an indelicate pause trailing behind her like a fox-fur stole. It had the desired effect.

'Oh my God, that's terrible! I'm so sorry. I'm so, so sorry.' Suzy did look genuinely upset.

'Sympathy's great, honey, but it won't fund my treatment.' Christie was nothing if not direct. 'I need to sell my painting and Conny's the only guy in the world I can sell it to. So I've got to get Mr Viejo here in front of him before he gets put on that plane. I'd have sorted something out with Conny directly, but when I knew him, we didn't have mobile phones or social media, so I just didn't have a way to get in touch.'

It sounded entirely plausible, and I could tell that Suzy

wanted to help her. She also appeared to be torn. Her face became pensive in a way that I'd forgotten it could be; in the way that people who didn't have huge reserves of social capital could become pensive when they were forced to consider the possible consequences of a misjudgement. Eventually, after a long pause, she spoke.

'OK guys, you can go now,' she said to the security guards. 'I'll sort it out from here.'

'You sure, miss?' asked Mo.

'Yeah, it's fine. I can deal with it.'

Mo and Daniel duly departed. Then Suzy turned to us.

'Look, I've got to be careful. This might look like a shitty job to you, but it's a damn sight better than the Travelodge and,' she looked at me pointedly, 'given my current financial position, I can't afford to lose it.'

'They wouldn't take you back at Alison Jacques?' I asked. This was a rhetorical question and, in retrospect, the sarcasm it implied did not reflect well on me.

'You might struggle to believe this, Gabe, but I had to fight to get a minimum wage job in here on a zero-hours contract. That's how it is for people like me. It's taken me *nine months* of trying, but I've finally got myself a proper contract, regular hours, and a half-decent salary. So, however much sympathy I might feel for you, Ms McGraw, to be honest, I can't afford to do anything that might mean I lose those things.'

'And I'm not asking you to, honey, I swear.'

'You say that, but Mr Gerou has booked out the whole of the top floor for his party – do you know how much a booking like that generates for this hotel? – and he wants absolute privacy. If he thinks I've sold him out he will complain to my bosses and they will throw me out with the trash in a heartbeat. And that cannot happen. D'you get me?'

There was an urgency and determination to her voice that I remembered from the first few times we met, before we were an item. It spoke of an overriding concern to protect herself and an absolutely unshakeable belief that such self-preservation was necessary. I'd tried to coax her out of that way of thinking because I genuinely thought it was counter-productive – it put off the very people she needed to impress if she wanted to establish herself in the art world – but somehow every time she was 'let go', or a temporary contract failed to be renewed, it seemed to redouble her conviction. Christie seemed to sense this – or at least, if she didn't, she seemed to sense that Suzy needed some reassurance that we understood the stakes for her.

'I understand that honey, honestly I do.' She put her hand on Suzy's arm and looked at her with a seriousness I'd not seen in her before. 'And I want you to know that I won't let you get into any trouble. I absolutely promise you. If this goes wrong, it's all on me.' Pause. 'And him.'

I don't know if it was the reassurance or the possibility of getting me into trouble that changed her mind, but the frost in Suzy's stare melted slightly.

'He's got an interview here with the *Daily Telegraph* at four-thirty,' she said. 'In reception. He says he'll be down here for about an hour. But he'll have his own security detail with him, so he doesn't get pounced on by less friendly elements – they've been co-ordinating it with my guys.' Suzy raised a cynical eyebrow. 'For a man who's spending so much of his time insisting on his innocence, he's spending an awful lot of his money on keeping prying eyes at bay.'

'Great. Thanks, honey. Can I just ask—?'

'That's it. That's all I can tell you. And you definitely didn't hear it from me.' She fixed me, in particular, with an especially fierce stare. 'Now for God's sake, sit down, shut up and stay the hell out of my way.'

# THIRTEEN

Christie returned to the Dorchester, while I decided to stay in reception in anticipation of Conny's arrival. Suzy seemed willing to tolerate my presence as long as I was prepared to tolerate the fierce scowl she would pointedly direct at me every time she walked through reception. It was a busy hotel, and she was clearly a fastidious manager, so there was a lot of scowling: it wasn't much fun, but I kept reminding myself that our marriage was over and what she thought of me was no longer any of my concern. I had moved on. If she couldn't, then that was her issue, not mine.

But I found myself spending much of the next hour or so looking at her – how she reacted to hotel guests and interacted with her staff. The Suzy they saw was different from the one I had grown accustomed to. It gave me a strange nostalgia for the early days of our relationship. I had bumped into her at the National Gallery one wet Wednesday afternoon and recognised her from the Courtauld. As the slightly older postgraduate student, I offered to take her on a tour of my favourite rooms. She loved it so much that we agreed to do it again the next week. Then the next. It became a weekly appointment for both of us. We would stare at those paintings for hours as if their beauty was somehow only for us. The memory of it still makes me emotional.

At the time I remember being worried that I was using my art-world connections to make her interested in me, as though I was somehow duping her. Looking back, I can't believe how naïve I was.

I was brought back to the present by the arrival of a dapper young man with floppy hair and a rather flustered manner. Suzy took him to a seat next to some coffee and biscuits in a secluded part of the hotel lobby, then made her way over to me.

'No sign of Mr Gerou yet, but that's the guy from the *Telegraph*,' she said.

She made to head back to her other duties, and I knew that I should have let her, but my nostalgia got the better of me.

'How are you, Suze?' I asked.

'I'm fine.' She snipped at the words, as though clipping them with a pair of scissors. 'Just about keeping my head above water. No thanks to you.'

'I can't believe we've met like this.'

'What are the odds?' she replied, with a heavy dose of cynicism.

'Maybe it's fate.' Something in me genuinely wondered at the time if that might be true.

'Yeah, maybe fate's giving you another chance to give me the money you owe me.'

I sighed. This was not an argument I intended getting into.

'I hear you're dating again.'

I hadn't heard this at all.

'Oh really? Well, I'd love to know who told you that.'

It was phrased to sound like it could have been a denial, but there was a self-satisfied smile on her face as she said it, which caused my heart to sink.

'Is it anyone I know?'

'That's not something that needs to concern you any more.'

She pulled away and headed back to the reception desk.

'I hope he makes you happy,' I called after her, but she didn't turn back.

About twenty minutes later the lift doors opened and out stepped a phalanx of swarthy-looking men in the midst of which could be seen the instantly recognisable features of Constantine Gerou.

I'd forgotten how short he was – I reckon he was no more than 5'3" – yet despite this, he was one of those guys who somehow seemed to dominate the room just by entering it. I guess money can do that to a person. And being surrounded by half a dozen minders probably helped too. They were all young and muscular, but he seemed to have selected them so that none was more than a few inches taller than he was. Marching through the lobby they looked oddly Lilliputian next to Daniel, who was waiting to greet them.

If Conny was worried at the prospect of being grilled by a journalist, he certainly didn't show it: his face betrayed none of the careworn anxiety that I might have anticipated in a man quite literally on trial. He still appeared to be wearing the same self-satisfied grin I remembered from the time he managed to secure *Hold Me Closer* (1981) from under Mimi's nose for a knock-down $315,000. Although, to be fair, that smirk did seem to be a pretty much permanent fixture on his face.

He took great pride in his appearance too. I calculated that he must have been in his mid-seventies, yet with his incongruously jet-black hair swept back into a ponytail, and his dapper suit, he had the appearance of an ageing roué who still considered himself to be something of a catch.

Our strategy had been for me to immediately make my way over and introduce myself before Conny had a chance to get into conversation with the journalist, but this was clearly going to be easier said than done. For a start, someone I assumed to be his publicist took him to a secluded corner, with his back to the rest of the lobby area. At this point Mo and Daniel erected some temporary screens to cordon the whole area off – something I had not anticipated, and Suzy had not warned me about. Then his entourage fanned themselves out about six feet in front of the screens to form a security phalanx which, despite my best efforts, proved impossible to penetrate.

My gentle enquiries about whether it would be possible for me to speak to Conny when he'd finished his interview were met with a dismissive stare. Conny's own security maintained a firm grip on the cordon sanitaire that they had created. The situation appeared hopeless.

I waited half an hour in the hope that something might change, but still Conny remained behind the screen with the young journalist, while his publicist brought him a steady stream of coffees. Eventually, having spent the previous two hours drinking coffee myself, my own need for the bathroom defeated me. Realising I was unlikely to get any joy from Conny's guards, I approached Daniel in the hope of a more sympathetic response.

'Is there a gents' toilet I can use?'

Daniel looked at me, sceptically. 'There's one here I can let you use,' he said eventually, before guiding me past Conny's security barrier and towards some toilets located just off the hotel lobby behind where Conny was sitting.

I was still in my cubicle when I felt my phone vibrate in my pocket. Seeing that it was Christie, I took the decision to answer it.

'So, have you spoken to him yet? Has he agreed to buy?'

'It's not that simple. There are people; protocols. He's still doing his interview.'

Christie was not impressed. She started to berate me for not trying hard enough, and I sought to defend myself as best I could. At some point I guess I heard that someone else had entered the bathroom, but I was too busy trying to explain the complexities of the situation to Christie to really take much notice. What had seemed simple in New York now felt a lot more difficult in reality. Even if Conny might theoretically have been interested in buying our painting, I just didn't see how I could gain access to him to find out. None of his entourage looked overly interested in assisting their boss to add to his collection of Erik von Holunder paintings. Their focus seemed wholly on maintaining his privacy. And, as Suzy had attested, that seemed to be their boss' priority too.

I explained all this to Christie. Or at least, I tried to explain.

'Are you kidding me?' she said. 'We travel three thousand miles to try and find one guy in a city of nine million. I get you within fifty feet of him – and you still can't close a deal?'

'It's not the distance, it's the set-up. There are people, there's security—'

'Jesus! It's like you were expecting Conny to find you and then beg you to sell him the picture. Of course there are obstacles. I'm paying you to overcome them.'

'Look, this is still a great painting. Maybe I can find you a different buyer.'

'I don't want a different buyer. It has to be Conny. We both agreed that. He's the one in the photo with the painting. He's the one with the dirty money he needs to get rid of.'

'Those allegations are just that – allegations.'

'Please don't tell me you think he's legit.'

I certainly didn't think that, but there was something else niggling at the back of my mind.

'I've got to be honest with you, Christie. Seeing him here has changed something. I mean, I've seen him before, but not for a few years. Seeing him now, though… I don't know. I don't think this man is an aesthete. I think he's an investor. You and I know that you're selling one of the best paintings of the last fifty years, but Conny? I don't think so. I don't think he'd know a piece of great art if he came home and found it in bed with his wife.'

I unlocked the cubicle door to make my way to the wash-hand basins. But something was blocking my path.

Constantine Gerou.

He was flanked by two of his minders, and none of them looked particularly happy.

'So this is why they suggested I come in here. Mr Viejo,' Conny said, with his trademark smirk. 'I thought it was you.'

I didn't know what to say, but I felt my stomach perform an adroit somersault before sinking into my shoes.

'So, you think I can't appreciate great art?'

# FOURTEEN

Conny was an ageing man who had been liberally availing himself of the free coffee that was on offer. I probably should have guessed, therefore, that at some point he would need to go to the bathroom too. For reasons that would become apparent later, he had been directed into the toilet that I had already gone into, rather than being allowed to return to his suite on the top floor. Had I foreseen this happening, I might have chosen my words more carefully, or at least expressed them more judiciously. Now, however, I was faced with having to rescue a situation which Conny's face suggested might not be recoverable. And so I did something that it felt like I had spent rather a lot of my time doing in the few days since I had first met Christie: I floundered.

'Ah, Mr Gerou! Fancy meeting you here... What are the chances, eh? It must be what? Five? Six years? Too long, anyway. Good to see you again.' I proffered my free – but as yet unwashed – hand. Conny looked down at it with the kind of withering disdain that I had not seen directed towards one of my body parts since I had emerged, naked, from the bedroom of my flat during an ill-fated attempt at reconciliation with Suzy. His hands remained firmly in his pockets.

'I think you might want to wash that before expecting me to touch it,' he said (which, coincidentally, was also pretty much what Suzy had said that night.)

'Oh, right. Yes. Of course.'

A voice came out of the phone in my hand. 'Well, it sounds like you've managed to make contact after all. I'll leave you two to sort out the details.' And with that, Christie ended the call. I made my way over to the sink and began to wash my hands. An awkward silence fell on the room.

'I'll just dry myself,' I said nervously.

'Great,' Conny said drolly. 'And then you might want to explain to me what the hell you're trying to pull here.'

I remembered him as a chain smoker back in the day, and the timbre of his voice still betrayed that fact. It sounded as if his vocal cords had been peppered with ground glass and buckshot, then left to marinate in a vat of Metaxa.

I took a deep breath and tried to explain the situation as best I could. I had spent much of the previous two hours perfecting my pitch to the point where I had convinced myself that Conny would be salivating to get his hands on *Susanna & the Elders* within moments of me starting to talk. However, in my head Conny had been intrigued to start with. Now, though, he was standing in front of me fixing me with a look that suggested he was taking a perverse pleasure in my discomfort. Despite this, my mind was so agitated I found myself ploughing on with my planned opening gambit, regardless.

'Mr Gerou, I have one of the great figurative paintings of the last fifty years to sell, and I have come here directly from New York to sell it to you, specifically – because you are the only collector I know with the discernment to fully appreciate it.'

Conny's face told me I had somewhat neutralised the impact of this speech by what he had overhead me saying not two minutes previously.

'You can spare me the sales pitch, Mr Viejo. I just want to know what all this is about.'

He retained his suave demeanour but the two men at his side suggested that this was only because he could outsource any sense of threat that he wanted me to feel. I paused for a moment to assess how I might answer his question. Then, over the following ten minutes or so, I sought to explain everything – well, not quite *everything*, obviously, but everything that it felt relevant for him to know. I also reminded Conny that, even when I hadn't been aware he was in the room, I had described it as 'one of the best paintings of the last fifty years' so he could be confident that I believed that to be true. I then addressed the delicate issue of why the sale was being forced through now and, given the urgency of the situation, emphasised that the vendor would be offering it at a hefty discount in order to secure a prompt cash sale. I remained tactfully silent on the issue of his own potential motivations for wanting to complete the purchase quickly with used bank notes and, given what she'd told me, also decided it would be best to keep Christie's name out of my story for the moment.

It would be wrong to say that Conny's look became warmer during my little monologue – but neither did it become cooler, and he let me speak without interruption. These facts alone gave me encouragement, and I grew in confidence to such an extent that I found myself reverting to my pre-planned script. This finished with a big rhetorical flourish that I was convinced would win him over.

'And so, Mr Gerou, this is it. This really is it. This is the lost Von Holunder masterpiece whose existence has long been rumoured, but never actually proven. And I'm offering it to you – to you, and no one else – not out of some misplaced sense of obligation, but because you are perhaps the only person still alive who can vouch for its authenticity.'

With this Conny's face suddenly changed. Despite his best efforts he couldn't prevent his nonchalant smirk giving way to something else; something that hinted at intrigue. It only lasted a moment before he sought to reassert the supremacy of his unruffled smile, but that moment was enough for me to know that if I played the next moment right, I would have him hooked.

'And how can I do that, Mr Viejo?'

'Because not only are you *in* this picture but you also saw the finished painting.' I reached into my pocket and, with a theatrical flourish, withdrew the photo of Conny and Erik in front of *Susanna & the Elders*. 'And were even photographed doing so!' I got down on one knee and proffered the photo to him with mock humility. It was time for my big finish. 'Mr Gerou, I am offering to you *Susanna & the Elders*.'

Conny looked at me askance. He didn't say anything immediately, but you could sense from the look in his eye that this was because he didn't want to seem too keen. No buyer is more vulnerable than when they let the seller know that they really want to buy what is being offered. The professional buyer, like the professional poker player, gives nothing away.

They slow everything down, refuse to be rushed, and remind themselves of the questions that need to be asked. I could see the cogs in Conny's mind clicking and whirring as he went through this process. Finally, after what seemed like an age, he rearranged his features into those of a sceptic, and spoke.

'So how come you've got it?'

This was not an issue I wanted to explore with him in any detail.

'Essentially, the vendor was gifted the painting by Erik himself, who otherwise would have thrown it out. For that reason, it was never registered and so has never been sold. But now the vendor is ill and needs money to cover medical bills. They've asked me, as the world's leading authority on Von Holunder's works, to vouch for its authenticity. Having examined the painting thoroughly and been given the photo of you and Mr Von Holunder alongside it, I am happy to do so. And, just to be clear, I appreciate the time pressures that you're facing here, so I can confirm we're able to complete a sale within the next twenty-four hours – for cash.'

Conny tried to look unimpressed. He stepped away, leaving his two minders in front of me, and stared at the photo I'd given him.

'I remember that afternoon. It was one helluva day. Boy, we put some cognac away that day, I can tell you.' He chuckled to himself, but not in a way that suggested I was being invited to join him. 'Your problem is that I also remember who took that photo.'

I couldn't be sure if he meant it, or whether it was a bit of bluster designed to try and extract the information from me. For that reason I decided to play it cool.

'And who was that?'

Conny muttered something in what I took to be Greek and immediately the two minders rushed forward, grabbed me and slammed me against the bathroom wall. They held me there, my feet dangling six inches off the ground, while Conny sauntered slowly over and looked up at me, his face wearing the same self-satisfied grin it had worn as he'd walked across the hotel lobby.

'The same woman you were talking to on that phone two minutes ago: Christie McGraw.' He savoured the words as he might have done the good cognac that he shared with Erik that afternoon. 'And I think it's her who's trying to sell this painting.' His voice was slow, quiet, and ominously soft, like the tread of an intruder along a carpeted corridor. 'Which presents us with a rather interesting situation, don't you think?'

'Look, either you want the painting, or you don't. It's that simple.'

He chuckled again, this time more raucously, so that he sounded like he had a sack of broken glass rattling inside his chest. 'Oh, I want to see the painting, certainly... But I also want to see Ms McGraw.'

From the tenor of his voice it was impossible to tell whether he meant this benignly, or with a more malevolent intent, but given my current situation, pinned to a toilet wall by two minders, dangling six inches off the ground, it seemed safest to assume the worst.

'I'm afraid that's not going to be possible,' I said as coolly as I could manage under the circumstances. 'Even if I knew where she was – which, of course, I'm not able to confirm.'

Conny turned away again and muttered something in Greek, with a weariness that I mistook for indifference. Immediately a hard fist delivered a solid blow to my solar plexus. I felt the wind punched out of me and I doubled up involuntarily, blood flooding into my face as I gasped for air. The minders let me go and I dropped to the floor, writhing in agony on the tiles, unable to breathe and genuinely fearing that I was about to die, despite everyone else's apparent lack of interest. Conny looked down at me, then flicked my body with his foot, like a lion toying with a dying gazelle.

'Come to my rooms at seven this evening with your painting – and you'd better bring Ms McGraw too. No Christie, no deal.'

I coughed and gasped, still fighting to find my breath. 'OK. OK. I'll try.'

'Don't try, Mr Viejo. Make it happen. Oh, and I hope I've made it clear, that you better not try and pull a fast one on me. I'm *very* intolerant of people who try and fuck me over.'

He dropped the photo inches from my face and then the three of them sauntered out of the bathroom, leaving me breathless and shaken on the floor.

# FIFTEEN

When I finally recovered my poise enough to phone Christie with the news, she was adamant that she couldn't meet Conny.

On the basis of my own experience, I could understand why she might be concerned. It wasn't necessarily that you feared *him*; it was that you found yourself worrying about the things that he could make happen. Powerful men often have that effect on people. I guess that's what makes them powerful.

But Conny had been clear: unless he met Christie, he wasn't going to buy the painting. Whatever misgivings she may have had therefore, I reminded her of the reality of her situation.

'Christie, that suite you're in, that shopping trip you've been on, those debts you've cleared – it's all being paid for by the proceeds of a deal that you haven't actually completed yet.'

'That's my money from you!' she protested. 'It's nothing to do with Conny.'

'But if you don't complete the deal with Conny, that life-saving treatment you still need the money for…well, it isn't going to happen.'

I didn't want to get into an argument about my own needs in the situation, but if Christie was a motivated seller, then I was very definitely a motivated agent. The fact was that I was currently $135,000 down on the deal and it was in no way clear to me that I could recover that money if the deal with Conny fell through.

'I don't care what Conny wants,' she shouted down the phone. 'I'm not taking orders from that man. He's the one who should be taking orders from me!'

I was concerned enough by the implication of this comment to immediately get a cab over to the Dorchester in order to argue my case in person.

She didn't want to talk about it, but I was desperate enough to hold my ground for once. Eventually, as we sat among the Corinthian columns and classical wall and ceiling mouldings in her suite overlooking Mayfair, the truth came tumbling out.

'I haven't seen Conny since '92, and I said some things then that he didn't take too kindly to. Nothing insulting, but some home truths I thought he needed to hear.' This was new information to me, and I could tell that it caused Christie some concern. 'We were breaking up. It's never an easy thing to do. And for a guy like Conny – well, he's a proud guy and I don't think he's used to hearing people say those things to him.'

'Wait a minute – breaking up? You mean you actually went out with him? It wasn't just a friendship – it was an actual relationship? A romantic one?'

Her eyes dipped. 'Yeah. It was after Erik died, of course. Conny waited a respectable period then made a move.'

'But why? I mean, I can see why he made a move on you,

but you – why'd you agree to go out with him?'

'What? You think that he was beneath me?'

I did, although Christie didn't seem to find the idea as ridiculous as I did.

She avoided my gaze as she spoke.

'He was my last connection to that world: the world of Erik, and the Dakota, and opening nights at the Guggenheim. I'd lost all that and I wanted it back. I missed it.' I could sense in her voice a diffidence that I was not used to hearing, as though she'd never shared her reflections on the question so honestly before. 'He was married by then, of course. But I didn't really have anywhere to live so I didn't feel as though I had much choice – and besides, I'd spent twelve years with Erik, so I was used to being on my own in a relationship. He put me up in a tiny apartment in the Lower East Side. It was hardly what I'd been used to with Erik, but it was better than what I had. He'd come visit every couple of months when he was in town on business, but…' her voice dropped wistfully, 'it wasn't the same. He wasn't the same.'

'The same as what?'

'He'd always been so generous – he'd bring me flowers whenever he came over to see Erik, get me something beautiful, a piece of jewellery or something, for Christmas and my birthday. But… I dunno – once he got me in the apartment he changed. He seemed to resent the expense. He'd always been such a gentleman when Erik was around. Then he wasn't.'

The possibilities this raised troubled me, and I wanted to be sure I'd understood her correctly.

'He wasn't a gentleman…?'

She paused as if considering how best to answer.

'Conny's fine as long as he gets his own way and you laugh at his jokes. He'll treat you like a princess and that feels wonderful. But he'll expect you to act like he's the king and if you don't, well, let's just say you see a different side to him.'

I felt the need to probe her about this. 'And this different side…?'

'You know some guys – they expect a behaviour sticker if they take you out and don't behave like an asshole. I said to him, "Honey, if you want a badge, become a security guard. I'm worth every cent you're spending on me and every bit of attention you're giving me".'

'I can see how he wouldn't appreciate that.'

'No, he didn't appreciate that.' She lifted her head and looked at me. There was an uncharacteristic brittleness to her stare. 'Or all the other stuff.'

'I guess if you're that rich, you get used to being told what you want to hear.'

Christie took a sip from her espresso, then turned to stare out of the window. 'We stuck at it for three years, off and on, but on my fortieth birthday I decided I had to make the break.'

'And I'm guessing he didn't take that well.'

'No, he didn't. He's a proud man, and it may have felt like I'd humiliated him.'

'Short guys can get touchy about stuff like that,' I said.

'I think it's more about his background, in Conny's case. He might have plenty of money now, but he was brought up poor. They had nothing. And he was the youngest of eight, so he had to fight for everything he's got; and he fought hard, and he fought dirty, believe me. So he never gives up anything. Not ever. That's how he's had to be. Always fighting.' She left a pause before raising her voice slightly in a defiant rhetorical flourish. 'So, if I'm honest, he's not a guy I'd be comfortable being alone in a room with.'

This revelation changed my perception markedly. But it didn't change the underlying economics of the situation.

'I get all that, I really do. But Christie, you need another $125,000 to stay alive. And Conny's not going to give it to you unless you agree to meet with him.'

'And maybe not even then.'

'Maybe not. But you were the one who insisted: it has to be Conny. And if it has to be Conny then I'm afraid...'

She paused for a moment. Then she looked at me directly.

'I want you in the room with me. All the time.'

'Of course.'

'All. The. Time.'

'Absolutely.'

'Nothing's going to happen to me. You promise?'

I felt the tightness that had been building in my chest begin to relax.

'I promise. A hundred per cent.'

Consequently, the two of us found ourselves standing outside the door of Conny's penthouse suite at 7pm that evening with our hearts in our mouths and *Susanna & the Elders* under our arms. Christie was wearing one of her Azzedine Alaïa dresses, which still looked pristine – and still fitted her perfectly – after more than thirty years. I wasn't sure which of these facts astounded me more.

'This was one of Conny's favourites,' Christie had explained as she'd exited from her cab in the stunning crossover halterneck midi-dress in black silk. Looking at her, I could see why he liked it. On anybody else it might have looked a bit much for what was basically a business meeting, but on her it looked just the right kind of classy.

'Believe me – I know what Conny likes,' she'd reassured me, and I didn't doubt it for a moment.

The door was opened by one of Conny's minders, who showed us, silently, into one of the side rooms of the suite.

'Wait here,' our escort said sternly. 'I'll come and collect you when Mr Gerou is ready.' He then disappeared without waiting for questions.

# SIXTEEN

The room felt huge, as one might have expected for a penthouse suite in the Walled Garden, but its size was offset by the large packages that it was currently housing, all marked as diplomatic baggage.

In my head I guess the phrase 'diplomatic baggage' had always conjured up images of smart attaché cases with perhaps an understated label tied with string to the handle declaring that the case and its contents were the property of Her Britannic Majesty. This, however, was not what we were surrounded by. The packages ranged in size from perhaps two feet by four feet, to some which seemed as tall as me. What they all had in common was that they were all flat. Whatever the height and width, none was more than eight inches in depth. I couldn't see the contents because they were all wrapped in white hessian with a Greek crest and 'HELLAS' stamped in blue on the front, but they did not appear to be the diplomatic papers which Conny had insisted in court that he would be assiduously reviewing during his London sojourn. A more cynical mind than mine may have concluded that he was trying to evacuate some of his favourite artworks from the country as well as his cash, and that more cynical mind belonged to Christie.

'Oh my God! He really is on the run. I wonder which pictures he's chosen to take with him.' She began to rummage through them. 'Do you think he'll have any of me?'

Given the size of Conny's Von Holunder collection, I was pretty confident that among this cornucopia of thirty or forty frames there would be at least some featuring Christie. In light of my experience in the bathroom earlier that afternoon, however, it was not a theory I was anxious to verify. Christie, on the other hand, didn't even bother to check the door before she headed to the largest frame in the room and began trying to remove its hessian shroud.

'I'm really not sure you should be—'

'Relax! He'll be ages. Believe me, I know Conny – he'll keep us waiting twenty minutes just to make a point.' And she continued her battle with the huge hessian shroud.

It interested me that she needed to know; that it mattered to her whether Conny – whose collection of artworks could be numbered in the high hundreds – had selected anything featuring her among those few that he had chosen to take with him.

Somehow, she managed to remove the staples that were holding the hessian together over the frame without damaging either them or the hessian itself. She wriggled the hessian sheath down the side of the frame to reveal what I instantly recognised as Erik's 1983 painting, *Within Arm's Reach of Desire*.

This was a rare chance for me to see it in the flesh. Conny kept it in his private collection so it was seldom on public display. I'd only ever seen it once before – on that fateful night with Suzy at the Redfern, as part of Erik's retrospective – but it had been one of the paintings that had made an impression on me then, and that impression was immediately reignited by seeing it again.

In it, Christie wore a pair of figure-hugging hot pants and a denim shirt tied off under her bust, leaving her taut midriff exposed. The top three buttons of the shirt were left undone, and she leant forward teasingly so that her cleavage was visible.

But the thing that really made that picture was what Christie was doing with the Coke bottle in her right hand. Unusually for a Von Holunder portrait of Christie, her head was angled away from the viewer towards the bottle which she held up invitingly to her lips. She was pouting exaggeratedly as though straining to reach the bottle, the contents of which were almost-but-not-quite being poured into her mouth. Her lips seemed to be gently kissing the mouth of the bottle in the manner of so many soft drink ads of that era.

But rather than closing her eyes in imagined ecstasy, as an ad photographer might have got her to do, Christie was looking out of the corner of her eye back at the viewer. It was not a look of wilful defiance as in the earlier pictures, nor of gentle insouciance as in the later ones. Instead, there was something knowing in her eyes that hinted – and more than hinted – that she was fully aware of the effect she was having on the viewer, but which also suggested she was gently mocking it, and even gently mocking the idea of using sex to sell something as perfunctory as a sugared beverage.

Looked at in isolation, critics tended to regard the painting as something of a double bluff. Erik had been accused (most notably by Craig Owens in a piece for *Art in America*) both of laughing at Coke's advertising strategy and, at the same time, of using exactly the same strategy to sell his own painting. This may or may not have been fair, but seen within the context of his broader career, I had always understood *Within Arm's Reach of Desire* to be Erik's pivot painting; the one which signalled a shift from his mid-career, with its obsession with Christie as a young girl, to his later career where he began to see her more as a fully grown woman.

She'd turned thirty by this point and she no longer seemed at war with the viewer in the way that she had been in the earlier portraits. But more than that, she no longer seemed at war with her sexuality. She was aware of it now in a way which she hadn't been in 1975's *Juvenile Heart Attack*, for instance, and (whether through careful calculation or weary resignation) she seemed to have made her peace with the effect she could have. In *Within Arm's Reach of Desire* she had worked out how to control and calibrate her power for maximum effect so that, looking at it now, I still couldn't quite tell if she was mocking the viewer for staring at her, mocking the collector for paying so much for it, or mocking Erik for being so obsessed with her.

'Oh, I absolutely love this one,' Christie said, and I noticed her anxiety ease. The memories of the disappointment of her visit to MoMA were banished and her face surrendered to a look of wistful satisfaction. 'The title comes from the Robert Woodruff quote, of course,' she said.

I knew this. Coke's former president was every ad-man's hero, and the phrase '*Coca-Cola should always be within an arm's reach of desire*' had entered copywriting folklore. He wanted Coke to represent fulfilment so that people would want to buy it. But at the same time its fulfilment had to remain tantalisingly out of reach, or else you wouldn't need to buy it again. The phrase brilliantly captured the promise that was perpetually offered yet never quite delivered.

Looked at like that, it seemed entirely natural for Erik to put Christie and a Coke bottle in the same picture.

I turned my head from the painting to the real-life Christie standing next to me.

'He's really captured you there. There's something about you, even now, that he's brought out in this painting.'

'You really think so? What do you think that is?'

She turned to look at me as though, for once, she was actually interested in my answer. I didn't realise why at the time, I just thought that maybe my attempts at charm were starting to get to her. In any event, I took a moment to compose a reply that I thought might nudge me further into Christie's affections.

'Well, you're within arm's reach of the viewer in this picture, but, of course, we can't actually touch you. You're teasing us. You're *almost* drinking the Coke; you're *almost* showing your breasts. We can't quite touch the thing that we want. It's still just a picture. I guess I think you're still like that now – even in the flesh.'

She looked at me deeply for a moment, and then her face broke out into a broad smile. 'Well spotted, young man. I mean, I've been pawed at by more men than I dare to count, believe me. You're standing right next to me now – you could reach out and grab my ass like the rest of them—'

'Oh, I would never do that. I hope you know that.'

'Don't be stupid – of course I do! But it wouldn't matter if you did. Because what I realised when I saw this painting was that it didn't really matter.'

'Oh, but I think it does. It absolutely does,' I interjected quickly.

'I get that. In one sense. And maybe it was just a coping mechanism, but I came to think that it didn't matter *ultimately* because there would always be something about me that was fundamentally ungraspable.'

'And that was the thing they really wanted.'

She nodded. 'I think that's true of all the best women. Certainly all the interesting ones. The guys who grab us never get what they *really* want. I take some pleasure from that. The girls who complain are the ones who are dull enough to be worried that their ass might be the only thing they've got worth grabbing.'

And that was Christie in a nutshell: stunningly, gloriously right, and at the same time horribly, tragically wrong.

# SEVENTEEN

Thankfully, Christie had managed to replace the hessian over the frame and reapply the staples before our escort returned. But when he did, it was not to show us through to Conny. Instead, he walked in and, without acknowledging our presence, headed straight over to a selection of frames that were leaning against a sideboard. He grappled with the hessian sheath on a couple of them and stood, staring at what he had revealed. He eyed the door nervously, before shaking his head, grabbing one of the frames – apparently at random – and heading back out of the room with it.

Moments later we heard a menacing female voice cut through the air. 'What the fuck's this? I asked for the Hodgkin – this is a Bowling! Bring me the fucking Hodgkin!'

There was a pause, during which muttered voices could be heard before the female voice once again sought to establish order. 'Jesus, Conny! Do any of your people know anything?

Can they not tell the difference between a Howard Hodgkin and a Frank Bowling?'

This seemed quite a high bar to set for someone who was basically being paid to intimidate people on behalf of his boss. I'd been working in the contemporary art market for fifteen years and I wasn't sure that even I would be able tell the difference between works by the two masters of British abstract expressionism.

But while my mind was exercised on this issue, it soon became clear that Christie's was focused on something else. She froze, apparently unable to speak for a moment.

'Are you alright?' I asked, concerned.

Her response made no sense to me at first. 'Is that Loo-veh?' she asked.

'What?'

'Loo-veh? The lawyer.'

That was when the penny dropped. 'Oh, you mean *Love*!'

Love Menolo was the daughter of a famous Swedish beauty (hence the two-vowelled pronunciation of her Christian name), and a father who had run Drouot's, France's most famous auction house. She was, indeed, a lawyer and, given her paternity, it was perhaps not surprising that her legal expertise was focused on the art market. What exactly her legal expertise involved her in was a matter of much conjecture in the art market itself. Most of her cases seemed to have links with suspected fraud, but whether she was preventing it or enabling it was never wholly clear. She'd been refused a licence to practise law in at least three countries that I knew of, for reasons that had never been made public, but she had never been convicted of a crime. The simple fact was, if you needed something done 'discreetly' – perhaps a painting disposed of, or its bona fides defended – then Love was the lawyer you wanted to do it. Consequently, her services were in greater demand in the art community than her reputation in the legal community suggested they should be.

It made perfect sense that she knew Conny: they were both involved in the art world, and both seemed comfortable operating close to its penumbral fringes if a suitably lucrative opportunity presented itself. But two things caused me concern. First, what was she doing with Conny now? If Conny was utilising her services then it would have to be because of something to do with art, rather than his extradition, and I assumed that that could only be related to our proposed sale of *Susanna & the Elders*. Given their respective reputations, if he and Love were operating together, it seemed to raise the risks associated with our deal to levels with which I would be uncomfortable.

The other possibility, however, was even more concerning. It was that Conny and Love *weren't* operating together. Love was usually based in Paris – her office was in the eighth arrondissement – and there was one other art-world figure also based in Paris (and also in the eighth arrondissement) who I knew would be interested in the conversation that Christie and I were about to have with Conny: Mimi von Holunder.

Was it possible Love was here on an errand from Mimi? I could feel my mouth drying out at the very thought, and a small wave of nausea rose in the pit of my stomach. Christie was way ahead of me.

'What does she know?' she asked me.

It was not a question I could answer, but it gnawed away at my bowels.

Conny's minder returned, looking suitably humbled, and

153

cast the Bowling painting to one side. He then took one of the others, removed the hessian sheath protecting it, and checked it against an image on his mobile phone. The Abstract Expressionists were outside my area of expertise, but even to my untrained eye it looked special. I guessed that it was Howard Hodgkin's *Chinoiserie* (although, to be honest, a lot of Hodgkin's output from the 2003-10 period looked pretty similar, so I couldn't be absolutely sure). I knew that *Chinoiserie* had been sold by the Gagosian at Sotheby's in New York fairly recently. From memory, it had gone for about $450,000 – about twice the pre-auction estimate – so this was not a cheap painting. It raised the question in my mind of why Love wanted it, and even more, why Conny would be prepared to give it to her.

The minder put the painting back in its hessian sheath and took it back to Conny. We couldn't hear the details of the conversation, but Love seemed placated. Christie, however, was not.

'What is she doing here, Gabriel?'

'I don't know.'

'Well, for Christ's sake, find out!'

I went to the door of our room, opened it very slightly and peered cautiously through. Sure enough, there was Love, looking resplendent in a very sharp trouser suit. She was probably four or five years older than me, but she'd managed to keep her weight down more successfully than I had and it gave her a certain elegance, although, to be fair, her Louboutin heels probably helped too (Love's unique brand of legal assistance did not come cheap).

She was flanked by two of Conny's men, one of whom was carrying the Hodgkin. Conny was there too, in his shirtsleeves, with his collar unbuttoned, talking to Love in hushed tones. I couldn't tell what they were saying, but the fact that, for once, Conny wasn't grinning suggested that it was important. Then a thick-bodied man in a dishevelled brown suit emerged from another room in the suite carrying several large bundles of what appeared to be bank notes. I recognised him immediately as Rocco Danaos, who was a familiar figure in Conny's entourage. The precise ambit of Rocco's job was never wholly clear, but he always appeared to be very agitated while he was doing it, and today was no exception. The more charitable observers called him a chief of staff, but most of us saw him as Conny's fixer. The careworn look on his chubby, middle-aged face suggested that there was plenty for him to fix.

Rocco looked at Conny, who gave him a nod, and then he carefully began counting out the bundles into a small knapsack being held open by Love. There were six large bundles of two hundred-euro bank notes. I don't know how many notes were in each bundle, but together they looked like a significant sum of money. Five of the bundles went into the knapsack, which was then firmly zipped shut before the sixth was put directly into Love's outstretched hand.

Love passed the knapsack to one of her escorts, offered Rocco and Conny a firm handshake, then turned on her perfectly crafted heels and left, closely followed by Conny's two men. Rocco and Conny looked at each other and let out a sigh, but neither looked relaxed. Our escort was there too, standing at the entrance to another room in the suite.

'Is she still here?' Conny called out to him.

'Yes, sir. She's with some guy. They're waiting in the other room,' he replied, pointing in my direction.

I discreetly pulled my head away from the doorway.

'Well, let me get ready, and then bring them in,' I heard Conny say.

Christie was anxious to know what I had seen. I didn't know, and that made me uncomfortable. It didn't make sense that Love was receiving money if she was also receiving a painting. Nor could I understand why Conny had been prepared to hand over a valuable Howard Hodgkin without, apparently, receiving any paperwork in return. There was also a rather obvious question: if the one bundle of notes had been for her, then who were the other five bundles for – and why?

All I knew was that Rocco was famous for treating Conny's money as though it were his own, so if he had been so liberally dispensing it to one of Europe's most dubitable lawyers, it could only mean one thing: trouble.

# EIGHTEEN

Christie and I were left to stew in our own juices for perhaps a further twenty minutes, during which we exhaustively mined every conceivable justification for the scene that I had witnessed. While we didn't agree on much, the one thing we did both agree on was that Love's presence was a complicating factor we had not anticipated, and certainly did not welcome. It left a bolus of unease between us, which we tetchily chewed on while we waited to be summoned by our host.

Eventually, our escort returned, and we were wordlessly taken through to see Conny. The lounge area of his suite was luxurious and expansive, the decorative wall mouldings and intricate cornices giving it the feel of an Italian palazzo, but it was littered with various members of his entourage, who appeared to be arranged in a very specific hierarchy centred around who got a seat. I recognised one of the lucky ones as Mandalay Schunk, Conny's art buyer. It was a while since

I'd seen him, but he hadn't changed much – not even his wardrobe. He appeared to be the last man in the world still wearing a black polo-neck for professional purposes. With his creased, bronzed skin and swept back white hair, it gave him the appearance of an ageing Riviera cat burglar tempted out of retirement for one last job. Despite this, I was relieved that he was there. If Conny outsourced his personal safety to his minders, he outsourced his artistic taste to Mandalay, so the fact that he was in the room suggested that Conny was serious about buying our painting.

The only other face I recognised was Rocco's. He was seated by the door, tapping away on his smartphone, a film of sweat glistening on his brow. The pings on his phone indicated that messages were coming back at him almost as fast as he was sending them out. Judging by his face, none of them were bringing him any comfort. If anything, he looked even more anxious than he had done earlier when he'd been handing over the cash to Love, and I noticed him taking a blast from an asthma inhaler to ease his breathing. But even that was nothing next to the anxiety that Christie and I were feeling. Love's unexpected appearance complicated everything. The solid ground that we had thought we were treading on was shifting beneath our feet and I could feel the room spinning as I approached our host.

'Are you sure you don't want me to get one of the guys to check them over?' Rocco asked. His physique and appearance bore testimony to a life that could euphemistically be described as having been 'fully lived' but his voice sounded as though his inhaler was filled with helium rather than Ventolin.

Conny smiled. 'I think I can trust her. You're not carrying anything sharp, are you?' he asked Christie.

'Only my tongue,' she replied.

Conny let out one of his signature bronchial chuckles. 'That's what I always loved about you. Your sense of humour.'

Conny was seated behind a large mahogany writing desk adorned with ornate marquetry, which he appeared to be using as some kind of power projection device. One corner of the desk was piled with cartons of Sobranie Black Russians, one of which was open, and a lit cigarette hung from Conny's hand. I looked up at the ceiling to see that he'd had one of his men cover the smoke sensor with a rather elegant sock. He seemed to have showered and changed his suit since his conversation with Love. His sleeves were secured with gold cufflinks and his neck was now adorned with a Swarovski-encrusted Stefano Ricci tie. Having wondered if Christie had been overdoing it with her outfit, I now felt distinctly underdressed – although I was not naïve enough to believe that any of Conny's sartorial effort had been expended in order to impress me.

If that had not been clear before, it became apparent the moment Christie cautiously followed me into the room. Conny stood and greeted her with a warm hug, despite her apparent awkwardness. In her heels she was a good six inches taller than him, so the scene had a slightly comic quality, but Conny seemed transfixed by her, and this gave him a radically different demeanour. The anxious grimace he had flashed at Rocco in the hallway just a few minutes previously had given way to a warm and open smile. If I hadn't known him better, I'd have assumed that he was smitten.

'Christie! You are a marvel! As beautiful and elegant as I remember.'

His face cracked into a wide crocodilian grin. If his intention was to put Christie at her ease, he hadn't communicated this to his eyes. Something in the way they devoured her implied that she was right to be worried, although not perhaps for the reasons she'd initially assumed.

'Thanks. Good to see you too, Conny,' she said, uncharacteristically muted. 'I hope you'll be as enthusiastic about the painting we're going to show you.'

We were invited to sit on the other side of the desk. Mandalay, sitting in the seat to Conny's right, nodded at me wordlessly, but didn't rise or offer a hand. I was used to this, and not discouraged. Mandalay could be the most personable guy in the room over a drink, but when there was business to be done, he became unfailingly serious. His demeanour suggested he was in business mode.

Conny turned to the attractive young woman whom I'd assumed was his publicist and muttered something to her in Greek. She appeared unimpressed by this and flounced out. She returned a few moments later carrying a tray with a bottle of champagne, some glasses and a single red rose in a glass vase, before disappearing out of the room again.

'It's your favourite – Dom Pérignon,' Conny said, taking the bottle from its chiller and pouring Christie a glass. 'The 2008. I know the 2002 is more powerful, but this one offers greater acidity, so I think it ages better... Rather like you.' He flashed a coy smile at her and raised his eyebrows. 'Cheers!'

'Thank you. But I suggest we leave the champagne on ice until we've got something to celebrate,' Christie replied flatly.

'But surely we already do?'

'What would that be?'

'The resumption of our relationship.' Conny lifted his own champagne flute. 'To old flames.'

Christie looked sceptical. 'Our relationship ended, Conny.

And for very particular reasons.'

'I know it did. But couldn't it be restarted?' He searched her face for a sign of encouragement.

Christie's lips tightened. I could tell she wanted to say more than she felt she could. After all, we still needed to seal the deal.

'You can be my emeritus boyfriend,' she said in a rare attempt to be diplomatic.

'What does that mean?'

'It's Latin, Conny. E is for ex, and meritus means you deserved it.'

Conny chuckled a horrible, rasping laugh. 'Well *that's* not very ladylike – although I guess you never were.'

'Thanks. I'll take that as a compliment. And for the record, Conny,' she said as he moved behind her, 'it's not my job to behave like a lady. It's your job to behave like a gentleman.'

I could tell that she really meant it.

I decided to intervene and move discussions on to their intended purpose.

'Look, Mr Gerou, we're really appreciative of your time given the, uh, other pressures you're under at the moment.' Rocco stopped tapping, lifted his eyes for a moment, and shot me an unimpressed stare before returning to his phone. 'And I know that Ms McGraw is delighted to reconnect with you after so many years. But let's get down to business. We have a painting that Ms McGraw is keen to sell, and which we think you'll be keen to buy.'

Mandalay finally broke his silence. 'Well, let me be the judge of that,' he said, affecting disinterest.

I had never quite been able to place Mandalay's accent. He spoke French, Italian and Spanish fluently, and was reputedly even passable in Greek and Tagalog, but, despite his surname, had no German. He clearly wanted to sound American, yet there was a clipped severity to his consonants that suggested he'd learnt his English from one of the villains in the Bond movies of my childhood. Like many in the art world, he appeared to have been everywhere, but come from nowhere.

Christie and I stood, removed our painting from its pouch, and placed it on our seats, directly in front of Mandalay and Conny.

'Gentlemen,' I said, theatrically. 'I give you – *Susanna & the Elders*. The lost masterpiece of Erik von Holunder!'

Immediately, Mandalay leant forward, and he couldn't stop himself gasping in surprise. He was not disinterested now.

'And you say Von Holunder painted this?'

Conny appeared agitated. 'Of course he did! I watched him do it. It was '85, '86 – around then, anyway. I even saw the finished thing, although I don't remember it being as good as this. But to be fair, I had been drinking cognac all day. Show him the photo.'

I took out the old photo and placed it on the desk in front of Mandalay.

'You see?' Conny said, slapping Mandalay's shoulder with the back of his hand. 'There it is – in Erik's studio. How else do you think it got there, other than Erik painting it?'

'It's just that... How do I put this? This is not what I was expecting,' Mandalay said. 'The *Old Masters* series was pretty... variable – and Erik held this one back. The word was that he wasn't happy with it; that it wasn't good enough to show. But this! Well, to be frank, this looks better than most of the shit he did show.'

'So, you want to buy it?' Christie asked.

'Hey, hold on there! I need to check it out first,' said Mandalay, rising from his seat. 'May I?'

He removed a magnifier from his pocket and carefully placed it in his eye socket. Then he came round to the front of the desk and began to examine the painting. The room fell into a hushed and anxious silence, broken only by Rocco tapping out a soft, galloping rhythm on his phone, much to Christie's annoyance.

'Hey, Fred Astaire – you got a mute function on that thing?'

Rocco looked at his boss in surprise, but Conny only gave him a single, dour, nod. Rocco sighed, flicked a button on the side of his phone, and proceeded to continue his tapping in silence. Meanwhile, the young publicist sheepishly re-entered the room and began staring at the painting too, albeit from a greater distance. After a few moments she spotted something that amused her. She put her hand on Conny's shoulder and pointed at the painting.

'Is that you on there? Oh my God, you look so different! You're adorable!'

Her unsolicited affection seemed to aggravate Conny, who shook her off. There was a tart exchange between them in Greek and the young woman left the room again.

Mandalay continued to examine the painting with a diligence and thoroughness that suggested he was unimpressed by even Conny's insistence that it was genuine. His face was cold and expressionless as he drew the magnifier slowly over the picture, paying particular attention to the signature in the bottom right-hand corner. The room seemed frozen, and I became aware of the ticking of my wristwatch, which suddenly seemed to be disconcertingly loud. I noticed that my hands were balled into tight fists, and I felt a clamminess building on my palms. I had not anticipated this degree of suspicion from Mandalay, and it disturbed me. My cedit card bill and future career path were both resting on his decision.

I looked over at Christie and saw her leg was shaking. Even Conny's face was pensive. He nervously took a draw on his cigarette before stubbing it out in a makeshift ashtray. But as the delay lengthened, he grabbed the open packet and lit another.

Eventually it appeared that Mandalay's examination was complete. He stood up and placed the magnifier back in his pocket. His face still gave no clue as to his judgement.

'Well, that all seems to be in order – more or less,' he said.

Christie was not impressed. 'More or less?! What's that supposed to mean? It's either in order or it isn't.'

I managed to keep my mouth shut but was similarly aggrieved. It felt like he was questioning my bona fides.

'The painting looks genuine, at least superficially. The signature seems kosher, and your story certainly helps. It's just that…' He stopped talking and looked at the painting again with a pained expression.

'It's just that, what? You don't believe your boss?' I asked with a forcefulness that perhaps hinted at a mounting concern on my part, even though it was intended to convey the opposite.

Mandalay would not be flustered. He had been asked to establish the authenticity of the painting and that is what he would do, without fear or favour. The art world was full of embarrassed experts who had let emotion get the better of them. Mandalay had survived so long in the business precisely because he refused to make that mistake. Emotion didn't come into his valuations; they were driven by the facts, and there was one fact that gave him pause.

'The brush strokes here, in the middle of the painting – they seem different somehow.'

'Well *of course* they're different!' Christie replied. 'He was painting me. He painted them with a very specific tenderness to show how much he loved me. Isn't that so, Mr Viejo?' She turned to me in search of some support.

This theory was speculative, but it was the theory that I had come up with when I had first seen the painting in Christie's trailer, so it naturally appealed. It was also plausible. Given what was at stake therefore, I decided that now was the time to give it my enthusiastic backing.

'Absolutely,' I said, confidently. 'And that's what makes this painting so interesting. It causes us to reappraise Von Holunder's whole relationship with Ms McGraw. So many of his earlier paintings focus on her raw sexuality, but here, right towards the end of his life, when he's painting a scene that could have given him full rein to explore that again, we can see a much rounder, a much fuller portrayal of her womanhood. This is a very definite maturing of his style. Perhaps that's why he didn't show it?'

'What? Because it was better than the other eleven paintings in the series? That seems unlikely,' Mandalay replied.

'No, because he didn't want to risk Mimi seeing that Christie was more than just his mistress. Perhaps he didn't want to risk her seeing this and realising that actually it was Christie, and not her, who was the real love of his life.'

'Exactly!' Christie added, stepping forward and jabbing her finger on the desk.

Mandalay reflected on this for a moment. 'I guess so...but there's one thing I'd like to check. Just to be absolutely sure.'

He picked up the picture and flipped it over. Then he began

to pull the canvas away from the back of the strainer in the bottom right-hand corner. I was incensed.

'What the hell are you doing? You can't do that!'

'Relax! I'm just checking if it's been stitched. Surely you – of all people – know about that?'

I didn't and this was an embarrassment to me. It suggested that Mandalay knew more about Erik's work than I did. I flashed Christie a worried stare. For her part she appeared unconcerned by Mandalay's assault on her painting, so I resisted the urge to grab it from out of his hands.

'Of course we know!' Christie said. She turned as though addressing her explanation to Rocco, although he seemed wholly concerned with his phone. 'There were so many frauds about. And some of them were really good – really convincing. Erik was paranoid that not even he would be able to tell the real ones from the fakes, so he started stitching his initials into the back of the canvas after he'd finished it. That way, if there was ever a question mark about authenticity, he would have a sure-fire way to confirm one way or the other. He did it right in the corner and then glued it down so no one could see it, but it would be easy enough for him to check if he ever had to.'

'And here we are,' said Mandalay, peeling the canvas away from the stretcher to reveal some red letters stitched into it. 'EvH – Erik von Holunder.'

He now fixed me with a pitying smile.

'Don't beat yourself up about it, kid,' he said. 'Nobody knew. That was the point. If the fakers knew they'd just have copied him.'

This revelation was shocking to me. I'd studied Erik's work for so long and prided myself that there was nothing that I didn't know, yet it appeared that this crucial secret had evaded me. It would have saved me a lot of hassle later if I had started to wonder at that point what other secrets might have evaded me, but a combination of wounded professional pride and my crush on Christie blinded me.

'He only told me about it after I started buying seriously from him,' Conny added. 'He was falling out of favour a bit by then and I was keeping his market value up pretty much singlehandedly, so he wanted to make sure I didn't get stung.'

As a supposed expert in the works of Erik von Holunder I wanted to explore this more, but as someone trying to close a sale, I recognised that I needed to move the conversation on.

'OK Mandy, I think we need to discuss our proposed terms of sale.'

I had already indicated the fact that it had to be a cash sale and that we were amenable to completing within the next twenty-fours. Given that Conny's flight back to Greece was scheduled to leave in a little more than thirty-six hours, I hoped that our willingness to offer the latter would encourage Conny to consider a generous offer in regard to the former, but Mandalay appeared keen to flush out our position first.

'So, what were you hoping to get for it?' he asked.

I knew from Grandpa Jo that that was the one piece of information you should never give away, so I demurred.

'I'd be interested in your view as to what it's worth,' I replied.

'I tell you what,' Conny said, turning to Christie. 'Why don't you meet me in the restaurant for dinner in half an hour and I'll give you my offer then?'

'I think we need to seal the deal before we start celebrating it,' Christie replied.

'But if we don't go to dinner there may be no deal to seal.'

'I'm not really hungry,' she said.

'No dinner, no deal,' said Conny, gruffly.

Christie remained insistent: 'No deal, no dinner.'

Negotiations over dinner proved to be more acrimonious than discussions over provenance, but eventually the compromise position was agreed that Christie would have dinner with Conny but only once the sale was concluded and the money had been received. And, as this was a business deal that they were celebrating, she would be joined by her business associate – me – and Conny could bring a business associate of his choosing too, 'or anyone else you want to bring along,' Christie said, looking rather dismissively in the direction of the door out of which the young woman had disappeared. Conny was growing agitated at Christie's attitude, and this simply riled him more.

I decided to move things along. 'So, where does that leave us?' No one responded. 'I was thinking—'

'Well, quit thinking and just listen.' Conny stood up and attempted to loom over the table at me. Given his lack of height this was easier said than done. 'I don't know what you two are trying to pull here, but I'm not some mug who's wet behind the ears. And I gotta tell you, I won't be screwed over – not by you or anyone else.'

He looked accusingly at Christie. She was about to interrupt, but Conny proceeded regardless. 'I've got dozens of Erik's paintings and I know what they're worth.' His eyes narrowed. 'And I also know what they're *not* worth.'

'I don't doubt it for a moment, Mr Gerou,' I said. But Conny was not in listening mode.

'So don't think you can use me as some kind of cashpoint,

Christie, just because of our history. And don't think I'll pay over the odds just because I'm in the painting. I'm not running a charity here. I'm a businessman, and this is a business investment.'

I began hastily revising downwards the mathematics on our possible deal. Conny stubbed out his cigarette aggressively then stabbed his finger at me. 'Eight hundred thousand,' he boomed. 'Not a cent more.'

I tried to retain my composure. Out of the corner of my eye I saw that even Mandalay started slightly. Rocco immediately stopped tapping on his phone and cast a nervous glance in his boss's direction.

'I'm sorry, was that dollars?' I asked.

'Of course it's dollars. It sure as hell ain't pounds.'

I decided to accept the offer as gracefully as possible. 'Well, I'm sure that would be more than—'

'Absolutely no way!' Christie exploded.

All of us were stunned into silence.

'What the hell do you take me for, Conny? Some kind of sap? You think you can leer over me and shout a bit and I'll just go along, simpering, with whatever figure you pluck out of the air?'

Even Conny didn't know what to say. He sat back in his chair looking like a child being berated by the teacher.

'This painting is it – the great lost Von Holunder that everyone's been looking for for the past thirty years. And it's mine. Because I rescued it when the whole world was happy for him to throw it away.' She was quaking with an indignation that appeared so righteous even I wasn't sure if she really was serious. 'Let's not forget, *I'd Love to Turn You On* sold for a million dollars the last time it came up for sale and this is way better than that.' She was correct on both counts, although the last time Erik's 1968 portrait of Mimi (officially entitled *J'adorerais t'allumer*) had come up for sale was in 1992, when Mimi had bought it at a massively inflated price simply because she was determined that Erik's most expensive painting should be of her rather than of Christie. Christie, however, judiciously chose to omit these facts, and then continued with her tirade before anyone else had the chance to mention them.

'This painting is my last connection with Erik and that whole world. It's the only thing I have left of his. And you want me to give it away to you just because you think I'm desperate? How dare you! How dare you, Conny! I am worth more than that. I certainly should be worth more than that to you!' She stabbed her finger towards him accusingly.

Conny didn't know how to respond. It was clearly not the reaction he had been expecting, and to be fair, neither had I.

'So what do you think would be a fair price?' he asked.

'One point two million.'

'Dollars?' he spluttered.

'Well I sure as hell don't mean Chinese yuan,' Christie replied.

Rocco took another blast from his inhaler. The look on his face suggested that his medication might have been the only thing keeping him alive at that moment.

Negotiations progressed rapidly from that point. I had thought that they would be led by Mandalay and me, but the thing about Christie was that in her company you were invariably forced into the role of acolyte, whether you liked it or not. And Conny was clearly not a man used to being told no – and certainly not by a woman.

It was difficult to tell if his offer was driven more by his desperate need to offload some cash quickly before he and his diplomatic baggage were bundled aboard the plane back to Greece in barely thirty-six hours' time, or by his apparently uncontainable desire to secure a dinner date with Christie. In any event, he didn't appear kindly disposed toward Mandalay's attempts to convince Christie to accept the $800,000 on the table and I started to wonder if she could get the full $1.2 million. But she seemed just a little too desperate to secure a sale and have the cash handed over there and then if she could. It gave Conny a toehold in negotiations, which he slowly and stealthily built on.

There was an awkwardness, a stiltedness, to their bargaining that suggested a residual wariness on both sides. Cards were not being put on the table. Nothing in Conny's demeanour, or in anything Mandalay had said, suggested to me that either man had any reason to believe Mimi knew of our meeting, but she hovered above our conversation and prowled its shadows. The same was true of Love. No one had mentioned her name or acknowledged that she had been in the self-same suite barely thirty minutes previously, but she lurked in every glance that Christie and I exchanged. Like Banquo's ghost, the presence of the two women could be sensed rather than seen, but it was none the less real for that.

In the end Conny and Christie settled on a purchase price of $1 million. Under the terms of my agreement with Christie this would turn my initial $135,000 investments into a cool half-a-million dollars, which was a very nice couple of days' work indeed. And it would give Christie the $250,000 she said she needed and still leave her a further $250,000 for her disbursements (which were proving to be significant). But before they could shake hands on the deal, Conny turned to

Mandalay.

'You OK with that?' he muttered, clearly expecting a brief nod of agreement.

Mandalay paused and looked directly at me. 'That depends on Mr Viejo.'

Conny was as surprised as I was.

'I've already said I'm prepared to vouch for its authenticity, Mandy,' I said. 'I've written and signed a statement certifying that I believe this to be a genuine Von Holunder. And Christie has also provided a statement saying that she saw Erik paint this, and that she saw Mr Gerou and Erik discussing it when Erik was going to throw it out. That means you can turn this into a legitimate asset.'

'And you'll give us these statements as part of the deal?' asked Conny.

'Of course. Here – you can check them out.' I reached into my jacket pocket and pulled out two statements, before offering them to Conny.

To my surprise, Mandalay leapt up and snatched them both out of my hand.

'It's OK. I'll check those,' he said, and he proceeded to read through them both.

'That's all great,' he said eventually. 'I just need you to understand that there are certain...expectations that come with asking me to authorise the purchase of a painting like this for a price like that. As long as you're prepared to meet those expectations then I'm happy to give my blessing.'

I wasn't quite sure what he was getting at and, judging by the look on Conny's face, neither was he.

'You think I'm going to rip your client off?' I asked.

'Not at all.'

'Well then, I don't understand what you mean.'

'I just need you to understand that it's my reputation on the line too. I need you to understand that there are implications to that. I have to defend my reputation.'

'I understand that, Mandy. Of course I do. I would never want to damage your reputation, I promise you.'

'Good. As long as we understand each other, then I'm fine with it.'

I wasn't sure we understood each other at all, but I just wanted to get out of that room with a deal agreed. I was already imagining phoning Jasper with the good news about my offer to buy my way into his gallery.

'So we're good?' Conny asked.

Mandalay fixed me with his smile once again. 'We're good.'

'For a million dollars?'

'With Mr Viejo's report and Ms McGraw's statement, then yes. I guess so.'

'And you?' Conny asked Rocco. 'You can make this happen?'

'It's your money,' shrugged Rocco. 'If Mandy's happy, then I'll see what I can do.'

'Then we have a deal,' said Conny, smiling.

'Great!' said Christie enthusiastically. 'Well, if you just give us the money we can go and leave you with your painting.'

Conny snorted. 'What? You think we have a million dollars just lying around the room in cash?'

That was, of course, exactly what we thought, but Conny's manner suggested that this idea was patently absurd, so both Christie and I suddenly became reluctant to explain that that was the basis on which our whole plan had been formulated.

'It'll take time to put that kind of money together,' Rocco explained.

'Time? We haven't got time,' Christie explained. 'I'm supposed to be flying out the day after tomorrow. As, I believe, are you,' she added archly.

'If you want it in dollars – which I assume you do – I'm going to need to talk to some people,' Rocco said. I sensed from his manner that 'talking to some people' would be neither an easy nor an inexpensive process.

Christie looked at me anxiously, but actually I was reassured by Rocco's comment. Coming from Greece to London, it made sense that their cash was probably in euros and sterling, neither of which would be of much use to Christie in the US.

'Relax, honey,' said Conny, putting a soothing hand on her shoulder. 'We'll have it ready for tomorrow. I promise.'

'Tomorrow morning?' Christie asked.

Conny unleashed another rasping guffaw, that turned into a bronchial cough. 'I think you'll find I have other business to attend to in the morning. We can meet up when I'm back from court.'

'That'll be fine, Mr Gerou,' I said.

Rocco didn't look too happy about his boss' assurances and immediately began texting again, this time even more frantically than before.

'So, would you like to join me in a celebratory glass of champagne now?' asked Conny.

'Thanks for the offer, Con, but we have a dinner reservation we have to get to.' This was news to me – but not unwelcome. 'Come on, Mr Viejo. Let's take this with us.'

I helped Christie put *Susanna & the Elders* back in its pouch, a rising sense of excitement building within me at the prospect of a dinner date with her. But Conny was not quite ready to give up his pursuit.

'Well, here's my card. Just so you've got my number if you need it,' he said, offering her a business card.

She looked at him sceptically. 'Oh, I've got your number, honey. Don't you worry about that.'

She turned on her heels and left – with the painting, but without Conny's card, which was left hanging forlornly from his outstretched hand.

# NINETEEN

'Well, he certainly seemed to like you,' I said as the lift doors closed behind us and we began our descent back to the hotel lobby. I tried to say it in a light-hearted way because I thought that she'd be flattered, and I didn't want her to think that I was jealous of him. But when she responded there was a slight edge to her voice that I hadn't anticipated.

'He desired me – there's a difference.'

'Is that a problem?'

'You betcha. I can do without his desire, thank you very much,' she replied through pursed lips.

This confused me and I felt the need to probe for an explanation. 'But Christie...the way you're dressed, the way you are, the whole aura you give off. You must know that you're going to provoke a certain amount of desire in a man.'

She turned to me and raised an eyebrow. It was sardonic rather than playful, as was her voice. '"Provoke"? Are you sure that's the word you want to use there?'

I felt myself blush. 'Well, maybe not. Probably not. But are you saying that you don't want to be desired?'

'I didn't say that – of course I want to be desired. Who doesn't?'

'Then I'm not sure exactly what you're—'

'Listen, kiddo, women want to be desired – even if they say they don't. Hell, *especially* if they say they don't.' She raised her index finger to silence the objection that she sensed was about to come from me. 'But that isn't enough. Guys think it should be...that you should be flattered that they desire you. But think about it from our perspective for a minute. If a guy takes a shine to you, then nine times out of ten, he can pretty much have his way with you, whether you want him to or not. Even Conny can make things happen – he can create a world around you that narrows your choices. Guys can do that. So yes, women want to be desired – but we also want to be *respected*. And the respect has to come first. You have to earn the right to desire a woman.'

She left a brief pause before adding, 'You know the thing that disappoints me most about men? It's not the fact that it's so easy to "provoke" them into desiring you. It's the fact it's so damn hard to make them respect you.'

And with that, the lift doors opened and she strode out into the hotel lobby.

She immediately set about trying to find Suzy. By the time we did, Suzy was getting ready to leave for the night. After what had clearly been a long day, I assumed she would be keen to get off promptly at the end of her shift, but the moment she saw us she took her coat off and began engaging Christie in conversation.

'Oh, Ms McGraw! How did it go?' she gushed when she saw her. 'Have you got what you wanted?' She exchanged a conspiratorial glance with Christie to indicate that she had kept the precise details of our business with Conny secret from the other hotel staff, several of whom remained in and around the hotel lobby.

'Call me Christie, please. And yes, I think we're there. We agreed a deal at any rate. We've just got to hope they can come up with the money tomorrow.'

This was more information than I was comfortable sharing with Suzy.

'Anyway, we don't want to stop you getting off,' I said. 'I'm sure it's been a long day.'

'For goodness sake, where are your manners, Gabriel?' Christie turned to Suzy. 'Would you like to join us for dinner? You were so helpful; I don't know what we'd have done without you. The least we can do is buy you dinner to say thank you. You'll do that, won't you, Gabriel?'

If there was one thing I liked less than Christie's profligacy with her own money, it was her profligacy with mine.

'Can I have a word?' I asked, steering her away from Suzy and towards a quiet corner of reception.

'Are you out of your mind?' I demanded when I was satisfied we were out of earshot.

I genuinely couldn't see what purpose could be served by inviting Suzy to have dinner with us. It would simply provide an opportunity for her to ask us lots of questions which Christie (probably) and I (certainly) didn't want to answer.

'What? She was very helpful this afternoon. I think it's pretty obvious we owe her one.'

'Well, given the significant depletion of my finances to

178

which Suzy has recently contributed, can I just say that that point feels a lot less obvious to me?'

But Christie wanted another favour from Suzy, and dinner at my expense was, in Christie's view, the ideal way of getting her to agree to it.

'I think it would be best if we left *Susanna* here for the night. Don't you agree?'

'No!'

Knowing Suzy as I did, it felt precarious at best for Christie to entrust the fate of a painting that we had just had valued at one million dollars to her care. But Christie brushed aside my objections.

'I don't want to be schlepping a million-dollar painting back and forth across London without any kind of protection. Hotels like this...well they always have some kind of secure storeroom for the guests to keep their valuables in.'

'I'm sure they do, but you seem to be ignoring the one salient fact here – we aren't guests in this hotel.'

'Which is why we need to get your ex-wife on our side. Unless you want to carry this around on your own for the next twenty-four hours?'

I remained silent.

'Look, for the price of a meal, it'd definitely be worth it. If we throw in a few glasses of wine I'm pretty sure she'd agree. You saw how much she liked me.'

This felt supremely optimistic to me, but Christie was not for budging and I certainly didn't fancy the prospect of travelling back to Wood Green on the Tube with a million-dollar painting under my arm, so I reluctantly acquiesced to her plan.

Behind all of Christie's bluster and chutzpah, the reality

was that her plan was no more complicated than plying Suzy with drink and hoping she'd eventually become amenable to breaking the hotel's rules as a favour to us. For her part, Suzy seemed keen to join us, although it was clear that this was more because of the chance it afforded her to spend time with Christie than because she wanted to reacquaint herself with me. On that basis, it seemed Christie's idea was at least worth a try.

Having agreed to that, I hoped that Christie would give me a reciprocal undertaking not to mention anything about the money I had given her, or its source. I was worried that any injudicious reference to my Argentinian bank account would reopen a whole chapter of my life that had been painfully – and expensively – closed, and the gains I had lately secured might all potentially disappear. However, as I was about to explain the sensitivities of my recent divorce settlement to her, Suzy came up and whisked us over to a table in the hotel's own restaurant.

'You can get your snap here,' she said. ('Snap' as a synonym for 'food' was another Suzy word.) 'We've just been awarded our first Michelin star!'

'Oh that would be wonderful!' said Christie. 'Wouldn't it Gabriel?'

The memory of my bill from the meal at Le Bernardin's suggested that my credit card was about to be pushed perilously close to its limit.

'Well, I'm not sure we need to go to all the expense of a Michelin star. Not until we've actually sealed the deal.'

'Relax. I get a thirty percent discount with my staff pass, so you're not really paying for me,' Suzy said with a wink in my direction.

Given the fastidiousness with which she and her lawyers had spent the last two years trying to part me from my assets, it seemed somewhat ironic that she clearly regarded her offer to save me a few quid on the price of our meal as a generous olive branch. But it was one that, under the circumstances, I was happy to accept.

The restaurant was called the Mastic Tree and Suzy had managed to secure us a plum table in a beautiful alcove next to the titular tree itself, the aromatic resin of which perfumed the air with the scent of pine and olibanum. The tree appeared to be growing out of the floor of the restaurant, but Suzy assured us it was rooted in a pot located under the tiling. Within a few minutes she and Christie were chatting away like old friends, much to my frustration. There was an easy familiarity to the way they spoke that was uninhibited by my presence and I found myself resenting it, and the fact that Suzy seemed so much more adept at getting Christie to open up than I had been. It meant that I found myself on the outside of the conversation, looking in at the two women locked in a shared intimacy from which I was excluded.

For her part, Christie seemed able to access a warmth and playfulness in Suzy that I no longer could. I'd always felt up until that point as though our divorce was somehow my failure – that I had failed to make our marriage work. But that night I began to wonder if actually I could ever have made it work. Listening to them, I could hear that, although they came from different continents, they came from the same world, and so understood each other's battles intuitively in a way that I did not, and perhaps never could have.

Eventually, Christie decided that Suzy had had enough of the Chateauneuf du Pape for her proposition regarding the storage of *Susanna & the Elders* to seem eminently reasonable so she started to explain to her that Conny couldn't complete the deal for perhaps another twenty-four hours. That meant that Christie was stuck with a highly valuable painting for the night and, as a vulnerable lone female, she didn't want to have to transport it back and forth across London; nor did she want to have sole custody of it, even for an hour or two.

'So, I was just wondering, is there perhaps somewhere safe and secure within The Walled Garden itself where we could keep the painting? Just for the night? I saw on your website that you have a secure storeroom, for instance. Might that be suitable, do you think?' she asked, innocently.

'Depends,' Suzy replied. 'How much is the painting worth?'

'Does that matter? I mean *really*?'

'We've got a limit of a hundred grand on individual items. It's our insurers. Sorry.'

'Well, honey, this is worth a little more than that, but I'm sure that as a friend—'

Suzy wasn't quite drunk enough to avoid the obvious conclusion that agreeing to store an item above the insurance limit on behalf of a non-guest could well prove to be a 'career-limiting' decision for her.

'Then it's a no, I'm afraid. I've got to stick to the limit, whoever's asking. We wouldn't let Mr Gerou put any of his 'diplomatic baggage' in there and he's a paying guest. But he couldn't certify it was below the limit, so my boss wouldn't let me. Sorry, but it's more than my job's worth.'

Christie smiled politely and poured Suzy another glass of wine, as she continued her diplomatic efforts. While Suzy was clearly pleasantly sozzled, her critical faculties had not entirely deserted her and there was one issue that was troubling her.

'What I can't understand,' Suzy said, turning to me, 'is why this has suddenly become an issue now. I mean, it was stored under a bed in a trailer park for thirty years. Why is one more night at the Dorchester such a problem?'

'It's not a problem, as such—' I protested.

'But it clearly is. You've brought it all the way from the States without any security, but you won't take it a couple of miles between us and the Dorchester. I don't understand.'

'I don't think there's anything for you to understand, Suze. Christie's just asking you for a favour, as a friend—'

'And maybe if I understood what was going on here, Gabe, then I'd be more willing to consider being friendly,' she said, adopting the patronising tone that had wound me up so much in our divorce negotiations. 'At the moment though, you're asking me to break the rules for you, but you won't explain why. I *might* be willing to do that as a favour – although let me make it quite clear that it would be a favour for Christie, not you – but not unless I understand what the hell's going on.'

I swirled what was left of the wine around my glass and gave Christie a brief, plaintive look.

'Do you want to be responsible for this for the next twenty-four hours?' Christie asked me, rhetorically.

It appeared that, Chateauneuf notwithstanding, we were going to have to take Suzy into our confidence rather more than I had anticipated.

'The thing is, Suze,' I began, leaning forward and speaking softly and slowly, 'until an hour ago this painting was worthless. More or less. It didn't exist. Not officially. We had to get Mr Gerou to agree to buy it from us in order for it to come into existence. When it didn't exist, there was no point in anyone stealing it because they wouldn't be able to sell it – not without the provenance that only Christie, me and Mr Gerou can provide between us. It had literally no value. But now that it does exist, and people other than us know that it exists… Well, that changes things. Because Erik's widow – Mimi – will also want this painting. Except that she won't want to pay us for it. And she may not have to pay us for it – not legally.'

'I'm confused.' Suzy's face betrayed the truth of this. Her brow was furrowing in a desperate attempt to force her brain back to sobriety. 'If you sell the painting to Mr Gerou and Mimi finds out, won't she just demand it off him?'

'Let's just say that, with a bit of help from Christie and me, Mr Gerou can construct a very plausible cover story to suggest the painting has been in his possession legitimately for over thirty years.'

She looked at me askance. '"Plausible"? So not actually true, then?'

Christie and I flicked a glance at each other. I stared intently at the wine glass in my hand as I twirled its stem.

'I don't think it's untrue, either. Not strictly speaking.'

Suzy left a generous silence as her brain sought to assimilate these new facts.

'Jesus, Gabe. You really are a piece of work, aren't you?'

'I hardly think that's fair. I'm helping a woman in distressed circumstances to maximise what little leverage she has in a very difficult situation.'

'Is that what you call it?' I could hear faint traces of her Birmingham accent again. 'If it was my brother doing it the management here would expect me to report this to the police as an attempted crime. But you – somehow, because of your breeding, you make it sound like you're a boy scout on bob-a-job week.'

My supposed breeding had been a bone of contention with Suzy throughout our marriage and divorce. I anticipated from her voice, therefore, that she was about to mount her high horse and ride off to the moral high ground, comparing as she did so my imagined fate to that of her (entirely hypothetical) brother. Christie's presence however, meant that she now had a more pressing issue to address. Because what she now understood was that Christie and I had in our possession a painting that had recently gone from being worthless to being worth rather a lot.

'Conny can't really afford to be sentimental about the prospect of a candlelit dinner with Christie,' I continued. 'What he needs – or so we believe – is to get rid of a large amount of cash in exchange for something he can turn into a legitimate asset relatively easily. There's a photo and some supporting documentation which would back up his claim that he's had this painting since it was painted, pretty much, so Mimi can't claim it off him. Suffice to say, no one else can claim that. We have to sell it to him.'

'So what's the problem?'

'The problem is that it doesn't really matter to him who he buys it from. It could be us, but it could be anyone else. As far as he's concerned, the important thing is for him to get rid of the cash and get the painting. An hour ago there was no incentive for anyone to even contemplate a theft, but now that he's said he's prepared to part with a rather large amount of money to get this painting, there's at least one roomful of people who would have every reason to contemplate stealing it. And those people know other people, who know other people, some of whom know Mimi. So I think you can see, Suze, that popping a highly valuable painting in the back of an

Uber with only a sexagenarian woman riddled with cancer for company might not be the best idea.'

I thought this had convinced her that a little bending of the hotel's rules was perfectly justified, but there was one thing that was clearly bugging her.

'OK. But can you explain to me why you're so invested in this? I mean, a week ago you'd never even met Christie. Why are you so anxious all of a sudden about whether she can sell her painting?'

This was not an area that I was keen for us to explore.

'Let's just say that your ex-husband here is a co-investor in this deal,' Christie explained. 'Isn't that right, Gabriel?'

I closed my eyes briefly and let out a sigh. The knot that had been slowly tightening in my stomach as Suzy had begun circling the issue of money, tugged itself tighter still. The temperature rose in my cheeks as my face flushed and I felt a thin film of sweat seep onto my brow. Although I felt sure she had done so innocently, Christie had just done the one thing I had been anxious for her not to do.

Suzy slowly turned her head toward me and raised her eyebrows. 'A co-investor? Is that true?'

'Well, yes...after a fashion. A very small co-investor, obviously. More of a silent partner, really.'

I glowered at Christie in a way that I hoped would communicate to her that she needed to steer the conversation away from this particular subject and back on to what we were supposed to be focusing on.

'Don't be so modest!' she interjected, playfully slapping my hand. 'I couldn't have done it without you. You know, he put $125,000 of his own money into this deal!'

My look having failed, I kicked her under the table, which

finally succeeded in admonishing her.

'Ouch!' she cried, looking at me aggrieved. The look I gave her at that point obviously betrayed me. 'Oh, sorry… Was I not supposed to mention that?'

'It's fine.' I said. But I knew that it wasn't. I felt my heart fall into my stomach and I was pretty sure it wasn't because of the wine.

Suzy was certainly sober now. '$125,000! And where did you get that from? I thought the divorce had left you penniless. At least, that's what you've always insisted.'

'Well, I can't understand that. I definitely got the money. Look.' Christie brought up her bank account on her smartphone. '$125,000 from Mr Gabriel Viejo.'

Suzy took the phone off Christie and clicked on the transaction. 'From an account with Banco de la Nación Argentina. Well, I never.'

I was expecting one of Suzy's unexpurgated explosions of anger, yet what I actually got was a rather smug grin. This amplified the sense of unease in my stomach, and I began to notice a vague scent of sweat emanating from under my arms. Suzy was no poker player. Her face indicated that she felt she had a winning hand and she proceeded to play it with great relish.

'So, Gabriel, am I right in thinking that you are currently $125,000 out of pocket on this deal?'

I shifted uncomfortably in my seat. 'Yes.'

'That and the ten grand you paid to get me and the painting over here,' interjected Christie. 'Don't forget that.'

'And how much are you out of pocket, Ms McGraw?' asked Suzy.

Christie looked confused. 'Well, nothing. I don't have any

money – except what Gabriel's just given me.'

'So if this picture went missing now you wouldn't lose anything?' Suzy said.

'Well, no,' Christie replied.

'But you, on the other hand,' Suzy said, returning her gaze to me, 'would be $135,000 down with no legal recourse, I'm guessing, to retrieve that money?'

I wasn't sure where this was leading, but I knew I didn't like it. The idea that the painting might go missing after I had paid Christie for it but before Conny had paid me, was not one that I had entertained. But when I did, it began to dawn on me that Suzy was probably right.

A ball of nausea began to grow in my stomach. I had been so focused on what would happen if I ended up stuck with *Susanna & the Elders* because Conny didn't want to buy it that I had neglected to consider what might happen if he did want to buy it, but I didn't have the painting to sell him.

'That's more or less the case,' I admitted. 'But I can't see—'

Suzy lifted her hand to silence me. 'So actually, it's *you* who really needs this painting to be kept safe until tomorrow, not Christie.'

'Well, it's not quite that simple,' I protested. 'Christie needs her share of the sale to fund her cancer treatment. Without that—'

'I get that. But she actually won't be any worse off. In fact, she'd still be a hundred and twenty-five grand to the good irregardless' (another Suzy word) 'of whether you lost the painting or the whole deal collapsed because Mimi suddenly turned up. Maybe that's not enough to fund all her treatment, but it's not a bad start.

'You, on the other hand…'

I tried to pull my mind into focus. In all the scenarios I had run through in my head back in New York, this was a low-risk deal for me, and yet, here I was in London, and it suddenly appeared as though all of the risk was on my shoulders. I couldn't work out how that had happened, until I realised that in none of the various scenarios I had gone through in my head back in New York had my vengeful ex-wife's unexpected appearance featured. Through a mixture of skilful extraction of information from me, and unfortunate indiscretion from Christie, Suzy now found herself in a position of considerable power. While she couldn't get her hands on my money, one phone call and she could make sure that I didn't get to keep it either. I felt the colour drain from my cheeks.

'Are you trying to blackmail me?' I asked.

'Oh, so when you try to – what did you call it? – "maximise your leverage", then that's just good negotiation. But if I try to do it, it's blackmail.'

'That's not what I said.'

'Don't worry, I might not care about you any more, but I do care about Ms McGraw here. I know if this deal falls through now, then that's going to cost her a lot more than a few hundred grand.' She paused and reapplied the smug grin to her face. 'That's why I'm going to give you a chance, Gabriel.'

'A chance? A chance for what?'

'To do the right thing. I'm going to give you the chance to do what you should have done years ago: to tell the truth.'

# TWENTY

I wasn't prepared to admit to anything in front of Suzy. While the matter had been adjudicated, without taking legal advice I couldn't risk saying anything that would allow her to reopen the divorce settlement. Whatever affection she might have had for Christie, Suzy's animus toward me remained far greater. One call to Mimi and the deal would be sunk and all the money I'd spent so far – $135,000 – gone, along with my professional reputation. Regardless of the safety of the painting therefore, my overwhelming need was to keep Suzy sweet.

I was also given an extra nudge by Christie, whose face indicated she was reappraising her assessment of me as a reliable business partner. In order to preserve my financial stake in the deal therefore, I agreed to set out the details of how I ended up with $200,000 in an Argentinian bank account to an independent witness: Christie. But I was not prepared to do that with Suzy in attendance. Frankly, if I admitted to Suzy what I had done then I'd probably lose all of my inheritance money in alimony, fines and/or legal fees anyway so there barely seemed any point in granting her the satisfaction. Yet if I told Christie what I'd done without Suzy there, then she could tell Suzy whatever she wanted afterwards, but it would be impossible to prove.

So the compromise was agreed that Suzy would leave the table and I would tell Christie The Truth.

Suzy took the painting and headed off to place it in the secure storeroom while Christie poured me another glass of wine and settled back.

'So,' she asked. 'Are you a liar?' I left a pause, my wine glass fascinating me once more. 'I'm guessing from the fact that you've agreed to all this, that there's at least some truth to what she's insinuating.'

I took a sharp swig of the wine to fortify myself before beginning to tell my tale.

'It's not what you think… I mean, it's not as simple as Suzy makes out. She claims I was hiding money from her as part of the divorce settlement.'

'And were you?'

'No, not really…' I trailed off. I couldn't look at her, but felt her eyes boring into me. 'I think "hiding" is a very judge-y word to use. It implies a degree of intention on my part that I genuinely don't think was there.'

Christie arched an eyebrow in my direction. This time I met her gaze.

'Look, the simple facts are that by the time we found out Grandpa Jo was dying, Suzy and I were pretty much over. We were still legally married – just about – but we both knew where things were heading. Suzy had lost her job again, so she flew out to Argentina to see Grandpa one last time, and she ended up staying out there for a couple of months. Well, that was pretty much the end of us.'

'But old Jo left you an inheritance. I remember you mentioning something about it.'

'Yes, the proceeds of the sale of that Francis Bacon sketch I told you and Liga about.'

She raised her eyebrows. 'Nice.'

'Yes, but at the time I wasn't sure about it.' Christie shot me a sceptical look. 'Genuinely. It had been years since Grandpa Jo had mentioned leaving me anything and I didn't know what was in his will. At the point I completed the divorce papers and sent back the initial financial declaration – the Form E – I honestly didn't know for sure if I'd be getting anything, so my form couldn't mention anything about the money. I didn't really lie. I made a full disclosure of the facts as they were at the time. That's the truth of the matter, I swear.'

'And when the facts changed?'

I lost her look again. 'When my lawyer filled out the final declaration for me – the D81 – he just used the information I'd put on the Form E. It seemed like an unnecessary complication to start mentioning the hypothetical proceeds of a sale that hadn't actually happened. So I just left it as it was.'

'You didn't think to mention the money that was heading your way?'

'Because I didn't know how much would be heading my way. Or even if anything would be. The auction had been scheduled, there was a reserve price and everything, but the sketch hadn't actually been sold. And I didn't know for sure that it would be.'

'And maybe because you were worried the courts might not

let you keep all the proceeds from the sale if they knew?'

'Yeah... I guess so.'

She let this revelation settle before finally putting me out of my misery.

'Relax, kiddo. I'm not interested in other people's divorces. People always claim that they got a bum deal and the other side robbed them. I'm sixty-seven in a couple of weeks and I've still never met anyone who tells me they got a better deal than their ex. The only people who ever seem to come out of it well are the lawyers.'

'So what are you going to tell Suzy?'

'What she wants to hear, I guess.'

My eyes returned to the wine glass in my hand as a silence grew between us.

It was eventually broken by Suzy's return, along with a waitress who brought our meals. Despite the Mastic Tree's Michelin star, Suzy doused her salmon roulade with salt before turning her attention to the matter of what I had – and hadn't – told Christie about the precise circumstances of my inheritance.

'So?' she asked, looking at Christie with a quizzical stare.

Christie went through a brief summary of my revelations in what I felt were fairly neutral terms. I remained silent throughout, despite the temptation to provide some further caveats to Christie's assessment. When she reached the end, she seemed to offer Suzy what she wanted: an acknowledgement that her suspicions were more or less right. But she also left me with a small degree of dignity intact.

'So did Gabriel accept that I am legally entitled to a share of that money?' Suzy asked when she had concluded.

'No,' I interjected.

'Gabriel doesn't accept that he withheld any relevant information from his financial declaration,' Christie replied. Suzy let out a loud harrumph. 'But he does accept that there was a risk that the court might have decided otherwise.'

Suzy turned to me. 'Gabe?'

'Obviously, I am neither confirming nor denying anything she's just said. I'm happy to rest on the decision of the court – which, let me say, I think is a fair one overall, whatever the legal technicalities.'

Suzy was not impressed with this. 'Legal technicalities!?' And she proceeded to set out her version of the story of Grandpa Jo, Francis Bacon and the sketch of Muriel Belcher. Suffice to say, this was very different to mine.

'Your grandpa loved me, Gabe. Frankly, I think he preferred me to you.'

'That's ridiculous! But even if it were true, it's completely irrelevant. He didn't leave you anything in his will. He left it to me.'

'Because he thought that I would benefit from it through you. As far as he was concerned, we were still married. He knew it was safe to give it to you because I was around to make sure you didn't squander it.'

'"Safe"? He knew it was "safe" to give the money to me?'

'Yes, because of what had happened.'

'Oh, for God's sake! Not this again.'

'Yes, this again. I'm sorry if me bringing up your drug addiction embarrasses you, Gabe, but I think it's relevant.'

Christie nearly choked on her glass of water. 'Drug addiction?'

'I was not a drug addict!'

'You cadged some cash off him which you said was to invest

in a painting, but instead you blew it on cocaine,' Suzy said.

'I got that painting for a good price and, yes, I celebrated a little with the cash I had left over. That's hardly being a drug addict.'

'You checked-in to rehab! Which, can I just say, Grandpa Jo also ended up paying for.'

'You *took* me to rehab. I didn't need to go, and I only agreed to stay because you said you'd pay for it. It was you, let me just point out, who ended up telling my grandpa a whole pile of bullshit about my "addiction" so that he'd feel obliged to pay. If I'd known you were going to do that, I'd never have agreed to go.'

'I said I'd get it paid for so that you could just focus on getting better. I didn't say I'd take the money out of my own bank account. I don't have that kind of money.'

'And don't you make sure everyone knows it?' That seemed to shut Suzy up for long enough for me to get back to the main point. 'None of this affects the central fact that Grandpa Jo left the money to me, not me and you.'

'Only because I stopped him from changing his will?'

Christie chipped in. 'You stopped him changing his will?'

'Yes! After the whole rehab thing he mentioned that he was worried about leaving Gabe any of his money in case he just blew it on drugs. I managed to convince him that, as we were getting married, I'd be around to take care of Gabe and make sure he didn't get into trouble again.'

'But what you don't mention, Suzy, is that the will which he didn't change was written before we were married – before we'd even met – and the money didn't come through 'til after we were divorced. So the inheritance isn't a matrimonial asset.'

'Are you kidding me? Let me just remind you that it was

me, not you, who flew over to Buenos Aires to look after him when he was sick. You stayed in London.'

If she had paused long enough to let me speak, I would have pointed out that this was simply because I was working when Grandpa Jo became ill, whereas Suzy wasn't. Somebody had to make sure the mortgage on our London townhouse was being paid. But Suzy just ploughed on.

'He was delirious on morphine by the time I got there, so he couldn't process that the two of us were separating. But if he'd still been compos mentis, I guarantee you he would have amended his will to ensure that I was a direct beneficiary. I earned it for those two months, I can tell you! But the fact is that, even without changing his will, Grandpa Jo died believing that I would benefit from that sketch through you.'

I wanted to intervene, but the story of the alimony that I 'stole' from her was the one thing that was guaranteed to get Suzy regaling whatever audience she could find with all the enthusiasm of a latter-day Elmer Gantry. What HMRC would make of all my financial skulduggery did not bear thinking about, Suzy said (although, perversely, she seemed to have thought of little else for the past two years).

Fortunately, having sat through this for five minutes, even Christie seemed to be wearying.

'Gee, honey, that all sure sounds bad. I can't believe someone like Gabriel here – who I've always found to be the perfect gentleman – would behave so badly. But I gotta tell you, it's not clear to me that he's actually broken any rules.'

I thought this might deflate Suzy, but it only seemed to wind her up more. 'That's the point! He doesn't have to break any rules because the rules are stacked in his favour.'

This was a favourite hobbyhorse of Suzy's – one that she

had regularly mounted during our years together: the idea that 'the system' was rigged against people like her, and in favour of people like me.

'That's ridiculous!' I protested. 'The whole point of the rules is that that they're there to ensure that everyone gets treated fairly. They're not there to make sure that you get whatever you want. The rules might say that you're entitled to my grandpa's money – although, just to be clear, I don't concede that they do – but the fact is, that was my grandpa's sketch, not yours.'

'Exactly!' Suzy replied, as though I had somehow proved her point, rather than undermined it. 'And the rules say that Mimi should inherit *Susanna & the Elders* one hundred per cent and Christie should get nothing. But we both know in a fair world that wouldn't be true.'

This is what it came down to. It's what all of our arguments came down to. Suzy believed that somehow her background had cut her out from ever accessing the good things in life, whereas my background had given me the golden ticket. It still riled her that, thanks to a canny bit of business by my grandad, we had ended up with a Bacon sketch, whereas when her grandad had died all he'd left her was a bill for four weeks rent that was due on his council flat. But rather than acknowledge that her war with me and the world was based on her own disappointment with how life had turned out for her, she tried to pretend it was driven by a desire to see a fair outcome for others.

The argument could have gone on all night but at that moment I noticed a commotion in the reception area as Conny, two of his minders and the young woman I recognised from his suite, emerged from one of the lifts. Conny was scowling while muttering something into his phone. He looked anxious and was growing frustrated. Eventually his anger boiled over.

'Look, I don't care how difficult it is, Love,' he shouted into his phone. 'Just find him and give it to him! The judge has to make his decision tomorrow. They're coming to take me to the airport in less than thirty-six hours – I'm running out of time!'

The mention of Love Menolo's name prompted Christie to shoot me a concerned glance across the table. Suzy missed this brief flickering of the conspiracy between us. Instead, she seemed primarily concerned with Conny's female companion, who had changed into a fetching off-the-shoulder number and redone her make-up. If I hadn't been more concerned about the exact nature of Conny's dealings with Love, her efforts might have struck me more than they did. They seemed to have caught Suzy's attention, however.

'God, she's so beautiful. I hate her,' she said, looking after the woman forlornly.

Another of my many frustrations with Suzy was that, for a feminist, she seemed to pay an unduly large amount of attention to how other women looked, and to assume that they were invariably more attractive to men than she was. This felt unfair, both to them and herself. She was only a couple of years younger than me, but she had kept her looks and her figure much better than I had. To me Suzy was more beautiful than Conny's companion, but I didn't know quite why. Thankfully, Christie seemed to know precisely.

'Actually, she's just pretty,' she said, following Suzy's look across the lobby.

Suzy started. 'Really? You think so? What's the difference?'

'Prettiness is about perfection; beauty's about imperfection.

It's the grit in the oyster; the flaw in the diamond. They're worthless without imperfection. Prettiness – well, it might look nice, but it's just bland. Beauty on the other hand…that's about seeing the scars of life in someone's face. Not physically; I mean in their eyes. It's about seeing those scars and still seeing hope in the way they look at you. Because hope only counts if you know life won't be perfect, and still hope anyway.' She sighed. 'You can be pretty at twenty-one, but to be beautiful you really need to be forty.'

Suzy started to answer back, but I just smiled. My attention was elsewhere and soon the moment, like Conny and his entourage, disappeared into the night.

# TWENTY-ONE

We'd just finished our meal when I noticed the lift doors open and Mandalay stepping out. He cast several nervous glances around the hotel lobby as he strode across it towards the bar, where he took up a stool. I couldn't help noticing, however, that his attention seemed wholly focused on our table. He appeared to be trying to make eye contact with me but didn't seem willing to walk over and just talk.

I went through all of the possible reasons why Mandalay would want to speak to us but be nervous about doing so. None of them were good.

After a few minutes, having clearly got tired of waiting for me to respond to his casual nods, he stood up and beckoned me over with his finger. I gave my apologies to Christie and Suzy and made my way over to him, trying to look as casual as possible, even as I could feel my heartbeat quicken.

He guided me over to a table away from the bar and invited

me to sit. I cast a nervous glance back at Christie, but she remained locked in conversation with Suzy.

'So,' I said, placing my palms on the table-top with what I hoped was an air of authority. 'What can I help you with?'

He looked at me uncertainly for a moment.

'That was quite a sales pitch you gave up there,' he said. 'Congratulations on the deal.'

'Thanks,' I said. 'Not quite the price we'd hoped for, but hey…'

'It never is with Conny.' He wasn't smiling as he said this.

A waitress arrived with a coffee, which she placed in front of Mandalay. With great deliberation he added some sugar and then stirred it slowly for longer than felt necessary. His attention seemed wholly focused on the small cup in front of him even when, eventually, he spoke again.

'I just wanted to check that we understand each other,' he said. 'You seemed a bit confused up there, so I wanted to make sure that there was no misunderstanding.' He looked up at me. 'About my part in the deal.'

I looked at him askance. 'I didn't realise you had a part. I thought you were just there to confirm that the painting we're selling Conny is genuine.'

'Exactly.'

I wasn't sure what he expected me to say. 'Yes…well, thanks for doing that.'

'It's not a problem…' His eyes returned to his drink. 'As long as we understand each other.'

This again. 'I'm not sure that we do,' I said, acknowledging my confusion.

Mandalay winced and sat forward in his chair. He cast another glance around him before speaking slowly and softly.

'You need this deal to go ahead. But the only way Conny will hand over the money is if I tell him the painting's genuine. That puts me in a rather powerful position, wouldn't you say? If I were to have any doubts about the painting's authenticity, then it would scupper the whole deal.'

He leant back to allow the implications of this to sink in, taking a casual sip of his espresso as he did so.

'But you don't have any doubts. Do you?'

'No. Not at the moment.' He left a generous pause while he stirred his coffee again. Then he looked me in the eye. 'But I might have.'

I felt the pace of my speech quicken as the solid ground on which I thought I had been standing seemed to crumble beneath my feet.

'This isn't about those brushstrokes, is it? We told you why they were different. You said you were happy.'

'I said I was happy today. But tonight I go to sleep. Maybe tomorrow I'll be unhappy.' He leaned forward across the table to meet my stare. 'Unless...'

Mandalay had been part of the furniture of Conny's entourage for so long, without, as far as I was aware, ever being tempted to stick his hand in the till that it had never occurred to me for a moment that we might need to worry about him doing so now. But it appeared that we did. I was determined however, not to make this any easier for him. I waited for a moment for an explanation that didn't come.

'Unless what?' I asked.

'Do I need to spell it out?'

I gave him a deadpan look in an attempt to make it absolutely clear that yes, he did.

He paused for a moment, closed his eyes gently and took

a deep breath in. Then he opened them again and looked directly at me.

'Five per cent.'

I felt myself gasp inwardly, but just about managed to hold it in. 'Of what?'

'Five per cent of the purchase price. That's my fee.'

'Your fee? Your fee for what?'

'For not having any doubts.'

I could sense the blood rising in my cheeks. 'Fifty grand just for telling the truth – that's ridiculous.'

'Oh, it's not for telling the truth. It's for *not* telling the truth. If you want me to tell the truth I can phone up the police right now and tell them the truth.' He withdrew his mobile phone and held it out as though waiting for me to give the word so he could start dialling.

I felt as though one of Conny's minders had just punched me in the gut again. That was not what I wanted to happen and he knew it.

'Five per cent. Tonight. To silence my doubts about those brushstrokes.'

I couldn't make sense of it. For over twenty years Conny had made sure that Mandalay had enjoyed a very comfortable life. But it was all based on trust: Mandalay looked after Conny's interests with total dedication (and absolute discretion), in return for which Conny looked after him with a greater degree of generosity than any regular art buyer would reasonably expect. So inserting himself into one of Conny's deals behind his boss' back felt like a massive risk for Mandalay to take and, whatever else I thought about him, Mandalay did not strike me as a natural risk-taker.

'It's all going to shit here,' he explained when I put this

point to him. 'The extradition fucks everything up. For all of us. They're talking about trying to get to Venezuela. What the hell am I going to do there? No, I've got to get out and get myself set up on my own.'

'You're really going to do this? You're going to dump Conny after all these years?'

Mandalay shrugged. 'I gotta. And to do that requires money. You're going to be making loads of it – you know that painting's worth nowhere near what Conny's paying – so I think me asking you for a small slice of the very large pie is fair to us both.'

Try as I might, I couldn't think of a way to complete the deal without Mandalay's say-so. He was Conny's buyer, so it was natural Conny would defer to him. And Conny was scheduled to be flown out of the country in less than thirty-six hours so there simply wasn't time to find someone else to vouch for *Susanna & the Elders*, even if I could get him to accept the advice of someone other than Mandalay (which I doubted I could.)

'OK Mandy, so here's what I propose. The simplest arrangement is that we pay you out of the proceeds of our sale. We get the money tomorrow night and hand it straight over. Everybody's happy.'

Mandalay chuckled. 'In cash, up front. Tonight.'

'I can't do that, Mandy. It's not possible.'

'Well, I'm not prepared to take a chance on Conny finding anything out about our arrangement here. I get the money tonight or those brushstrokes are going to come back to haunt you tomorrow.'

I sighed.

'There's a flight to Paris at just after six o'clock tomorrow morning,' Mandalay continued. 'If you tell me I'm getting my money, I'll book a ticket for that flight now – right here in front of you.' He waved his phone again. 'And the second the money hits my account I'll book an Uber and head straight over to the airport. You won't see or hear from me ever again. And neither will Conny.'

The cold, emotionless stare with which he had looked at *Susanna & the Elders* earlier that evening was now directed towards me. It was not the stare of a man who was open to persuasion.

'I shall refer to my client and get back to you,' I said. 'But I gotta tell you, Mandy, this feels like we're being mugged.'

'No one's mugging anyone,' he said patiently. 'You're charging Christie a fee, yes? Well, this is mine. Think of it as an enabling fee. I'm charging you five per cent so that you actually get to access the other ninety-five per cent.'

And when he put it like that, I really couldn't see that we had any choice but to agree.

# TWENTY-TWO

When I arrived back at our dinner table Suzy had gone to the bathroom, so Christie and I were alone. I didn't know how to break the news to her that Mandalay was threatening to pull the plug on the deal, but when I did her face fell.

'Mandalay? Mandy said that to you? Jesus! I though he was the one straight guy in the whole room.'

But, whatever our qualms, it was clear to both of us that we were going to have to pay him his $50,000. This was not loose change. Christie was still some way short of having the money she needed for her remaining three rounds of chemotherapy, so she was adamant that she couldn't provide the necessary cash. And we both agreed that there was really no point in asking Conny.

This left just one – uncomfortable – possibility as a source of the required funds: me.

Even after paying out $135,000, there was still $75,000 left in my Banco de la Nación Argentina account. While I had always wanted to avoid carrying too much risk myself, Suzy had already established that that was precisely the position I was now in. As far as Christie was concerned therefore, it was entirely reasonable to expect me to stump up the cash.

'After all, you're going to be walking away from this with a very large sum of money in exchange for doing very little,' she said.

'Very little?' The stress that I had put myself under on Christie's behalf didn't feel like 'very little' from my perspective.

'Sure. You didn't even get me the best price,' she said. 'I pretty much had to negotiate the deal myself. Some agent you are.'

And with that she sent me back to Mandalay.

Once he'd confirmed that the money had arrived in his account, he disappeared in a cab and normal service was able to resume between me, Christie and Suzy. After the hiatus of Mandalay's unexpected intervention, Christie felt like celebrating our success, so the three of us found ourselves back in her suite at the Dorchester downing Jägerbombs that Christie had ordered on room service. This was actually the compromise position. She had originally suggested that we go out to a nightclub and Suzy had enthusiastically agreed, but I had to be awake and sober for a catch-up call with my publisher at 9am the next morning and I knew from my previous experience that the latter requirement would be imperilled by the former course of action.

If my intention in restricting our party to Christie's hotel suite was that it would limit the opportunity for things to descend too far into bacchanalian revelry (which it was), this was to prove a forlorn hope. By the time the third set of Jägerbombs was delivered to Christie's door by the hard-pressed hotel staff, Christie had discovered a karaoke app on her TV and was insistent that Suzy join her in what might charitably be called a rousing rendition of The Weather Girls' 'It's Raining Men'. Suzy (who, if truth be told, had needed little encouragement) drained a small bottle of prosecco from the minibar and turned it upside down to use as a microphone, and Christie grabbed a hairbrush for hers. They gyrated and swayed as though playing the Madison Square Garden, although I was their only audience.

Looking at the two of them performing together, I became conscious for the first time of how much Christie had changed in the years since she'd posed for Erik. Up until that point the thing that had struck me most about her was how much she had defied the ageing process; how recognisable she still was as the sensual and arresting young woman of Von Holunder's paintings. Seeing her next to Suzy however, both of them bumping and grinding together in mock provocation of me, what I noticed was how much she had aged since Von Holunder had portrayed her as the epitome of womanhood in *Ecce Femina* (1979). But I found myself not caring because the way that she stared at you – the arresting, demanding-yet-longing look that had caused every college frat boy for a decade or more to put a print of her on their bedroom wall – was still the same. It was the look of a woman who, despite the inevitable ravages of time, still seemed to embody something that I yearned for. The way that she looked at you was still the same way as the way that she looked at the viewer in all of Erik's best paintings of her. It was a look that accused you, but at the same time forgave you. It forgave you for looking. And even for desiring.

And what I realised then – the one observation that made absolute sense, even in the dense fog of Jägermeister within which it was shrouded – was that Suzy's look had always felt like an accusation, a judgement against me. But one without forgiveness.

Judgement matters, of course. But judgement without the offer of forgiveness is just judgementalism, and what I wanted more than anything else in that moment was the forgiveness that Christie's look seemed to offer. I wanted to wallow in the forgiveness of her stare.

This sense of yearning grew within me as the alcohol continued to flow until I found myself in such a confused state of sexual longing that I decided I needed to tell Christie how I felt. The first stage of this was to sober up, so I decided to leave Christie and Suzy chatting in the lounge while I went to the bathroom.

The moment I tried to stand up I realised I had been more affected by the alcohol I'd been drinking than even I'd realised. This should have given me cause to consider how wise my proposed plan of action was, but I stupidly ignored all the warning signs. Eventually I managed to stumble to the bathroom. Fearing I might collapse at any moment, I left the door open to ease access for any medical assistance that needed to be called. I wasn't deliberately listening to what Christie and Suzy were saying, but when the subject turned to why our marriage ended I couldn't help tuning in.

'The thing you've got to realise about Gabe is that he's a total narshishist,' Suzy said, the Jägermeister having taken a decisive hold.

'Gabriel? Really?'

'Absolutely. Total narshishist. Believe me.'

'I don't think I've seen that side to him,' said Christie with a degree of precision that told me that, once again, she had somehow managed to remain more sober than Suzy and me.

I was drying my hands by this point but held back from walking in on them and, in a moment of masochistic self-abasement, decided to let Suzy tell her story uninterrupted.

'Ahhhhhh, you don't. Not at first. I din't. All I could see was that he was at the centre of the whole scene that I wanted to get into, but he made me feel that I was the one who mattered. It blew my mind.' I could hear her acting out her head exploding. 'Blew my mind. That someone like that – that *posh* – would take me – basically, a piece of shit from Birmingham – would take me to press nights at the Tate and private viewings at the Saatchi Gallery – stuff like that – and make me feel like I mattered. God, it felt good.

'But then – then we got married and I saw... Narshishist. Totally....' There was a pause as she tried to form a thought in her head, 'I saw that he only did all that stuff so that I would make him feel good about himself by being impressed. He didn't choose me *despite* the fact that I knew nothing about his world – he chose me *because* of it.'

I hoped that Christie might come in with a defence of me at this point, but she just let Suzy continue.

'I couldn't work out why the other girls – the posh girls – weren't falling at his feet. But to them he wasn't all that. Not at all. They weren't as easily impressed as I was. *That* was why he chose me. I was easily impressed. See? Total narshishist.'

I wanted to rush back in and protest, but Christie cut in before I had a chance to think of what to say.

'I think that's true of a lot of men, honey,' she said. 'They don't want to be loved; they want to be worshipped. It's certainly true of Conny.'

'You're so right,' Suzy replied, animatedly. 'That's what I love about you, Christie. And I do love you. Honestly, I do. I love you so-o-o-o much. Things just seem to come alive whenever you turn up somewhere.'

'And I love you too, honey,' Christie replied, flatly.

'Thank you,' Suzy said, sounding as though she was on the verge of tears. 'Gabe always said that he loved me, but I never felt it. Not really. Not when there wasn't an audience,' she said. 'His love was like our central heating. He turned it on before people arrived and pretended it was like that all the time.'

Her words hovered in the air like cigarette smoke, stinging in my eye. It felt particularly cruel that my love could mean so little to her now, having meant so much to her once, and this prompted me to finally re-enter the lounge area.

'I cannot believe that you'd say that—' I said, storming back in.

'Jesus!' said Suzy, jolting in alarm at the sound of my voice. 'How much of that did you just hear?'

'A narcissist, am I?' I replied.

'Look, I'm sure you've been called worse,' Christie said.

'I most certainly have not!'

'Well you bloody well should have been,' Suzy replied. 'You didn't want a lover; you wanted a fan club. Just like the rest of 'em. You're all the same.'

This kind of remark was typical of her. She could see the whole world with complete clarity, and yet she was totally blind to herself.

'Don't you ever think that it's not all our fault?' I said. 'That maybe sometimes it's women who make life hard for men?'

'Are you kiddin' me?' Christie interjected. 'Erik always said that the worst thing about having a mistress was having to go and see *Cats* twice. If that's all he'd got to complain about I don't think he had it too bad.'

Maybe it was all the alcohol, but I found myself stifling a chuckle. Suzy was right about Christie: the night came alive when she was around you. She lit up the darkness like a night with too much moon.

Suzy, however, was clearly intent on undermining me. I decided I needed to find a way to get rid of her so that I could make my declaration quickly. I raided the minibar to find a soft drink then, having removed the last bottle of water, suggested Suzy try and get it restocked for us. She'd commented as we'd arrived that she knew the Dorchester's duty manager because he'd previously worked for her at the Walled Garden so I hoped that, rather than just phoning down to the front desk, she'd want to go downstairs and speak to him directly to see if she could squeeze some extras out of him. In this regard at least, Suzy did not disappoint, and I finally found myself alone with Christie.

I had no idea what I was going to say, but it seemed to make sense to start with the thought that was uppermost in my mind and see where that took me. The memory of it makes me blanch even now.

'I don't want you to leave,' I said, standing before her. 'I don't want you to go back to New York.'

'What? Why ever not?'

'Because… I think I'm falling in love with you.'

She looked at me with a mixture of sympathy and disappointment. It reminded me of the way my mother looked at me when she walked into my room once and caught me quickly hiding a copy of *Big 'n' Bouncy* under the bedclothes. It was hard to tell if Mum was disappointed with me, or disappointed with herself for being disappointed with me. Whichever it was, I felt similarly chastened by Christie that night.

'Oh, honey,' she said, her big round eyes fixing me with an almost maternal compassion.

'Don't say it! Please don't say it!' I replied.

'Don't say what?'

'What you're going to say.'

'How do you know what I'm going to say?'

'I can hear it in your voice. I can see it in the way you're looking at me.' Sometimes Christie's eyes spoke more loudly than she did.

'Don't say "it would never work"? I don't need to say it. We're both grown adults. I think we both know—'

My heart sank, but I was determined to fight her on this point. 'No, we don't. We could make it work. There's something between us – don't tell me you don't feel it too – there's something between us that I've never felt before. Not even with Suzy.'

Christie arched an eyebrow. 'Yeah, well I'm not sure that's quite the benchmark we should be aiming for here.'

I flopped down on the seat next to her. She paused, took a deep breath and placed her hand gently on top of mine. 'I'm sorry, honey, but it *would* never work between us. It might feel like there's a lot of sexual tension now, but once we'd slept together the relationship would just fizzle out because there'd be nothing beyond that to hold us together.'

I knew that what she said made sense, yet I still didn't want it to be true. I opened my mouth to protest but couldn't think of anything to say so I just sat there for a moment with my mouth wide open in what must have looked like a silent howl of pain. Christie decided to put me out of my misery.

'I'm telling you, Gabriel; we'd have unbelievable sex twice and then you'd lose interest.'

Being honest, that seemed like a good deal to me. '*Twice*? That's a very specific number.'

'Trust me, honey, it'd be so unbelievable the first time you'd come back and do it again, just to check you hadn't dreamt it. But after that...well, I think you'd want someone more your own age. Someone you could settle down and start a family with.'

I wanted to believe that she was wrong, that there was something in the magic that she seemed to have that would have held us together. But I could see from the way her look had changed that I'd broken the spell. By making explicit my desire to sleep with her, I was guilty of trying to pull her into an orbit she had no desire to be in. With Christie, as with Bette Noir at that basement club in BoHo, you sensed that she was happier being admired from a distance. Get too close and I feared the magic would fade.

But what a magic it was. And in that moment, I'd have taken the offer of 'unbelievable sex twice' in a heartbeat. It had felt a real possibility at one point. However, her look now suggested that it was more of a rhetorical flourish. We'd had a blast that night, but the air between us had changed and in my heart, I was worried that I knew what it was.

'You don't think I'm like Conny, do you?'

'What? Are you kidding me? Oh honey, you're not at all like Conny. Not at all... I like you.'

'I meant the thing you said about respect. I mean, I know I desire you, but you know that I respect you too, don't you?'

I fixed her with a very deliberate stare. 'I want you to feel respected—'

She patted my hand. 'I know you do, honey.'

But something in the way she looked at me implied that I had somehow blotted my copybook with her. I started to become desperate.

'I want to feel that I've earnt the right to desire you. I have done that – haven't I?'

She said nothing. Which actually said rather a lot.

# TWENTY-THREE

Autumn in England is so often tinged with melancholy, but it felt particularly acute the next morning. Despite the amount of alcohol I'd drunk the previous night, I somehow still managed to rouse myself at a reasonable hour and complete the call to my publisher. I tried to convey something of the enthusiasm that I felt towards Christie and suggested that my interviews might require that we re-frame the narrative to give her more prominence. But I was doing so knowing that Christie herself had inspected me and, like Suzy before her, found me wanting. There was a sadness to this knowledge that I couldn't shake, and which somehow conveyed itself to my largely uninterested publisher.

After I'd hung up, I set off to find my way back to the Dorchester, the noise and hubbub of London adding to the fog in my brain. Christie had asked if I would spend the day with her and act as her tour guide around London while we waited for confirmation from Conny that our funds were available. The previous evening (when I had been drunk and 'in love') it had felt like an unbelievable opportunity to spend extra time in her company, but by the next morning (when I was hungover and full of regret) I understood that my declaration the previous evening had been a terrible mistake.

I had confused my desire for Christie with a love of her. I think men do that a lot, especially when we've been drinking. I'd probably done it with Suzy, too – confused the longing I felt because of her outward appearance with a love of the inner person. But I guess that part of the tragedy of a forbidden longing is how illegitimate our agony always feels to us. The other part, of course, is knowing how ridiculous it appears to others. And in the cold light of day, I knew I'd made myself look ridiculous to Christie, just as I had to Liga back at the drag night in BoHo.

I got off the tube at Hyde Park Corner and walked back through the rain-sodden park, the long sobs of autumn's violins pulling at my heart. I felt like an absolute heel, but I'd promised to get back early to the Dorchester in order to accompany Christie and felt honour-bound to keep my word. In my heart however, I knew that, for all its unforgettable saturnalian revelry, something had died between Christie and me the previous night, and our meeting that day was to bury it. I grasped my coat tight against the cold October wind, gazing at the forlorn autumnal sorrow of the trees around me. The brittle mass of amber, gold and topaz signalled that their leaves would be falling soon and I couldn't help but think that I knew how they felt.

When I entered Christie's suite at around eleven, I found Suzy asleep in a bathtub half-filled with prosecco, wearing only a bra and knickers and Christie's pair of Alain Mikli sunglasses. She had a traffic cone perched on top of her head and the words 'Just (Re)Married' written in bright red lipstick across her chest. It was a measure of Christie's undoubted ability to sniff out trouble that for a moment I wasn't sure whether that was a joke or not. The smell pervading the bathroom indicated that someone had spent at least some of the time since my departure liberally vomiting – and, judging by her sprightly appearance as she sipped on her grapefruit juice, I was guessing it wasn't Christie.

'Is she supposed to be back at work now?' I asked.

'Not until this evening, apparently,' said Christie, gazing at the sleeping figure compassionately. 'And anyway – I phoned in on her behalf and told them she quit her job.'

'You did what?!' Even by Christie's standards, this felt like quite a step.

'I quit for her,' she said as though it was the most natural thing in the world for her to do.

'But Christie, you heard her yesterday – she needs that job. Did you discuss this with her beforehand?'

'Kinda. Although obviously it wasn't a completely coherent conversation by that point. But it was making her miserable. You could see that. And so uptight. Jeez, that woman was busting your balls. Anyway, when she was barfing down the john – in tears, I might add – I told her not to worry about going into work; I'd sort it all out. And that seemed to cheer her up.'

This seemed quite a tenuous basis on which to submit someone's resignation for them, but another, more pressing issue was uppermost in my thoughts. 'Christie, we have a million-dollar painting in secure storage in that hotel. How are we going to get it out if Suzy doesn't work there any more?'

'Relax, kiddo. I said she'd do her shift tonight, but that would be her last one.' She took a set of keys off the sink unit and jangled them under my nose. 'So we can make sure we get our painting before she hands her keys back. And besides, once they found out she'd stored a million-dollar painting in there and it wasn't even a guest's, they'd probably have fired her anyway. I'm really doing her a favour if you think about it like that.'

I shook my head, but realised it was pointless to argue. What was done was done. I tried to content myself with a reminder that Suzy was not my responsibility any more, and it would be her problem to deal with the fallout, not mine. Later, of course, I came to understand things differently.

It was Christie's first time in London and she took to it with the enthusiasm of a puppy. This was what I loved so much about her: the way she threw herself into everything with such abandon. It's not an exaggeration to say that for me she incarnated the idea of joyous freedom that I had once believed all adult life consisted of once you were able to escape from the restraints of school. Despite the weather, for instance, she insisted we go on an open-top bus tour. *'I've always wanted to – and I'm not going to let a bit of rain stop me doing something I've dreamt about for years!'* she said over my protests. And so we did.

London had dipped its streets in murk as if trying to keep their grandeur secret, but somehow, she could see through it. I remember thinking that she seemed to have that rare ability to penetrate the surface of what we could see to recognise the beauty within. She could imbue the sights with a meaning, and for the first time it didn't seem ridiculous at all that she'd once wanted to be the artist and not the muse. She had an eye for beauty.

For her part, Christie was awestruck by the whole experience. When we passed Buckingham Palace, she gasped and her face broke out into the widest, most joyous smile, as though its beauty had never been truly appreciated before. And maybe it hadn't been. I found myself ashamed that I had passed this building so many times and yet it was only now that I saw its true glory, and even then, not directly, but reflected in her face. I've seen a lot of art, and I've been moved by the best of it, but all its power was lost in the magic of that smile. The sadness was that I now knew that its radiance was not for me. The forgiveness that I'd seen in her look the previous evening was gone and in its place was not so much an accusation as a reluctant realisation: I was just like all the rest of them. I couldn't even blame Suzy for that. It wasn't that Christie had been poisoned against me; it was that I had revealed myself.

That's the thing that kills a guy. The feeling that he has opened up his heart to the object of his desire and, having taken a look inside, she concludes he's no better than all the rest. I so much didn't want to be that guy, but now had to confront the undeniable evidence in Christie's face that I was.

She said that she wanted to see some art while she was in London so I thought she might have got off the bus by the National Gallery, but instead, it was not until we got to Regent Street that she leapt up excitedly and made her way down the steps of the bus. I assumed this was because she wanted to go on another shopping expedition, but instead, she looked closely at the squares on her tourist map and said, 'How do we get to Cork Street from here?'

It was a five-minute walk and then we found ourselves wandering up and down the street trying to find something we wanted to see. But even I had to admit that Cork Street was no longer the centre of London's art scene as it had been back in the days of Erik's retrospective, and Christie's face betrayed a look of disappointment. I took a morsel of pleasure from the fact that for once it wasn't me that had prompted this.

I tried to find something that might cover Erik's period and stumbled upon *Large Abstracts,* which was about to close at the Redfern. But it was no good.

'Not doing it for you, eh?' I said as we drifted through the show.

She scrunched up her face. 'I think I need beauty,' she said.

'Well, what about this one?' I replied, pointing her towards *Lotus,* Paul Jenkins' 1957 oil and enamel on canvas.

'And people. Beauty and people. I think people give art its soul.'

'Do you not think there's a soul in his rather exquisite blending of colours?'

Christie gave me one of her trademark looks and I turned away in frustration.

'Oh, I'm sorry, did I roll my eyes out loud?' she said.

Nothing I did could impress her now. Everything felt somehow shameful and ridiculous.

I knew that the Redfern had sold some of Erik's works, and, of course, the gallery was forever seared into my memory because of the retrospective they'd hosted fifteen years earlier. I decided therefore that it might be worth trying to pander to Christie's vanity. I drifted away from her, found a gallery assistant and asked politely if they had any Von Holunders for sale. He looked at me with a hint of suspicion hidden underneath a nervous smile.

'Von Holunder? *Erik* von Holunder?' It appeared that he couldn't quite believe anyone still wanted to buy works by a man once regarded as the natural successor to Gustav Klimt.

'He's the only Von Holunder I know,' I replied, drolly. 'Or at least, the only one I know who paints.'

'Well...I think we have one...but it's not one of his best.'

This didn't surprise me. A lot of the really good Von Holunder's were held by Mimi or Conny, or (as our trip to MoMA had demonstrated) sitting in the storage vaults of major museums. They rarely came up for sale, partly because Mimi and Conny didn't want to sell the ones they owned, and partly because the major museums couldn't face the write-down on their balance sheets if they sold theirs. But I thought that Christie might prefer a second-rate Von Holunder to a first-rate Paul Jenkins, so I told the assistant to bring it out anyway.

What he actually brought out was an iPad on which he brought up an image of Von Holunder's reinterpretation of *Saturn Devouring His Son* (1984-5). This had been the first painting Erik had painted after the disastrous *Night of the Super Vixens* exhibition in 1983 and it had formed part of the *Old Masters* series. He'd painted it after returning to Paris, where he had retreated to lick his wounds after his critical mauling, so for once it did not feature Christie. Instead it depicted the figure of Saturn, who, fearing that he would be overthrown by one of his children, just as he had overthrown his own father, ate each one upon their birth.

While opinions varied wildly about Von Holunder's work, pretty much everyone agreed that his reinterpretation of *Saturn Devouring His Son* was a disaster.

Its execution was clumsy, and the draftsmanship was also poorer than in his earlier paintings (and significantly poorer than in *Susanna & the Elders*). Yet, removed from its original context, it struck me that the painting had something to say.

Erik had been criticised for all the highly sexualised portrayals of women, and this was a painting in which women didn't appear at all. While he had been critical of the critics after *Night of the Super Vixens*, this painting could also be seen as a response to their criticism: they'd said he was too obsessed with sex and desire, so instead he'd painted something that said nothing about either. But it seemed they still weren't happy.

I called Christie over. 'Come here. Look what they've got for sale.'

She drifted over and peered at the screen but immediately recoiled in a visceral disgust that I had not anticipated. 'Ugh! That old thing. I told him he should have thrown *that* in the dumpster, not *Susanna*.'

It was the first time I'd heard her express anything other than uncritical admiration for one of Erik's works and it took me by surprise. Looking at the painting, though, I could see why. It is of course difficult to know what a human child might look like when it is being eaten alive by its parent, but I wasn't convinced it would look anything like the hapless child in Erik's painting. The shock and anguish of the child that Rubens so deftly conveyed in his portrayal of the same tableau was sadly lacking in this version. Of course, the same might be said of Goya's rendering of the scene, but Erik's Saturn had none of the febrile panic and self-disgust of the Spanish Master's earlier work. Instead, there appeared to be an almost casual arrogance.

Clearly trying to generate some interest from us in a

potential sale, the gallery assistant chipped in with his opinion. 'This certainly isn't one of Von Holunder's more fêted works, but I think it helps complete our picture of him. Critics have censured him for showing Saturn looking so unconcerned. But, of course, that was his whole point. Von Holunder felt they were destroying him, and they didn't seem to care. This painting is often seen as his attempt to show them what that felt like.'

It seemed a fair point to make, but it gave me a new understanding of why I felt instinctively that this was not a good painting.

'Yeah, I guess that's why I have a problem with it,' I said, trying to dampen the young assistant's expectations. 'I'm not sure it *does* convey what it feels like to be devoured by the press.'

Christie looked at it, her face filling with sorrow at memories it evoked.

'He just didn't seem to know what to paint any more,' she said. 'He lost confidence in himself, in his intuitions. He always felt that he knew what would sell, and then he didn't. He hadn't changed, but somehow everything around him had. He just couldn't cope with it.'

'It must've been a tough time,' I said.

She gave me a guarded look and we moved away from the gallery assistant.

'It was about that time he changed,' she continued when we were out of earshot. 'We'd had this fairytale, or what felt like a fairytale, but he was starting to get old – or rather, he was starting to *feel* old. I think I'd always kept him feeling young, but suddenly he couldn't...' She searched for a delicate way to make her point. 'He couldn't continue with the physical side of our relationship.' I think this was the only time I ever saw her blush. 'I think that's part of the reason he became so obsessed with porn – he was trying to stimulate himself, to get his mojo back, but it was no good. The more he watched the less aroused he became, and the less aroused he became the angrier he became. Especially with me. I guess that's why I hate that painting so much. It reminds me of that time, of how unhappy we'd become.'

I didn't know what to say. This was the first indication she'd given me that life with Erik before 1987 was ever anything less than blissful. I was concerned for her of course, but part of me was also thinking about the closing chapters of my biography. 'And this anger towards you. Was it ever—'

She turned and looked me straight in the eye. 'He'd always liked a drink, but by that point he'd started doing a bit of coke too – I mean, we both had. It was fun... Until it wasn't.' A heavy silence fell upon us both and then she said something which shocked me. 'You always feel like you can stop when you have to, but then you realise that you have to – and you find that you can't. And that's when you realise you're out of control. It's scary. So, so scary. That's what I put it down to: he was scared. He was scared he'd lost control. He couldn't cut down the coke and the booze, and he couldn't stop the porn, and he couldn't get it up any more. He was frightened of what he was becoming, but he couldn't stop it. He couldn't stop it happening.

'He'd been a god once. He'd been Saturn. But then everything changed, and he couldn't change it back. That just made him desperate.'

I wanted to probe her about what exactly 'it' consisted of, but before I could do so she moved the conversation on.

'That was when it first started to occur to me that maybe we wouldn't be together forever – which is what I'd always kinda assumed.'

'I'm sorry, Christie.' I couldn't think of anything else to say.

'Yeah, whatever.' She tried to appear nonchalant, but I could see the distress in her eyes.

While the traditional narrative was that *Saturn Devouring His Young* was a representation of what art critics do to artists, there was one thing that had never made sense to me about that interpretation.

'Christie, do you mind me asking, is that supposed to be Conny as Saturn? I mean, it kind of looks like him, but surely it would have made more sense to show Saturn as an art critic, rather than a buyer. Conny was buying Erik's stuff, after all. He wasn't the problem.'

Her face hardened, but she avoided eye contact. 'He suspected Conny was devouring his young.'

'I don't understand. Did he even have kids at that point?'

She let out a sigh before she spoke. 'Conny was spending a lot of time in New York by then. He was trying to get connected to the right people so he could build a good collection, y'know? I guess Erik and I were part of that whole circle he wanted to be part of. But when he was here, he took to hanging round with this young woman. Well, she was a girl really – eighteen, nineteen, I guess. I only met her a few times, but she was with him a lot.' She looked straight at me. 'And I mean a lot. After maybe six months of this, she suddenly disappears, like, totally. No one sees her, no one hears from her. Anyway, Erik hears a rumour that Conny had got her pregnant.'

'And had he?'

'Well, that's the thing; Conny wouldn't say. But when we

bumped into her a few months later she definitely wasn't pregnant and seemed pretty keen to avoid the topic.'

'And you thought Conny might have had something to do with that?'

Christie let out another sigh. 'Erik was a Catholic – I mean, not a *Catholic* Catholic, obviously. Not the kind who believes in things. He was more of a European Catholic.'

'The kind that doesn't believe in things?'

'The kind that doesn't believe it all, but who has very strong views about random shit. And that was part of the random shit that Erik had very strong views about. I think he'd liked the girl and he was upset to think…y'know.'

'It must've affected their relationship – Conny and Erik's, I mean.'

'For a while. I mean, I think Erik got over it in the end, but there was a period when he was definitely angry with Conny. I could tell.'

'And that's when he painted that painting?'

'Oh no, he'd already painted it – with dear old Dore Ashton as Saturn, would you believe? She'd ripped *Night of the Super Vixens* apart. But then the story came out about that poor young girl, and he repainted it the next year with Conny instead. That's when it stopped being about the critics and became about something else: a certain way of seeing women which Erik didn't approve of. He could be surprisingly puritanical about that kinda stuff.'

'Didn't it make you think twice about getting together with Conny later?'

'If only. I didn't know what to believe at the time. Conny had always seemed like such a charming guy. But later…well, let's just say, I came to see that picture as a prophecy, a warning.

One I stupidly ignored.'

'A prophecy?'

Christie paused. I could see a torrent of words bubbling up behind her lips, but she carefully controlled their flow out of her mouth. 'I don't know what he did to that young girl, and what he did or didn't make her do. But I know what he made me do; let's just leave it at that.'

'Oh my God, Christie. Did he…?'

'I said, let's just leave it at that.'

I wanted to say something, but the words just would not come. Robbed of speech, I felt a powerful urge to put my arm around her, but something in her eyes told me that I shouldn't. They appeared to contain a warning not to get too close. I thought it was her resilience that I could see in that flinty stare, but I wonder now if it wasn't actually her vulnerability. In any event I demurred, which I've always regretted since.

'You haven't had much luck with men,' was all I could think of to say.

She let out a brief, weary, laugh that sounded full of regret. 'I don't see it like that at all. Not at all. They were both flawed, but don't try and make out they were the same.'

'They both made you unhappy.'

'Erik worshipped me. He wanted me to be worthy of his worship and was frustrated when I wasn't. He wanted me to be better than I was. Conny wanted to conquer me – to devour me – and got frustrated when I wouldn't give in. He wanted me to be weaker than I was. There's a world of difference.'

'So why'd you go out with him? Conny, I mean.'

'I didn't have Erik by then. I didn't have anything, except a criminal record.'

'Yeah, Mimi mentioned that.'

'I bet she did.'

'What happened? I mean, you don't strike me as...' I couldn't bring myself to say it.

'I wasn't,' she said. 'Until I was. I mean, when Erik was around I just used to share stuff with friends. Everybody did, it was a social thing. But after Erik died, I couldn't afford to give it to them any more, so they'd pay me for it. Just a few friends. Then quite a lot of friends. Then the police turned up and I realised I didn't have any friends. What I had were customers.'

'I'm sure that's not true. I'm sure—'

'Not one of them stood by me. Not one. Conny was the only one there for me when I came out of those gates. He was all I had to hang on to. I couldn't afford to ask why. I was just so grateful. I guess I confused devouring with rescuing.'

I could see from the way she looked at me that Christie felt she had said too much. She gathered herself and headed out onto the street to hail a cab back to the Dorchester.

# TWENTY-FOUR

Christie seemed tired in the cab, and for the first time I became aware of her mortality. This cancer wasn't just something that sat waiting for her in the future; it was eating her up now. I'd always known that in the factual sense, but I'd never really felt it the way I did when I looked at her face in that cab. Something about our visit to the Redfern had drained her too. After the disaster of the previous evening, I decided it was best to leave Christie to her thoughts. I could see there was something needling her though. Eventually she put me out of my misery.

'Why is Suzy working at a hotel?' she asked.

I genuinely didn't know. 'I think you'll have to ask her that.'

'I did. She said you got her fired from her last proper job – her last gallery job, I mean.'

Even by Suzy's standards, this was quite a claim. 'I did not get her fired.'

'She said her boss was an old friend of yours and he fired

her ass the moment you announced that the two of you were getting divorced.'

'That's hardly the same thing as me getting her fired.'

'Isn't it?'

'And besides, I got her that job in the first place. In fact, I got her pretty much every gallery job she got after leaving the Courtauld. She wouldn't even have heard of half of them if it weren't for me.'

These were the facts that Suzy was rather less prone to telling people. I'd known Ernesto since we'd been at the Courtauld together. (His dad was a mate of Charles Saatchi, which helped burnish his CV.) He got left in the lurch by one of his curators and asked me if I knew anyone who could help him out at short notice. I'd put Suzy forward and she got the job. I left it at that. I never asked him to fire her (just as I'd never asked him to appoint her), although when we separated, I did mention it to him, just so he'd know. It was to avoid any potential embarrassment, really, for both of us.

'I did not get her fired,' I reiterated.

Christie raised her eyebrows and then turned to look out of the car window.

When we arrived back at the hotel, she went straight to her room to lie down. This seemed so uncharacteristic it surprised me, and I said so.

'Yeah, well, it surprises me too,' she replied. 'But let me tell you, honey, old age is the most unexpected thing that happens to a person.'

She had filled up my life so fully over the previous week it seemed almost incomprehensible to me that within twenty-four hours she would be gone from it, perhaps forever. And such had been her boundless *joie de vivre* during those first few days together, it would be difficult for me ever to think of New York again without imagining her living in it. Even when she was just lying down for a recuperative rest the world seemed somehow diminished by her absence.

Suzy was awake and dressed by this point. She was certainly more subdued than she had been the previous evening but there was something about her complexion that allowed her face to recover its glow without the aid of make-up. I'd always liked that about her: a little bit of eyeliner, maybe some lip gloss, and she was good to go. She was still young enough that her beauty looked effortless. It was something that I couldn't help but admire in her, even though I knew it was ridiculous to do so.

Without Christie to mediate between us, neither of us really knew what to do. Unlike the previous night, Suzy wasn't in the mood for an argument. This was a relief to me and made me feel safe enough to tentatively mention her job, or rather, Christie's resignation of her job on her behalf. Suzy seemed surprisingly unconcerned.

'Yeah, she said she was going to. I phoned my boss up while the two of you were out just to let him know I'll do my shift tonight. But that's it. After that, I'm leaving.'

'But why? I thought you needed that job.'

'For the same reason I left you. I deserve better.'

This seemed quite a shift from her take the previous day, but I knew from my own experience that a night in Christie's presence could do that to your perspective: it could make you see how small your life had become and transform your sense of what was possible. Somehow her irrepressible energy dragged you along in its wake and made you feel that you could be more than you were. I think, ultimately, that's what I loved most about her.

Suzy and I conducted an ornate dance around each other for the next hour. It wasn't that we weren't talking to each other; more that we managed to navigate our way around the suite without ever actually needing to talk to each other. Eventually, however, we both found ourselves in the lounge area sipping our respective coffees. Christie's question to me back in the cab was lurking at the back of my mind.

'Look, I hope you don't mind me asking, Suze; it's just that, I didn't expect to see you back working the hotels.'

She looked away. 'Neither did I.'

There was a sorrow in her voice that, for once, drowned out the anger. She looked at me as though weighing up what she wanted to say.

'How are you?' she asked eventually.

'Me? Oh, I'm fine. You don't have to worry about me.'

She was looking at me properly, perhaps for the first time since we'd re-met. 'I mean, really.'

I gave a half-hearted laugh and looked away. 'Fine.'

'You don't seem fine.' There was a sliver of genuine concern in her voice that I'd forgotten she could feel towards me.

'Don't I?'

'No. You look stressed.'

'Well I've just been through a very stressful divorce.'

She smiled at me and we had the briefest moment of connection, something I'd not felt for three years or more. It illuminated her face and for a fleeting instant I could see her as she had been – as the woman I'd fallen in love with. Perhaps sensing this, and regretting it, she quickly returned her attention to her coffee.

'What about you?' I asked.

'I'm good actually. Things seem to be turning round for me.' She sounded surprised even as she said it.

'New boyfriend OK?'

She gave a rueful smile and shook her head. 'Why does it bother you so much – whether I'm going out with someone? I mean, we've been separated for two years.'

'Who said I was bothered?' I asked. 'Is it anyone I know?'

'No. Wait, maybe yes… I dunno. You've definitely met him, but I don't think you know him, as such. But yes, he makes me happy. I'm not going to apologise for that.'

'Is he an art guy?' I was hoping to God it wasn't Jasper. I had always seen that he found her attractive, but it would complicate our business relationship no end.

'No. I've given up on art guys,' she said. 'I don't think they're for me.'

Then she stopped herself and looked up as a thought appeared to occur to her. 'Or maybe it's that I've realised I'm not for them.'

'I'm sure you're being hard on yourself.'

'I don't think so,' she said. 'It's like fish knives. I used to think fish knives were posh until I met you. Then I realised that they're not really – not proper posh.'

'I don't quite see—'

'I wanted to be a fish knife, I think. When I was growing up. I thought that would get me into the world of posh people. And I think I did – become a fish knife.' She turned to look at me directly. For once she spoke without malice. 'But one of the things I learnt from being with you is that proper posh people – like all your arty friends – they don't have fish knives, and they look down their noses at the people who do.'

I wanted to explore this further with her, but before I

could, Christie's warm and honeyed tones burst out from the bedroom.

'What the fuck!'

Suzy and I immediately sensed that something was wrong. Our eyes met in a moment of mutual panic.

'Hey, you two! I think you need to come in here. Now.'

We rose from our seats and dashed into Christie's bedroom. She was propped up on pillows watching the news. It had been on in the background in the lounge where Suzy and I had been, but the TV had been on mute, so we'd not really paid it any attention. Christie, however, was pointing in horror to the TV screen in front of her. She looked even more ashen-faced than she had in the cab, so I knew that whatever it was that she wanted me and Suzy to see, it wasn't going to be good news.

I turned my head to see the beaming face of Constantine Gerou staring out at me from the television set. Beside him Rocco and various other members of Conny's entourage were holding back the assembled members of the press as they sought to shove cameras, microphones and smartphones into his face. And at the bottom of the television screen the headline ran across on a ticker, 'BREAKING NEWS: Extradition of Greek businessman and diplomat Constantine Gerou collapses at the High Court.'

I had to see the headline appear and disappear twice before its implications began to sink in. Slowly, a logic trail began to form in my stunned mind: Conny's extradition had collapsed. This meant that he no longer faced being sent back to Greece. But if he no longer faced extradition then he no longer faced the prospect of his diplomatic baggage being ransacked by the Greek authorities. This in turn meant that there was now no possibility of any unexplained cash sums being found in his possession, which meant that there was no need for him to dispose of any cash. All of which pointed to one very obvious conclusion: Conny no longer needed to buy *Susanna & the Elders*.

At the point this realisation hit me, my heart sank into my stomach and my bowels rose up to meet it. I felt the colour drain from my cheeks and a thin film of sweat began to form on my forehead. I wasn't sure if I was going to defecate or vomit. It felt like I might do both. In the end, I fainted.

# PART 3

## JUDITH BEHEADS HOLOFERNES

### OCTOBER 2019 - FEBRUARY 2020
### LONDON

*Art is a lie that points to the truth*
**Pablo Picasso**

# TWENTY-FIVE

It took a while for the hotel reception to arrange a cab for the three of us. My collapse had given Suzy a great excuse to splash water in my face and slap my cheeks, so I assumed she'd be happy. Part of me suspected that the only reason she'd bothered to revive me was so that she could say *Told you so* to my face. But actually, as she sat back in the cab, I could see a look of real concern on her face. 'Oh my God, Gabe. What are we going to do?'

Her use of the word 'we' in this context was both reassuring and surprising. Our conversation back at the Dorchester suggested that, for all her surface hostility, there was still something in Suzy's heart that thought fondly of me. The truth, of course, was rather different, but then again, the truth is like *Sky News* – it's there, right in front of you on a screen wherever you go, but no one ever pays it any attention. In any event, the only answer I could offer to Suzy's question was, 'I don't know, Suze. I really don't know what we're going to do.'

As we crawled through the London traffic, I simply couldn't think of any way we could rescue the situation. Of course, the collapse of our deal with Conny would be a major blow to Christie, but I had risked everything on this going through. It wasn't only the $185,000 that I'd paid out that would be lost; one phone call, one text message from Conny to Mimi – or indeed to the police – and my reputation in the art world would be destroyed. Trying to sell a painting of doubtful provenance 'off book' for cash... Well, even with the Viejo name behind me, there was no way I could come back from that.

I had to get my money back.

By the time we pulled up outside the Walled Garden, Conny was standing at the entrance looking very pleased with himself while his solicitor (not Love, but a Hong Kong-Chinese extradition lawyer who announced herself as Audrey Lam) read out a statement to the assembled press corps on his behalf. The statement was predictably irate about the injustice of the whole ordeal and the impact of it on Conny's mental and physical health. It denounced the Greek authorities and also the British legal system's complicity in the 'unjustifiable witch hunt against a wholly innocent man'. It went on to point out that – despite his complete innocence – Conny's extradition would have been automatic had it not been for unspecified 'technical irregularities' in the Greek government's paperwork. There was something of a scrum on the hotel's steps as the journalists jostled for position, so I wasn't sure if Conny had seen us loitering at the back of the crowd. He certainly didn't make eye contact until Ms Lam reached the end of the statement. 'Given that this whole nightmare has shaken my confidence in my ability to be protected by the

British and EU legal systems from the vindictiveness of the Greek government, I shall be leaving the UK at the earliest opportunity, in order to seek asylum in a friendlier jurisdiction.'

Having read the statement, Ms Lam promptly turned around and walked briskly into the hotel, closely followed by Conny and his minders. A volley of questions exploded from the assembled journalists, and there was a surge of flash pops and whizzes from photographers' cameras, but it was clear that neither Conny nor Ms Lam would be providing further clarification.

Mo and Daniel took up positions in front of the entrance to make sure that none of the journalists could gain access to the hotel. On this basis, it wasn't obvious on what grounds Christie and I could claim admittance, given that neither of us were guests either. While Suzy went over to negotiate with Mo and Daniel, Christie turned to one of the journalists. His press pass, which hung on a lanyard around his neck, suggested he'd been sent over from Greece, so she clearly figured that he might have the inside track on what was going on.

'I don't understand. How did the case collapse?' Christie asked him, frantically. 'I thought he *had* to be extradited.'

'Yeah, he should be,' the world-weary reporter replied. 'But you know what people like that are like. The rules don't apply to them.'

'But isn't it automatic if the Greek government request it?'

'The statement says that the case has collapsed on "technical grounds".' He rolled his eyes. 'You can read into that whatever you want.'

'And what do you read into it?'

'Officially it means that someone in the Greek government has found some irregularities in the paperwork they've submitted to support the extradition request, so they've had to withdraw it. They say they're going to submit it again in a couple of days, but you heard him – he'll be gone by then.'

'And unofficially?' asked Christie, peering over the top of her sunglasses (which she had insisted on wearing despite the overcast weather).

The journalist leaned forward, flicking a glance behind him. 'The word is Gerou somehow managed to get some bribes through to a couple of people in the Greek Justice Ministry so, "technically", no one gives a shit about having him extradited any more.'

Suddenly the presence of Love Menolo in Conny's suite the previous evening, and the urgency with which her departure was orchestrated, made sense. His apparently generous offer of a million dollars for Christie's painting had only ever been a back-up in case his main plan failed.

At that point Suzy came back to us. 'Come on you two. We're in.' And she grabbed Christie and me and dragged us past the gaggle of journalists and into the Walled Garden.

Conny was still in reception talking to Ms Lam. He was arranging for one of his men to drive her away using the hotel's back entrance in order to protect her from any unwelcome attention from the press. In fairness to the young solicitor, she appeared as bemused as everyone else by what had just happened, so I assumed she must be legit. It made me worry slightly about exactly where Conny's minders might be taking her as they led her away.

Rocco had followed us in and called the lift, which now opened its doors. Christie stepped forward authoritatively, and called out, 'Conny! I think we need to talk.'

Conny turned round and fixed us with a smirk. He was

certainly feeling very pleased with himself. What he was not feeling, it appeared, was particularly well-disposed towards the idea of talking to us. He stepped into the lift accompanied by five of his minders so that not even Rocco could fit in. The doors closed and Conny and his entourage disappeared – along with any prospect of Christie being able to sell her painting, or me recover my money.

Christie turned to Rocco. I could see that she was struggling to hold it together. 'I guess this means our deal's off.'

His reply was more considered than I had anticipated. 'He likes you, Christie. Always did. But you don't get to be as rich as he is by being sentimental about an old girlfriend. And this is not the kind of business you discuss in a hotel foyer, if you know what I'm saying.'

A few moments later a second lift arrived, and Rocco got in. There was a rare glimpse of compassion in the look he gave Christie. 'Listen, I can't make any promises, but go up to his suite. I think he'd like to see you again, even if it's just to say goodbye,' he said, before adding, 'But I had to pull in a lot of favours to get that money changed into dollars so, personally, I think it would be a shame to see all that work go to waste.'

He gave Christie a courteous nod as the doors of the lift closed.

'Did I just hear what I think I heard?' I asked, turning to Suzy and Christie with an inquiring look.

'I think you did,' Suzy replied, as nonplussed as I was. It seemed that a door which appeared to have been firmly closed had actually been left slightly ajar.

'OK,' I said slowly. 'Do either of you think there's any way that Conny can be persuaded to still go ahead with the deal?'

Suzy looked at Christie, I looked at Suzy, and Christie looked at me. It seemed fanciful to all of us – you could tell that by our faces. But at the same time it seemed more plausible than it had done five minutes previously.

'I won't beg,' said Christie. Something about our interchange at the Redfern – and Conny's wordless disappearance in the lift – had steeled her resolve. 'I won't beg that man to give me anything. I'm through with begging.' Her cheeks were flushed, and I noticed her leg was shaking.

'No one's asking you to beg,' I said. 'Just go up there and see what he wants.'

'No,' she said. She sounded definite about it. 'If he wants something, let him beg me.'

'Of course. But if you want him to beg you for something then you're going to have to go upstairs and let him beg you.'

'No. You go. You're my representative: represent me. That's what I'm paying you for.'

'OK. But what am I supposed to do?'

'Find out what he wants. Then come back here and tell me.'

'And what if he doesn't offer anything? I asked.

'He will.'

'You think?'

'I do,' Christie replied. 'I'm pretty sure I know what he wants. I know what he's like. It's the only thing that makes sense.'

'What do you think it is?' asked Suzy.

Christie turned to me. 'I think you need to get in that lift, Gabriel, and find out.'

# TWENTY-SIX

I arrived at Conny's suite to find the whole of the top floor in a state of upheaval. Cases and crates were being packed and stacked at pace. Members of his entourage were striding purposefully around attaching stickers and luggage tags to the various items being left in the corridor. What sounded like a shredder could be heard rumbling in the background. It was clear that Conny wasn't intending to hang around any longer than necessary.

The door to his suite was open and, for once, appeared unguarded, but I knocked on it anyway. I could smell the scent of sweat, cigarette smoke and warm paper in the air. The rumbling stopped and a head appeared from out of one of the rooms. It was young, male and had the first traces of perspiration on its brow.

'Can I help you?'

There was something in the accompanying frown and

tone of voice which suggested that helping me wasn't really uppermost in his mind.

'I'm here to see Mr Gerou,' I said uncertainly.

The young man seemed sceptical.

'Uhm…Rocco suggested we come up…' I added, in an attempt to burnish my bona fides.

The head dipped back into the room. 'Mr Danaos?'

Rocco emerged from the room. 'What are you doing here?'

'You suggested I come up.'

'No, I suggested Ms McGraw come up.'

'Well, I'm Ms McGraw's representative. She's asked me to represent her.'

Rocco smirked. 'If you insist. But I think you'll be a bit of a disappointment.'

He led me toward the main sitting room area, where he indicated I should stop. He walked in and said, 'Mr Gerou – the guy's here.'

An unmistakable voice growled back its reply: 'A guy?'

'Yeah, I know. I have warned him.' There was a brief, furtive interchange between Rocco and Conny which I couldn't make out. 'Come through,' said Rocco eventually.

Conny was once more seated behind his desk, smoking a Black Russian. He nodded toward Rocco, who pulled the door closed behind him as he exited.

Conny sat back in his seat and took a slow, deliberate draw on his cigarette. He seemed determined to tinge this encounter with a layer of casual menace, which subtly charged the room. My head was telling me there was no reason for me to be nervous – I was eight inches taller than him and the best part of forty years younger – but despite this, I felt my stomach tighten and my heartbeat quicken.

'Do you need a seat?' he asked.

I certainly felt I needed one, as I was still feeling slightly faint, but I worried that taking one would look like a sign of weakness, so I decided to hold my ground.

'I'll stand, thanks.' I thought it might emphasise my height advantage.

'As you wish.'

I elected to get to the point quickly before I passed out again.

'Let me cut to the chase, Mr Gerou. Have we still got a deal or not?'

Conny lent forward and put his elbows on the desk before answering very deliberately. 'Well, that rather depends on you.'

I narrowed my eyes in an attempt to appear intimidating. 'Why does it depend on me? I mean, if there's no extradition then there's no need for you to get rid of any of your cash... Is there?'

Conny tried to look affronted. 'I love great art and I love beautiful women. And this painting is a great piece of art, featuring my favourite beautiful woman. Of course I still want to buy it.'

I wanted to believe him.

'But of course,' Conny continued, his look melting into something altogether more sarcastic, 'the situation is now changed.'

'I don't see why. The painting is still as good as it was, and all the guarantees regarding provenance are still in place. This is still a great deal for you.'

Conny chuckled in a way that suggested mild amusement. Even without his entourage, he seemed to have the power to make you perceive a vague sense of threat. I couldn't work out what I was nervous of, but something in his manner evinced in me the same reaction as a creak on the stairs in the dead of night.

'Of course, the painting is the same,' he said. 'But the man looking at it is not. I'm looking from a different perspective. And that means I can see different things – let's call them new possibilities.'

'And what would those be?' I asked, although I had a strong sense that I knew exactly what at least one of them was.

'Well, firstly, to keep more of my money.'

'This is a million-dollar painting! You said so yourself.'

Conny winced. 'But is it? Is it, really?'

'I think so. It's what I'd pay for it.'

'Maybe you would. But you don't have the money. I do.' He stood up and walked over to the window, which he proceeded to look out of. 'The first rule of valuation is that any asset is only worth what someone is prepared to pay for it.' He turned back to look at me. 'And I'm not prepared to pay one million dollars.'

This is exactly what I had feared.

'Let's be honest,' he said as he idly picked some fluff off the cuff of his jacket and ambled back towards me. 'It's pretty clear that you still need to sell, whereas I don't still need to buy. And it's also pretty clear that not many people are likely to want to buy your painting, given the issues with its provenance. But even if they did, one call from me to Mimi's people and you can't sell to anyone anyway. So the scales of the deal, which were evenly balanced, are now heavily tilted in one direction: mine. I think that means we need to agree to revise the purchase price.'

My stomach tightened further.

'Revise it to what?'

Conny ceased to be diverted by his personal grooming and fixed me with a cold, dead stare. The whole world seemed to hold its breath in that moment, but I guess it was just me.

'Five hundred thousand,' he said eventually.

To be honest, when I heard Conny's revised offer I almost wanted to collapse on the floor in relief and shower his feet with my tear-strewn kisses. It was enough. It wasn't as good a deal as I had thought I was going to get twenty-four hours previously, but I reminded myself that it was considerably better than the prospect of losing my $185,000, which had been my operating assumption ten minutes before. I could breathe again.

'Is that it?' I asked. 'Have we got a deal? At five hundred thousand?'

I wanted to check. After everything I'd been told about Conny – and had experienced first-hand – I couldn't believe that he'd been so generous in his negotiation despite there no longer being any need for him to be so. It seemed too good to be true.

Which, unfortunately, is exactly what it was.

'We *almost* have a deal,' Conny replied.

I looked at him askance, tensing as I did so. '*Almost?*'

He took another slow draw on his cigarette before answering.

'Yes,' he said eventually. 'There is just one more thing.' And the mischievous glint I had noticed at his first meeting with Christie reappeared in his eye.

Saturn was going to offer to rescue Christie. But once again it would look an awful lot like he was devouring her.

# TWENTY-SEVEN

'Absolutely not!' was Suzy's reaction when I returned to the ground floor and outlined Conny's revised terms. 'I forbid you – I absolutely forbid you – to do this, Christie.'

I had taken the two of them into one of the ground-floor conference rooms as I didn't want to break the news to them in a crowded hotel lobby.

I had anticipated Suzy's outrage and was determined to try to take the heat out of the situation.

'Look, I know we're all very emotional at the moment, but I would just ask if we could try and focus on what we're trying to achieve here. We all want the same thing.'

'Really? You think I want to fuck her too?' asked Suzy. I decided not to rise to the bait. 'We do not all want the same thing, Gabriel!' she continued, and at the time I believed she meant it. It was only later I came to realise that she was either lying or deluding herself. At root we did all want the same thing – it was just that for each of us that thing was a proxy for something else, and that was what was different. I genuinely don't think Suzy understood that. She liked to try and claim the moral high ground, but she was scrabbling around in the gutter just like the rest of us.

'Can you please calm down, Suze?' I asked. 'You're not even part of this deal. There are three parties to this – me, Conny and Christie – and I'm trying to find a way for us to do some business so that it will give all of us what we need.' Again, at the time I truly believed that.

'Do some business with each other? You are asking Christie to submit to rape to save your investment planning.'

I felt this needed correcting. 'I'm asking Christie to consider whether she's prepared to spend the night – one night – with Conny in order to secure the money she needs to stay alive.'

'Which amounts to the same thing!' The Brummie accent was in full force now.

'Look, I appreciate these aren't the terms any of us wanted, but it wasn't me who came up with them. I was just sent up there to find out if there was any way we could rescue the deal which, I think you'll find, I have done. I'm sorry it's not on terms which are more amenable to you, Suze, but I don't have a lot of leverage here.'

'Unbelievable, Gabe! You are fucking unbelievable!'

'What else can we do? If you're so adamant this can't go ahead, what do you suggest?'

'We can go to the police.'

'And say what? That we tried to offer a painting we don't really own to a businessman who's on the run for an off-the-books cash sale?'

'And say that that man was trying to procure sexual services in exchange for money.'

'Which he will deny! There was no one else there, Suzy. No one. Just me and him. I have no proof of any of this. But even if I did – even if I could go up there with a recording device and get him to repeat everything he just said to me – I'm sorry, but I just can't see a way in which our going to the authorities is going to get Christie the money she needs. Frankly, we're as likely to end up in prison as he is.'

'But it isn't right.' This was the nub of the matter for her. It always was. 'It can't be right that Christie has to prostitute herself in order to stay alive. We need to find another way. Have you not considered that possibility?'

Actually, I had thought about nothing else in the lift on the way back down other than how I might somehow rescue my money at the same time as rescuing Christie from the choice she now faced. Upon arrival on the ground floor, I had gone to the toilet and racked my brain for a further fifteen minutes before going to find Christie and Suzy.

The simple fact was that there was no obvious way to raise the money Christie needed within the time she needed to raise it. However repulsive it appeared, therefore, getting my money back and securing the money Christie needed for her treatment would have to involve agreeing a deal with Conny. And with the threat of extradition removed (at least for long enough for him to leave the country) Conny had no reason to agree a deal with us on anything other than his terms. In truth, it was a minor miracle that he was prepared to offer us a deal at all, even one with such punishing conditions.

'Look, there's a huge amount riding on this,' I said. 'We mustn't be too hasty. It's not only Christie's life that's at stake here—'

'No, it's her dignity, her self-respect. It's her ability to operate in society as a woman without being forced to pander to the whims of men like Constantine Gerou. It's about the ability of all women to retain their own free will and agency in a society—'

I could sense that Suzy was launching into one of her speeches, but, whatever the legitimacy of her feelings on the matter (and, for the record, I wasn't disagreeing with her overall assessment of the situation), it didn't seem likely to me that Conny was going to be won over by appeals to feminist theory. I was about to cut across her to point this out when Christie's voice, which had been unusually silent up to this point, rang out with calm authority.

'It's OK. I'll do it.'

There was a momentary silence while Suzy and I both struggled to assimilate what Christie had just said. My whole brain seemed to slow like they say it does in the final moments before a car crash. The reality of what she'd just consented to seemed so completely overwhelming that I wasn't able to process it in normal time.

Neither could Suzy. 'What? You can't be serious? Christie, you can't do this. You're worth more than this.'

Never meet your heroes – that's what they say. And the tears running down Suzy's horrified face betrayed the brutal truth of that.

But Christie was unmoved. She looked at me without a flicker of emotion. 'Tell Conny I'll do it.'

I didn't know whether to feel relieved or horrified, so in the end I felt both. My money was safe, but even I wasn't sure if I wanted it this much. I could taste the acid reflux coming up at the back of my throat.

'Are you sure?' I asked.

Christie's leg was trembling again, and I saw her eyes begin to glisten in the light of the room. But she refused to give Conny the satisfaction of her tears. 'Yes, I'm sure. I'll do it. But on my terms.'

'I'm not sure if Conny is going to—'

'This isn't just about Conny, Gabriel. It's about you too.'

'Me?'

'Yes, you. Like Suzy said, I'm currently a hundred and twenty-five grand up, even if this deal collapses. I mean, I know I don't have all the money I need right now, but even without it; I don't lose anything I hadn't lost already. But you – you're a long way down with no way of coming back if I don't go through with this. So if I'm going to help you get your money back, then I need you to do something for me.'

'Of course! Anything, absolutely anything, I promise.' I genuinely couldn't think of anything that she could ask me to do that I wouldn't have been prepared to do in a heartbeat.

'Great. Well, that's OK then. So here's what I want you to do...'

'Just say the word. Whatever it is.'

She looked at me sternly. 'I want to give you one last chance to do the right thing.'

This phrase was uncomfortably familiar to me. 'Do the right thing?' I said, forlornly.

'Yes. I want you to tell Suzy the truth about your inheritance. All of it.'

# TWENTY-EIGHT

We argued about it for ten minutes or more, all the time the self-satisfied smirk on Suzy's face growing wider and wider. In the end though, I had to concede defeat. I simply couldn't afford for the deal not to go through, and Christie wasn't for budging.

The one concession that I did manage to wring out of her – out of both of them really – was an agreement that nothing I said could be used to re-open the financial settlement that Suzy and I had reached. I was surprised how quickly Suzy agreed to this. She even agreed – no, she actually offered – to write out and sign a statement witnessed by Christie confirming that if I told her the truth about my inheritance, then she expressly committed that, 'at no point now or in the future will I ever take legal action against Gabriel Viejo to recover these or any other monies from him.'

That seemed to exclude any possibility of Suzy using

my confession to screw me over, so I couldn't see the harm in giving her the satisfaction of telling her that she'd been more or less correct in her suspicions. And getting the signed agreement off her would also mean that I could move the final $25,000 from my Argentinian bank account into my English one without triggering any renewed legal claim from Suzy.

The only thing I had to do for her in return was sign a similar statement, again witnessed by Christie, promising that I would never, either now or in the future, take any action 'legal or otherwise' to recover any money from her. As even I accepted that Suzy owed me nothing, and I had no intention of ever putting myself in a position where she might, this seemed like a small indulgence to grant her.

Despite this, for the first time in my life I felt like I could have actually benefited from the unique expertise of Love Menolo, which perhaps should have made me reflect more than I did on which side of the moral line I was currently standing on.

Once our respective statements had been agreed, signed and witnessed, I proceeded to set out again what I had told Christie the previous evening, but this time with Suzy listening intently. Having recounted this, I paused.

'So to summarise all that, are you saying that you did receive $200,000 from your grandpa that was not disclosed to my legal team despite repeated requests from them to you?' Suzy asked.

I sighed and played with the hotel pencil on the table in front of me. 'What you need to understand, Suze, is that it took ages for the whole estate to be sorted out. Eighteen months or more. I didn't know during all that time how much I'd be getting.'

'But when you did find out…?

The room began to feel stuffy, despite the air conditioning

humming gently in the background. 'The proceeds from the sale didn't actually arrive in my bank account until after we'd both submitted our final declarations.'

'And you decided to hide those proceeds offshore.'

'No. I still had a bank account in Argentina from when I was a child. I didn't *ask* for the money to be put in there. That was just the account Grandpa had nominated the money to go into, so the money never actually entered the UK. I wasn't hiding anything.

'I didn't really think about it at first. But then, your lawyers started asking about the sketch they claimed I'd inherited.'

'And you decided to lie about it.'

I couldn't bring myself to look at her. 'I didn't lie. Honestly... their letters assumed I'd inherited the sketch, rather than the proceeds of the sale of the sketch. All their questions were based on a slightly faulty premise, and I was just very precise in my answers.'

'Which meant that poor Suzy didn't get her share,' Christie said.

'But it wasn't hers!' I turned to Christie and looked at her imploringly. 'It was mine. Like *Susanna & the Elders* isn't Mimi's; it's yours, whatever the lawyers say.'

'But you didn't want to take a chance that the court might say different,' Christie replied.

'Like you don't want to take the chance with your painting! I'd agreed to everything her lawyers had suggested – even against the advice of my own – because I knew that I had that inheritance to fall back on. I couldn't risk losing that as well, and the advice was that there was a risk. The law isn't clear-cut. Anyway, Suzy didn't have the money to send a legal team out to Buenos Aires, so, from my perspective, as long as the proceeds of the sale stayed there and weren't brought into the UK, there was nothing she could do.'

'That's pretty smart,' Christie acknowledged. 'But I guess having $200,000 that you can't actually spend without living in Argentina is not really much of a benefit at all, is it? Not when you live in London.'

I paused. 'Not really, no.'

'So, would it also be true to say that one of the attractions of our little deal was that you could move some of your inheritance money from your Argentinian bank account through my New York account and on to your London account without anyone being able to link that money to old Jo's Bacon sketch?'

I felt myself blush. 'I guess so.'

'Because, if anyone did want to query exactly where all this money's come from all of a sudden, you could say with your hand on a Bible that every penny of it had been paid to you by Christie McGraw for professional services rendered – and rendered after your divorce. No matter how hard anyone looks, there'll be nothing in your English bank account transactions to link that money to the Bacon sketch, or anything else that happened while you were married.'

Christie looked triumphant, like the sleuth in the closing chapter of a low-grade detective novel. 'So Suzy can't claim it, but you can finally spend it. And with a very healthy little bonus from me to top it up, thank you very much.'

I couldn't bring myself to respond. Instead, I sat, twirling the pencil between my fingers while staring at a piece of paper that I wasn't reading. The silence between us expanded to fill the room until the atmosphere was as tense as a held breath.

'Well, that puts your offer to help me in a rather different light, wouldn't you say?' said Christie, eventually.

Suzy felt compelled to chip in. 'That's not even the worst of it.'

'Isn't it?' Christie seemed incredulous.

'No! The worst of it is that his grandpa didn't even pay Daniel Farson for the sketch in the first place.'

I wasn't prepared to allow this to go unchallenged. 'That's not true and you know it,' I said. 'Grandpa bought that sketch. There's a bill of sale. It was legitimately his.'

This was true: Grandpa Jo had bought the sketch off Daniel Farson, and our family had been incredibly proud of the fact that, as a consequence, we owned a genuine Francis Bacon. The precise nature of the transaction which brought it under Grandpa's ownership, however, was not something that we tended to dwell on too deeply.

'Oh, I'm sorry, Gabe, you're right. He did pay for it – it just wasn't in cash. Remind me again what it was…'

'You know full well what it was.'

'Yes, I do. It was a crate of scotch.'

Christie gasped. 'A case of scotch? To Daniel Farson? Jeez!'

'Exactly!' said Suzy.

By the early nineties Farson had lost or drunk most of the family fortune that he'd inherited ('enough to have bought a row of houses in London,' he claimed). He was largely unemployable on account of his alcoholism, which was only accelerated by Bacon's death in 1993. When Grandpa Jo met him on a trip to England in 1997, Farson knew he was dying, but was desperate for funds to tide him over until the release of his autobiography later that year.

Quite what prompted Farson to mention the sketch of Belcher to Grandpa was unclear, but the story went that he turned up at Grandpa's hotel one night with it tucked under his arm, asking for £20,000, and left thirty minutes later with a case of Bell's whisky which Grandpa Jo had purchased from the hotel bar, and his taxi fare home – but minus the sketch.

When Grandpa recounted this story (which he did frequently) it was told with his trademark twinkle firmly in his eye, and usually ended with him and his audience guffawing with laughter. It was clearly possible however, to frame the narrative in altogether less benign terms, and it was this less benign framing which Suzy seemed to be suggesting we focus on.

'He did nothing wrong,' I said.

'Nothing wrong? Are you kidding me?' Suzy replied. 'He took a highly valuable sketch off a vulnerable man and paid for it with what was effectively poison.'

'I think you're being over-dramatic.'

'How?'

'That sketch was not highly valuable when he got it – it wasn't even registered. It was Grandpa Jo who made it valuable. It was he who got Jeffrey Bernard to vouch for it. It was he who approached Martin Harrison to get it accredited. That cost him money. It was he who registered it. Farson must have had that sketch for twenty years, but he never bothered. That sketch was worthless when Farson turned up at my grandpa's hotel. He was taking a huge risk on it.'

'Not that huge. Even allowing for the hotel's mark-up, I bet the scotch didn't cost him more than a couple of hundred quid.'

This was not a battle I had envisaged having, so it was not one I had prepared for, and I could see from Christie's face that it was not going well for me. Something had changed in the way she was looking at me. Any remaining warmth that she might have felt towards me had gone from her eyes. I wonder now if that was the moment she made her decision. But at the time, all I wanted was for Christie to stop looking at me like she was. I wanted her to make me feel like she had when we were in New York, that night at Le Bernadin's.

'But none of that has anything to do with me,' I said. 'I did nothing wrong.'

'But you've benefited from what your grandad did wrong,' Suzy said.

'I have benefited from my grandpa taking a worthless sketch and turning it into a valuable one.'

'And that's how you see it,' Suzy said. 'As though it was just down to good luck and canny business. But haven't you ever noticed that stuff like that only happens to families like yours? No one turned up at our council house offering my mum a valuable artwork for the price of a case of scotch.'

Every meeting is a roomful of broken hearts, and every argument is just people trying to have their pain recognised while at the same time struggling to keep its precise shape and dimensions hidden. I never felt that as keenly as when I found myself in a room with Suzy. But I was weary with the arguing. I'd had thirteen years of it and nothing I could say could convince her to change her mind: I was always the privileged one and she was always the one fighting for the plucky underdog whom my family and I were oppressing. That was the thing that annoyed me most about Suzy – for her, everything was about virtue signalling and she signposted her virtue with all the subtlety of a golf sale at Nevada Bob's.

Fortunately, Christie was growing tired of the argument too. It was getting uncomfortably close to the socialism of which she clearly disapproved. So, having got me to confess my sins to Suzy and having satisfied her own curiosity as to the history of my grandpa's Bacon sketch, she pulled us back to the matter in hand.

'Conny's issued his terms,' she said. 'Now I want you to go back up there and issue mine.'

'If I'm being honest, I'm not sure Conny is going to be much minded to listen to anything you're going to demand of him, Christie,' I said.

But she was clearly determined not to capitulate to his whims entirely and when she articulated her terms, I felt there was nothing in them that Conny could reasonably object to.

Both parties were to meet in the hotel lobby at 8pm. Suzy was also to be there to act as broker for the exchange. There were to be none of Conny's minders present and Christie promised not to bring any 'muscle' either (not that she had any to bring): the only security was to be provided by Mo and Daniel, who would act under Suzy's direction.

Christie would bring the painting and Conny was to bring $500,000 dollars in cash in two suitcases. The suitcases were to have luggage tags attached in the name of Christie McGraw. Conny could check that the painting was the same one he had previously seen, and I would be given an opportunity to count the cash. Once Conny was satisfied that the painting was the same, and I was satisfied that the correct amount of money had been submitted, Daniel and Mo would take the painting and the cash and place them both in the hotel's safe room. The rest of us would leave at that point, so that at 8.15pm Christie could accompany Conny to dinner at the Mastic Tree restaurant, for which he would pay. Dinner would last until no later than 10.15pm at which point they would both retire to

Conny's suite.

There was to be no violence or threat of violence to be used against Christie, but (subject to that proviso being met) she agreed to engage in 'the full range of activities' that the two of them had enjoyed when they were a couple in New York. We would all meet again in the hotel lobby at 7am sharp the next morning. Suzy was to be allowed to check privately with both parties that the other party had kept to their side of the deal. Assuming that they had, Mo and Daniel would hand the painting over to Conny, the first suitcase of money to Christie, and the second to me. At that point Christie, Conny, Suzy and I would all be free to go our separate ways.

This sounded such a considered proposition and seemed so well thought through in order to protect the interests of all parties, I was almost tempted to forget the small matter of what was scheduled to happen between 10.15pm and 7am.

Christie wrote out her terms on a piece of hotel notepaper, which she then signed and gave to me with instructions to go back up to Conny's suite and establish whether he was prepared to accept them.

'And if his terms are non-negotiable, then so are mine,' she said. 'If he tries to change anything, you tell him the deal's off. And he's got to sign to say he accepts them – you better make sure he understands that. I want his signature on that piece of paper.'

'OK, OK, I understand. I'll make sure that's all spelt out to him.'

I couldn't see why Conny would object. He didn't know of Suzy's connection to me and Christie so it would look to him as though we were getting a genuinely neutral third party to oversee the exchange and provide the means of enforcing the terms of the deal on both parties. Suzy, who had calmed down slightly by this point, was still unhappy about this element of the plan, but Christie assured me that she would talk her round while I was up with Conny. All I had to do was hope to God that Conny would agree to Christie's terms.

# TWENTY-NINE

Going up to Conny's suite in the lift, I tried to comprehend why Christie had agreed to his proposal. I really had assumed she'd say no; that her pride wouldn't allow her to agree. Something about the fact that she had, saddened me. However cruel it sounds, it diminished her in my eyes. Yet I also understood the abyss she was staring into; that she had no real option other than to acquiesce if she wanted to stay alive. And in the end, that was what I put it down to.

So when I handed the sheet with Christie's terms on it over to Conny, I genuinely thought I was submitting her surrender on the best terms she could hope to get.

'Help yourself to a coffee if you want one,' he said, staring at the sheet.

My mouth was as dry as a desert, so I went over to the machine.

'And I'll have an espresso, if you're making one,' he added.

'Black, no sugar.'

I made our two drinks then walked back over and placed his espresso cup and saucer in front of him on his desk. His face gave no indication of what he thought of Christie's proposal.

'What is this?' he asked, sharply.

'I think it's pretty clear, isn't it? Those are Ms McGraw's terms for agreeing to your proposal.'

'What? She thinks she can dictate terms to me?' The false charm and air of fake bonhomie was suddenly gone, and for the first time he actually seemed in danger of losing his temper.

'I don't think she's trying to dictate terms. I just think she wants some guarantees. I don't think that's unreasonable.'

'Guarantees? About what? Does she think I can't be trusted?'

I didn't think it would help negotiations to point out that this was exactly what Christie thought.

'She just wants to make absolutely sure that she gets what she needs out of this deal, and she feels these terms are the best way for her to achieve that. She's still giving you what you asked for before she gets her money so it's not unreasonable for her to insist on an independent banker to hold onto her cash. You'll see from the document that that person will be protecting your interests as well as hers.'

Conny's face suggested that he still wasn't convinced. He called out for Rocco to come through.

'I'll need to take some advice.'

I noticed a rattling sound emanating from the cup and saucer I was holding so I quickly replaced them on the table.

Rocco entered and Conny passed the sheet to him.

'Whaddya think?'

The look that Rocco gave me suggested some annoyance with me, although I couldn't understand why. But he read through Christie's terms.

'They seem OK to me – if we can trust the broad who's overseeing the whole thing.'

'She's the hotel manager!' I protested. 'I don't think we can find anyone better at short notice.'

'She's a good kid,' said Conny, attempting to regain his poise. 'She's been very helpful. Very…discreet. Flexible. And she seems keen not to upset me, so I think we can trust her.'

'Then I'm OK with it,' said Rocco, handing the sheet back.

Conny leant forward, probing me fiercely with his stare. 'And if I agree to these terms then she'll agree to mine? All of them?'

'I think the document is pretty clear on that front. Or at least, as clear as social decorum allows.'

Conny sat back in his seat. 'OK. Then tell her I accept,' he said, trying to hand me back the piece of paper with barely a nod.

I couldn't stop myself sighing with relief. The promise of owning *Susanna & the Elders* might have been one factor in Conny's decision, but I'm pretty sure the prospect of one final night with Christie, one final victory to avenge for the defeat of being dumped all those years ago, was his primary driver. However, I wasn't going to let my relief stop me from following Christie's instructions.

'You have to sign the terms,' I said, pointedly keeping my hands in my lap.

'Tell her I accept,' he said. He twitched the sheet of paper in my direction.

'That's not enough. She wants you to sign. Like she has.' I took my Montblanc out of my jacket pocket, slipped off the cap and offered the pen to him. 'You have to sign.'

Rocco looked at me like I'd just asked the queen if she could lend me a fiver. 'Let me be clear. Mr Gerou doesn't sign contracts. Ms McGraw knows that.'

'It's not technically a contract,' I replied.

This was enough to cause Conny to erupt.

'Do you know how long I've been doing business with you people?' I didn't, but it didn't matter because Conny didn't leave a pause long enough for me to answer anyway. 'Thirty-five years! Thirty-five goddam years! Right from when I first went over to New York and started buying from Erik. And in those thirty-five years I have never once put my signature on a goddam piece of paper, and I am not about to start now – not for Christie McGraw or anyone else.'

They say that anger is just sadness which has nowhere to go, and I couldn't help but wonder what sadness was hiding in the twists and contortions of Conny's face as he roared his defiance at me.

An awkward silence descended on the room.

'I shall revert to my client,' I said eventually.

'You do that,' Rocco squeaked. 'And then tell her she's lucky Mr Gerou doesn't let her die in the gutter – trying to pull a stunt like that. She should be thankful he's a bigger man than that.'

'I don't think it's unreasonable for my client—'

'I'll show you out,' Rocco continued. 'We'll see you in reception at 8pm.'

I could see that I had outstayed my welcome and, accordingly, rose from my seat. Conny declined my offer of a handshake and instead grabbed his espresso. As I turned and walked towards the door, I heard the unmistakable sound of rattling ceramic crockery. And this time I knew it wasn't mine.

# THIRTY

As I made my way back down to reception from Conny's suite, the enormity of what we were about to pull off began to hit me. It was actually happening: the hare-brained, crackpot scheme that Christie and I had dreamt up in our semi-inebriated state on Drag Night at a club in BoHo was somehow going to be successfully executed. After the trauma of my divorce, I was finally going to be able to turn my life around. Life felt good – hopeful – for the first time in way too long.

Christie and Suzy were waiting for me when I returned to the hotel lobby, but I was concerned to see Christie seated, sipping gingerly at a glass of water, and Suzy kneeling at her feet and holding her hand.

'What's the matter?' I asked.

Christie shooed away my concern. 'It's nothing, honestly. I'll be fine.'

'I think she's had a bit of a turn,' said Suzy, furrowing her brow.

'I'm OK. Don't fuss! Just let me drink my water and I'll be fine in no time,' said Christie. 'How do I look? Is my hair OK?'

She looked pale, but not in any imminent danger. Yet looking at her sitting there, patting her hair, my overriding emotion was one of sadness. It wasn't that she looked ill; it was that she looked normal. She looked like any other sixty-seven-year-old woman might look: tired after an intense few days, and overwhelmed by a world that no longer felt reassuringly familiar. Her hair was fine, and I told her so, but I knew that she couldn't cope with me telling her the rest, so I kept my counsel while Suzy fussed around her.

Suzy was good at fussing. Maybe it was because her mum was a nurse, or because the hotel's customer service training was really good, but she just seemed comfortable and in control in that environment. She made me believe that everything was going to be OK in a way that she had never been able to when she worked in galleries. Even the staff members who came over to check if their assistance was needed seemed to respect and look up to her. Oleg, the Walled Garden's tall, liveried doorman, didn't so much as wince when, in a fit of pique, Suzy threatened to get 'yampy' with him if he didn't leave Christie alone and get back to his station on the front door. (Oleg, a grey-haired Ukrainian of a certain vintage, seemed to fancy his chances with the hotel's newly enfeebled guest.)

Thankfully, ten minutes later Christie seemed to have recovered her poise sufficiently to want to put the whole incident behind her. Suzy went off to arrange for a cab to take her back to the Dorchester, while I stayed with Christie and explained that Conny had agreed to her terms but refused to sign them. I thought this might cause her some concern, but much to my surprise, it only seemed to lift her spirits further.

'I knew he wouldn't,' she said, letting go a gentle chuckle.

'Well then, why did you ask me to insist? It got pretty frosty up there, I can tell you. I thought Rocco was going to pull the plug on the whole deal at one point.'

She was still chuckling to herself. 'Conny can't read.'

'What?'

'Well, not English at any rate.'

'But he never said.'

'Because that would mean admitting he couldn't do something. It would make him look weak.'

'But does it matter? He's Greek. I guess it's not unreasonable…'

'Yeah, I know. That's what I told him. He was brought up in a little fishing village and never really went to school. It's a wonder he can read and write in Greek, let alone English. I said he should be proud of that. But it matters to Conny because it matters. He's been doing business here for years and people assume he's learnt. He's desperate to be seen as successful – as better than the rest. He doesn't admit it to anyone.'

'So, how do you know?'

'I noticed it when we would go out – he wouldn't read the menu, he'd just ask if they had whatever he wanted; he'd always claim he'd forgotten to put his contacts in and get me to read him stuff. I wondered if he'd learnt by now but when we were up in his room, do you remember Rocco snatching that report out of your hand? I think Rocco and Mandy are the only ones who really know. The only ones Conny's told. I reckon they do his reading and writing for him.'

A number of things slotted into place in my mind, but the

news left me giddy. Before I had a chance to interrogate Christie further, however, Suzy returned to advise that Christie's cab was on its way. We had a little over four hours until the intended rendezvous with Conny and time was beginning to press, so this was a relief.

'I need a good soak in the bath and a quick pick-me-up. Then I'll be raring to go, I promise you,' Christie reassured us.

'Do you want me to come with you?' asked Suzy.

'That would be great, if you can. I'll need someone to do my zip up,' Christie said with a wink.

'It's not a problem; my shift doesn't start till eight,' Suzy replied. 'I'll just check everything's set up here for tonight. You wait there and I'll be back in a minute.'

Christie remained in her seat, and I stood by her. The idea that she had to spend that night with Conny broke my heart. Honestly, I wanted to call the whole thing off there and then and wondered, if I offered her that option, whether she would take it; whether the whole thing had just become too much for her. It made me think about her and the life she'd led. The life she'd been forced to lead.

There was no sign of Suzy returning so I decided to ask the question that had been lurking at the back of my mind since I first met her.

'Christie, do you mind me asking? Did you never feel exploited?'

I was half-expecting an eye-roll and an explosion of frustration at my naïveté. But instead, Christie took a slow sip of her water before answering very deliberately.

'Not at first,' she said. 'I was young, I guess. I was just excited to be in the heart of that whole world. I'm not sure I ever really looked at the pictures to be honest – I was just very aware of people's *reaction* to the pictures, and how much they were worth. I mean, the market was going crazy, and Erik was getting caught up in all of that. It felt like... I dunno... It felt like the value of the paintings was a reflection of *me*. As the value of the pictures started to go up, I think my sense of my own value did too.' She gave a shrug. 'But then the eighties happened, and everything started to change.'

'You mean the market?'

'I mean people's tastes. Which meant the market too. *Night of the Super Vixens* was in '83, I think. Jesus! We thought we were going to be the show of the season, but everyone turned up talking about the Paula Rego exhibition that had opened a couple of weeks before us. Neither of us saw that coming. Anyway, the value of Erik's work stopped going up, and then it started going down.'

'It must've been tough to stomach – with them being paintings of you.'

'I guess so. But actually, that wasn't the worst of it – after all, they were still going for six figures. No, what really got me, was that I realised that the painting's value wasn't my value at all. I didn't own it.'

'I don't get you.'

'What I mean is, people were buying these paintings as an investment and selling them on at a profit. But even if they held onto them, each time an image was reproduced – in an article, an exhibition catalogue, or on a poster, whatever – the copyright owner would be paid royalties. When works were collected together for a show, the owner would get paid just for loaning it. But I got nothing. Not even a sitter's fee. I just got an allowance from Erik, and as many gifts as he was prepared to let me have. But then he stopped making as much money, and…well, I began to feel like I was more of a burden to him.'

She spoke in sorrow rather than anger, but there was no doubt that it aged her. The spark had gone from her eyes, and, with it, something elemental about her.

'And, when I thought about that, it started to dawn on me: the value of all these paintings – paintings of me – was owned by someone else and there was no way for me to get at it. Not in my own right. It was all down to Erik's generosity. And then Conny's.'

Christie turned to look at me. 'I'm not a bitter person, but if I was, the thing that would've made me bitter is the fact that people like Conny – people who've contributed nothing to what an artwork looks like – those people get richer and richer for doing nothing more than owning it, while li'l old me – who's actually helped give those works their value – I get left with nothing.'

I really felt for her, because the fact was, she was right. Christie McGraw was more than a jobbing artist's model and everyone who knew anything about art knew that. Yes, Erik had spent eighteen years painting Mimi, and those paintings had established his reputation. But Mimi was little more than a rather beautiful marionette, dressed and manipulated into poses by Erik's imagination. Christie was different. It was her ferocious gaze and unpredictable manner that had helped bring those works to life. Erik hadn't created those looks; he had captured them, and it was these that made his post-1975 paintings more interesting – and therefore more valuable – than his earlier output.

I wanted to find a way to tell her all this at the time, but out of the corner of my eye I noticed an ashen-faced Suzy waving at me frantically from beside the reception desk.

'Hold on, Christie. I'll be back in a moment,' I said and made my way briskly across the hotel lobby. As I approached her, Suzy ducked into one of the conference rooms and indicated that I should follow her.

'Everything OK?' I asked.

'No, everything is not OK,' Suzy replied, her eyes frantic, her breathing heavy. 'Everything is not OK at all.'

I assumed that this was something to do with her abrupt resignation from her position; that something had gone wrong with her final pay calculation, or her boss was refusing to provide a reference. Something, at least, that I wouldn't have to worry about. But I was wrong. Very very wrong.

'It's gone,' she said.

'What? What are you talking about?'

'*Susanna & the Elders*. It's not there. In the secure store.'

This was very definitely something that I had to worry about. 'It must be there. Go and have another look. You must have missed it.'

'I've had another look, Gabriel!' she shouted at me. 'I've searched everywhere in that room and I'm telling you it's not there!' She looked on the verge of tears.

I was about to ask her how she could lose a highly valuable painting from a secure storage room located behind a staffed reception desk and overseen by state-of-the-art CCTV. But before I got the chance, her phone pinged. She looked at the message and her jaw dropped open in horror. Rendered mute by what she could see on her phone's screen, she turned it round and held it up for me to look at.

'*We have your painting!*' the message read. '*£20k. In cash (used notes). London Gateway Services. Two hours. Or else...*'

There was a photograph accompanying the message showing *Susanna & the Elders* with a black-gloved hand poised next to it holding an unsheathed Stanley knife.

'What are we going to do?' Suzy asked.

And I had to confess, I really didn't know.

# THIRTY-ONE

Three-quarters of an hour later I found myself heading north towards London Gateway services, my heart galloping in my chest.

Eventually Suzy and I had managed to come up with a plan. Given the timescale we were working to and the fragility of Christie's health, I accepted without any debate that the only possible source of the required funds was me.

Yet, even though I had $25,000 sitting in my Argentinian bank account, this was not a simple matter as, for understandable reasons, the thieves required us to produce the funds in cash in pounds sterling. Even if there had been a branch of the Banco de la Nación Argentina handily located within walking distance of the Walled Garden (which there wasn't) cash withdrawals of that amount of money always required at least twenty-four hours' notice and we'd got less than four hours until we had to present *Susanna & the Elders* for Conny's inspection.

This was when Suzy had what appeared to be an inspired idea. The Greek authorities had frozen all of Conny's assets, which meant that none of his bank cards worked. His agreement with the Walled Garden's management, therefore, was that he had to pay for his rooms in advance in cash, in sterling. Normally, small amounts of cash were banked swiftly by the hotel's staff, but on this occasion the amount of cash was so significant that Suzy had had to arrange a special collection to be made by G4S and she told me that she hadn't yet had the chance to set that up. The suites and penthouse that Conny had booked out were not cheap, so there was a significant amount of sterling currently sitting in the Walled Garden's safe. If I could transfer my money into the Walled Garden's bank account, then Suzy could legitimately take the equivalent of $25,000 in sterling from the safe and give it to me. This would make her look more fastidious than she was, and also save her bosses the expense of paying for a special pick-up.

But even this still didn't solve all of our problems. At the exchange rate that I could get at that time, we calculated that my final $25,000 was only equivalent to around £17,000. There was a heated exchange over text with the thieves as to whether this would be an acceptable amount, but eventually Suzy told me that they'd insisted it wouldn't be. Having already spent heavily, I was nearing my credit card's limit, but a quick call to my English bank and they agreed to extend me a further couple of grand. On that basis, Suzy agreed that 'as a special favour' (she actually used those words) she would give me a cash advance of the shortfall, on the basis that I would replace the cash she would give me from the hotel's safe the moment the transaction with Conny was completed. This was outside the Walled Garden's procedures, but we both calculated that I could replace the money first thing in the morning, before any of the hotel's senior managers would notice it was gone.

'And besides,' said Suzy with a twinkle in her eye. 'What are they going to do? Fire me?'

Suzy watched me transfer my last $25,000 to the Walled Garden's account using a money transfer service. This gave her (and me) a receipt confirming that the transfer had taken place, so she didn't have to wait for the money to hit the Walled Garden's account before she felt comfortable enough to extract the relevant amount of cash from the hotel's safe and hand it over to me. She then took my credit card details and gave me the £3,000 shortfall in exchange for a handwritten IOU note, which I signed. This was placed in the safe but would be removed and destroyed when I replaced the money after I received my share of the purchase price of *Susanna & the Elders* from Conny.

Having managed to execute that part of our plan flawlessly and without attracting undue attention from the hotel's other staff, we then had to work out how to get me and £20,000 in used bank notes to London Gateway services safely within the hour and a quarter that remained before our rendezvous with the thieves, and then get me and *Susanna & the Elders* back safely to the Walled Garden for our scheduled rendezvous with Conny at 8pm.

The only viable option was to use Suzy's car, which was parked in the duty manager's complimentary parking space in the Walled Garden's underground car park. My car was back at my flat and I wasn't prepared to get on a tube to Wood Green with twenty grand in used bank notes on me. I assumed all this, and the fact that she was the one the thieves had contacted, meant that Suzy would be going to meet the thieves, even if it was only to accompany me. Suzy, however, had other ideas.

'I can't,' she said. 'I said I would help Christie get ready. She needs someone to do her zip.'

'Oh my God! I think that's below even "I'm sorry, I'm washing my hair that night" in the annals of lame excuses.'

'Really? Christie's clearly ill and needs looking after. I have promised to look after her. I can't be in two places at once. I don't think that's lame at all.'

'But I'm not insured to drive your car any more.'

'What do I care? I'm changing it tomorrow anyway,' she said.

'But you're the one who's lost the painting – from a locked room. Don't you think you owe me one for that?'

Suzy was incredulous. 'Owe you one? Are you kidding me? After the scam you've just admitted pulling on me? I don't think I owe you shit!'

I wanted to argue this point, but she just dangled her car keys in front of me and tapped her watch. At which point I realised that she was right: the only person with something to lose in this scenario was me. Even if she hadn't already quit her job, I couldn't threaten to get her fired. I could hardly go to the hotel's management and claim that a painting that didn't exist had gone missing from a room it had no right to be in.

I wordlessly snatched the keys from her hand and headed to the car park.

It was now rush hour and the traffic out of London was as slow as I had feared, which meant that the journey seemed to take an age. But sitting in slow-moving traffic for so long gave my mind a chance to mull over the whole scenario I found myself in.

The uncomfortable fact was that I really was all-in on the deal now – and more than all-in. Every last cent of my $200,000 inheritance, plus the $10,000 of accrued interest, was invested in successfully selling *Susanna & the Elders*. In addition to this, I was now also nursing a hefty credit-card debt.

I perhaps should have reflected more than I did on quite how I'd found myself in this situation – on how I'd gone from doing a favour for someone who was seriously ill with no thought of reward for myself, to somehow being reliant on favours from my ex-wife in order to stop myself losing everything. But at the time the calculation seemed remarkably simple: if I could get the deal with Conny over the line, I would have $312,500 at my disposal. If I didn't, I'd be left with less than nothing. So at that point almost anything seemed justified in order to make sure that my current notional debts weren't crystallised.

I've subsequently learnt that this is called the sunk cost fallacy. But I didn't know that at the time.

By the time I'd reached the junction with the M1 another set of thoughts had begun playing out in my mind, however. *Susanna & the Elders* had gone missing from a locked room in one of London's most prestigious hotels. This fact alone had puzzled me, but when I asked her, Suzy had indicated that nothing else had gone missing – indeed she'd said she was 'one hundred per cent sure' that everything else in the room was still there because there was an inventory you could check against. This, and the fact that the thieves had contacted Suzy with a clearly established plan for a ransom to be paid, suggested that *Susanna & the Elders* had been stolen to order. They also seemed to be suggesting a timetable that fitted in with our need to return the painting promptly to the Walled

Garden that evening. My initial assumption, therefore, had been that it must have been stolen by someone connected to Conny's party, because they were the only people apart from the three of us who knew of the painting's existence and the proposed deal. But the further I inched up the M1, the more that explanation didn't make sense.

For one thing, it didn't explain how the thieves had managed to get through a locked door in a secure area of the hotel behind a fully staffed reception area and then walk out with a painting under their arm without attracting attention. Nor did it explain how they had managed to contact Suzy directly: the text message had come through on her personal mobile phone, the number of which Suzy closely guarded. She certainly didn't make it accessible to hotel guests.

The more I thought about it, the more it became apparent to me that the theft had to have been executed by someone working at the Walled Garden who was a close enough colleague of Suzy's to have her mobile phone number. But it also had to be someone whose presence in and around the secure storeroom wouldn't provoke any concern from other colleagues. Indeed, it probably had to be someone who had, or could easily gain access to, the key to the secure store, and turn off the relevant CCTV camera for a few minutes without anyone asking any questions. Someone involved in security, perhaps. Maybe someone who had recently been contacted by Suzy and asked to work an extra shift in order to supervise the exchange of a large amount of money and a highly valuable painting – the location of which would have been given to them as part of Suzy's explanation of the arrangements for the evening.

By the time I pulled up at the rear of the lorry park of London

Gateway services as arranged, I had narrowed the options for the thief down to two. When I saw the tall, muscular figure standing next to a white van, with dreadlocks poking out from the bottom of his balaclava, I was able to judge immediately which of my two suspects it was.

'It's alright, Daniel. I know it's you,' I called out. 'Don't worry, I don't want any trouble. To be honest with you, I've not got the time and I really don't want to have to explain all this to the police any more than you do. So you can still have your money, but let's just get this over with quickly, for God's sake. I've got to be back at the hotel in ninety minutes.'

# THIRTY-TWO

The drive back into central London was considerably quicker than the drive out had been, so I arrived back at the Walled Garden in plenty of time. I'd phoned Suzy from the car so she knew not to expect Daniel back.

When I sprinted into the hotel lobby, I found Suzy prowling reception, anxiously waiting for me, having just got back from the Dorchester. She quietly replaced *Susanna & the Elders* in the secure storeroom and set about her final night shift. After the stress of my journey, there wasn't much I could do now except wait.

I had a phone conversation with Jasper and let him know how much I might be able to put on the table now. He didn't make any commitment, but he allowed the conversation to stray onto what we might do together with the gallery, which I took to be a promising sign. It all felt exciting; a new start.

At two minutes past eight I saw a taxi pull up outside the

hotel and Christie emerge. I wasn't sure how she was intending to play the whole evening. Part of me thought that she might turn up in jeans and a T-shirt with no make-up, just to try and make a point to Conny. It made sense to me for her to comply with the strict letter of the agreement between them but to withhold the thing which he loved – which we all loved – about her, but which was nowhere stipulated as being a requirement of our deal: her glamour. It would have been typical of her uncanny ability to remain within arm's reach of desire.

But when she stepped into the hotel lobby and handed her coat to Mo, who was waiting to escort her, I saw that she was wearing the Reem Acra dress that had so entranced me at Le Bernardin's in New York. Even Mo, who was a good fifteen years younger than her, I'm sure, didn't seem to know where to look. Rather than treating this as the moment of her greatest humiliation, she was clearly determined to portray herself as the prize that was being fought over. It was a different, altogether more subtle way of denying Conny the total victory he craved, and I thought it would be sure to annoy him. This fact gave me some pleasure.

I got up and made my way over to meet her.

'You look stressed,' she said with concern.

'Yeah, well let's just say that our plan took a little unscheduled detour.'

A frisson of concern appeared in her face. 'A detour?'

'Don't worry. Everything's back on track now,' I reassured her, trying to relax.

But Christie pressed me, so I sat her down and explained as briefly and undramatically as possible what had happened.

'Thank you for doing that,' she said when I'd finished. She reached over the table and put her hand on mine. 'You didn't have to.'

The tenderness with which she held my hand for that moment felt like a parting gift.

'It was very generous of you, young man,' she added with a gentle squeeze, and the warmth returned to her gaze, as if I might not be the awful person she'd thought I was. It was ridiculous to think it even at the time, but it felt like a kind of redemption. I loved that feeling, and I loved the fact that it was Christie who had made me feel it. In the midst of everything that followed I couldn't stop myself returning in my mind to that moment and the joy it gave me.

We made our way over to Suzy, who was waiting for everyone to assemble at the rear of the lobby as agreed. Predictably, there was still no Conny. This was not unexpected, but the next ten minutes felt interminable. I was so close to becoming richer than I had ever been in my life, yet without Conny we couldn't complete the deal. I'd been confident that we'd set everything up perfectly, but every second that he failed to show I became less and less convinced that the deal was actually going to happen. By 8.15pm I had pretty much convinced myself that he wasn't going to turn up. By 8.20pm even Suzy and Christie were starting to get anxious. It was not until we reached 8.22pm and Conny finally emerged from the lift that I allowed myself to believe that the whole thing really was happening.

In fairness to Conny, he looked as though he had made as much of an effort as Christie had. In addition to his suit and Swarovski crystal-encrusted tie, he had also liberally applied some aftershave, judging by the pungent aroma that perfumed the air the moment the lift doors opened. When mixed with the altogether more subtle notes of Christie's perfume, it had the effect of making the lobby smell like a Zanzibari spice market.

Rocco followed behind Conny, wheeling two Smythson Greenwich cabin trollies.

'I got them in blue to match your eyes,' said Conny. 'I love that dress.'

'Thanks,' said Christie. 'I got it in black to match your heart.'

Conny let go a playful laugh and even his eyes managed to smile.

With the pleasantries, such as they were, concluded, Suzy took control of the situation. She instructed Mo to take the cases off Rocco and wheel them into a side room. I followed him and was allowed to open the cases and count the money.

When Rocco opened the cases in front of me, my heart almost stopped in my chest. I could feel my eyes widen at the sight of bundle after bundle of neatly wrapped used twenty-dollar bills. I had literally never seen that much money in my life. Suddenly the whole deal felt very real. I guess I thought it had felt real before, but seeing the money there felt as if I had actually crossed a Rubicon and entered a world that I had only really been looking in on from the outside until then. It seems ridiculous to say this now, but at the time I felt as though something in me had changed just by seeing that much money. Or rather, not just by seeing it, but by looking at it and accepting the Faustian pact that I was entering into in order to get my hands on it. For once in my life – a life I had largely spent apologising for what I thought and felt, and giving in to men like Conny – I was actually going to seize the day, but I felt somehow dirtier for doing so. Dirty on the inside. It made me wonder how Conny could live his whole life like this. Was it that men like him didn't feel the same kind of dirtiness that I did, or that they managed not to care? I was trying not to care but found myself unable to stop.

I wasn't sure how thorough Christie expected me to be in counting the cash. Given that all the parties would shortly be going their separate ways to different continents, so there would be no opportunity to rectify any errors, I felt the situation required me to be meticulous, but time was not my friend.

It would actually take twenty-five thousand twenty-dollar bills to make up half-a-million dollars. Even if I only took two seconds to count each one it would take a grand total of nearly fourteen hours to finish counting the money. We decided therefore that I would count the number of bundles and Mo would spend his nightshift checking the contents of each individual bundle. There was a banking machine behind reception that the hotel staff used to cash up and which could count and sort cash into bundles far quicker than humans could. It had the added advantage, Suzy assured me, of being situated in line of sight of two of the hotel's CCTV cameras so there was no possibility of any money going missing.

The bills had been wrapped in bundles with one hundred bills in each, each with '$2,000' stamped on it. I therefore calculated that there should have been two hundred and fifty bundles between the two cases. Having counted the bundles and confirmed they were all there, I split the money up. I put $125,000 in the smaller of the two cases for Christie, then I counted out the next $250,000 and put that in the larger case for me. The remaining money I split equally between the two cases before handing them both over to Mo. We returned to reception, and he took the two cabin trolleys back to the secure store.

'Was it all there?' Christie asked.

'As far as I can tell,' I replied. 'I split the money up as we agreed. I thought it would save us a job later. For reference, yours is the smaller case.'

Christie's eyes said *I bet it bloody is*, while her mouth said, 'Why, thank you, young man. How gallant.'

Mo returned from the secure store without the cabin trolleys but with *Susanna & the Elders*. Suzy offered it now to Conny for inspection.

'Have you not brought Mandalay with you?' Christie asked with a smirk.

'He's otherwise engaged,' Conny replied, scowling.

He flicked the painting over and checked the small corner of the canvas where the stitching was.

'Yep, this is the one I saw yesterday,' he said to Suzy.

'Great,' said Suzy. 'So can I ask, Mr Gerou, can you confirm that it's your intention to take possession of this painting from Mr Viejo?'

'Absolutely,' he replied. 'And I intend to take possession of this charming woman from him too.'

Suzy decided to ignore this. 'And Mr Viejo, can I ask whether it is your intention to hand it over to him?'

'Uhm...I guess so, yes. As long as I get my money.'

It was then that I noticed two serious-looking men moving at pace across the hotel lobby towards us. They arrived at our corner of the lobby and immediately took control of the situation.

'Hello. I'm DI Raglan and this is DS Munro of the Metropolitan Police.' Warrant cards were removed from pockets and flashed around. 'Can I just ask who this painting belongs to?'

I looked at Conny; Conny looked at me, then we both looked at Christie, but she was not making eye contact with anyone. A half-formed, but horrible possibility began to take shape in both Conny's and my mind at exactly the same time. In unison we both lifted our arms and pointed at the other. 'Him!' we both said.

'Interesting,' said DI Raglan. 'We just picked up on the microphone that you vouched for the authenticity of this painting,' he continued, turning to Conny. 'So it's your belief that this is a genuine work by Erik von Holunder?'

'I'm not confirming anything without a lawyer being present. Rocco, call Love.'

'As you like.' DI Raglan took the painting and checked the stitching at the rear. 'EvH. Certainly looks like a Von Holunder to me. And this photo,' he said as he withdrew it from his breast pocket, 'appears to show it in situ in Erik von Holunder's apartment at the Dakota Building.'

He presented us with a photo which I immediately recognised as the one that had accompanied Christie's interview in the March 1987 edition of *Village Voice*. Christie was standing by the fireplace, smiling warmly, but behind her, slightly out of focus and partially obscured by Christie herself, was a painting that bore an uncanny resemblance to the one that DI Raglan had just inspected.

'We spoke to Mimi von Holunder a couple of hours ago, and she claimed that the apartment shown in the photograph, and all of its contents as at thirteenth October 1987, were her legal property. Can either of you explain that?'

I had been so certain that any possibility of Mimi subverting our plan had been ruled out. But here were two policemen apparently intent on interrupting our sale, and in possession of information that it appeared she had provided. I couldn't understand who had tipped her off. Given that Conny was clearly under suspicion I couldn't see how it could be him, and there's no way Rocco, or even Mandalay, could have had access to that photo, even if they knew of the contents of Erik's will. This left one troubling, but inexplicable, possibility.

I noticed that Christie had been gradually stepping away from proceedings and moving towards the reception desk. Mo emerged from behind it wheeling the two cabin trollies behind him.

'Your cases, Ms McGraw,' he said, offering her the two cabin trollies. 'Your cab is waiting outside.'

Christie took the cases and began to head towards the hotel entrance. Both Conny and I shouted. 'Wait!'

DI Raglan and DS Munro looked at us expectantly.

'Stop her. She's leaving with my money,' said Conny.

'Oh, I think you're mistaken, Mr Gerou,' said Suzy with a smile. 'Those are definitely Ms McGraw's cases.'

'And you're certain they couldn't have got mixed up?' asked DI Raglan.

'Absolutely. We didn't take anything off Mr Gerou for secure storage. He asked, but we declined. We have a full inventory of the items which we keep in the secure store which my head of security would be happy to provide if you'd like to check? And we'd never give someone's baggage away to another guest. You can check the luggage tags if you don't believe me. They're in her name – aren't they, Mo?'

'Uh…yes. They're definitely in her name,' Mo said, dutifully, holding up the luggage tags for inspection.

DS Munro walked over and confirmed that the luggage tags were indeed in Christie's name.

'So,' said DI Raglan. 'Here we all are with a highly valuable missing painting and yet no sign of the legal owner – who has confirmed that she was unaware that either of you had it. And we have you on mic,' he said, looking at me, 'as agreeing to hand it over to this gentleman here in exchange for cash. Anyone care to explain?'

This was clearly a rhetorical question. He had on his face the kind of self-satisfied smirk that policemen have when they believe they've caught someone bang to rights. On this occasion the only issue appeared to be who had been caught bang to rights and for what. Neither Conny nor I felt like enlightening him.

'I suggest we continue this conversation back at the station,' said DI Raglan after leaving a suitably pregnant pause.

My heart sank. 'No, you can't; not now.'

'And why would that be?' asked DI Raglan.

The honest answer didn't feel like it would be helpful to my cause, so I ended up remaining mute.

Having not received an answer that gave him any reason to delay further, DI Raglan continued. 'I am arresting you both on suspicion of handling stolen goods. And on the basis of the conversation I've just heard, I am further arresting you, Mr Viejo, on suspicion of living off immoral earnings. You have the ri—'

'Living off immoral earnings?' Conny was incredulous. 'The man's been making a living for the past decade-and-a-half encouraging everyone to buy contemporary art, and you accuse him of living off immoral earnings for this?'

For the first time in my career, it felt like a good point.

'Well, if you've finished with me, officers, I'll just get on if you don't mind,' said Suzy. 'I'm due to meet my boyfriend for a dinner date this evening.'

She removed a concealed microphone and remote battery pack from under her jacket and handed them both over to DS Munro.

'Thanks for your help,' DI Raglan said to her. 'We'll come back to you if we need anything else.'

At that moment out of the corner of my eye I noticed Daniel entering the hotel lobby. I was gobsmacked. I'd assumed that our altercation in the car park was the last that any of us would see of him, but here he was, dressed to the nines and with a broad smile on his face. He appeared to be showing quite some nerve.

'Ms McGraw, let me help you with your bags,' said Suzy.

'Oh, that would be most kind. I struggle with these things now, at my age. Here, take this one,' and she handed over the smaller of the two cabin trollies to Suzy. 'This lovely young man said he's ordered me a cab.'

Christie smiled at Mo, who nervously grinned back at her, then she and Suzy headed briskly towards the exit.

As they reached the entrance, Daniel withdrew an envelope from his jacket pocket. I recognised it as the envelope that I had handed over to him two hours previously. He offered it to Suzy, but she just slipped it back into his pocket and pointed to her case. Then they enjoyed a slow, lingering kiss.

And with that, all three of them disappeared out into the street.

# THIRTY-THREE

The next few months were the worst of my life. Worse than my divorce – worse than my parents' divorce. Firstly, I was held in police custody for a couple of days while they decided whether or not to bring charges. They took photos, fingerprints and even a DNA sample. I was interviewed three times by two different sets of officers, although the interview questions were largely identical, as were my answers, which, on legal advice, consisted entirely of 'No comment'. I was then released on bail but told in no uncertain terms that I was not to attempt to make contact with Christie or Suzy, either directly or indirectly, and that I should decline any offers of contact from them. I wasn't supposed to contact Conny either, but as I didn't have his contact details and he didn't have mine this seemed a purely academic prohibition.

But even after my release, it was not the end of my nightmare. There then followed a period of several weeks while the investigation continued. My laptop and mobile phone were taken, all my passwords demanded, and my email, messaging and social media accounts all trawled.

My things were eventually returned to me and, outwardly at least, life began to return to something approaching normality. This was accompanied by a period of total silence from the police. And actually, that was the worst part of all. Because when you're in the eye of the storm you have something immediate, something definite, to focus on, whether that be the questions you're being asked or the practicalities you need to address. There is something you can do. But when faced with silence – no questions to answer, no correspondence to address, no allegations to rebut – you are held in a state of uniquely uncomfortable suspended animation in which your body is frozen, but your mind can still work. It's this that starts to eat away at you because your certainties start to dissolve, and you become locked in a world of endless liminality.

For instance, all my usual freelance work suddenly disappeared. I didn't realise how tightly woven into the fabric of the art world I had been, until I became a pariah overnight. Initially I tried to fight this, but the moment I sat down to try and compose a convincing explanation of what I'd been involved in and why it wasn't as bad as it may have appeared, I began to realise how hopeless the task was. Somehow the justification I'd initially constructed for what I was going to do – that I was selflessly helping a sick old woman who was down on her luck – fell apart the moment that secret money transfers from foreign bank accounts and trolley cases filled with used bank notes entered the narrative. Even without getting into a debate about the provenance of the Bacon sketch, I came to understand that plenty of reasonable people would choose to interpret my behaviour less charitably than I had done myself. And when those people had a raft of eager freelancers chasing them for work, they might reasonably conclude that the guy to miss out on a commission should be the one who had been caught apparently trying to launder money that he'd been hiding from his ex-wife, and indeed, the courts.

On top of that, my publisher began backing away from the project the moment my arrest became public. They couldn't pull out of the deal altogether (although God knows, they tried) but publication – and payment of all future tranches of my advance – was, in their words, *'indefinitely delayed'* while they waited for clarification on whether charges were going to be brought. Jasper, too, stopped responding to my texts and emails. Then I got a curt letter from his dad saying that they'd found an alternative investor for the gallery and were pursuing that option. After more than twenty years of friendship it was quite a kick in the teeth.

All of which left me with a problem. With any hope of further payments from my publisher and Grandpa Jo's inheritance money both gone, I was reduced to asking DWP for benefits and my father for handouts, just to keep the roof over my head. Neither was an easy conversation to have.

This only served to feed the rage that was burning furiously inside me. I couldn't believe that Christie had rinsed me over so thoroughly and had smiled at me as she was doing so. But every communication from my lawyers, every question from the police, made it increasingly clear that that is exactly what had happened. I had been trying to help her. She had sought to ignite the flame of desire within me and then used that to get around my better judgement and play me for a fool. I could forgive her a lot, but as I watched my reputation and career disappear, I felt like I could never forgive that.

And what made it worse was that she had done so on behalf of my ex-wife. I thought I had done everything possible to protect myself from Suzy's vindictiveness, but the one thing that I hadn't banked on was Christie being in cahoots with her. This made literally no sense to me. I mean, I could understand what Suzy was hoping to achieve – that much had always been pretty obvious – but why would Christie play along? And why, having fought tooth and nail to keep *Susanna & the Elders* out of Mimi's clutches, would Christie be quite happy to leave it behind and have it handed over to her for nothing?

I was kept waiting five long months for an answer, but eventually it came: not from the police, nor from my solicitor, but from Christie herself.

She turned up at my flat out of the blue on 29 February. I distinctly remember the date because my immediate reaction was to wonder if she had flown back over to propose. She was buried underneath an enormous full-length fur coat with matching hat and muff, which made her look like the wife of a Soviet-era Russian president. I couldn't understand it; it was nearly spring and not that cold.

'Christie! What the hell are you doing here?' I asked before remembering the protocol. 'You do realise, don't you, that I can't let you in, even if I wanted to – which I don't. The police have told me not even to talk to you. I can get in trouble if they find out we've been in contact. Not that I imagine you care.'

I fixed her with a cold, emotionless stare. If the forgiveness in Christie's eyes had been lost after that night at the Dorchester, then I made damn sure that I removed any hint of it from mine too that morning.

'Relax, honey. We've withdrawn our statements,' she

said, without any hint of awkwardness. This in itself was an interesting use of the plural. 'And Mimi's decided not to press charges. Have they not told you?'

They hadn't, although given the tardiness with which the police had communicated with my legal team up to that point, this was not altogether a surprise.

'Just as well I turned up then, isn't it? And of course I care. That's why I'm here,' she said, breezing into my flat uninvited.

Regardless of the legal technicalities, I was not going to pretend that nothing had happened. My anger towards her had been building for five months and her casual effrontery caused it all to spill out.

'Christie, what the hell are you doing? How dare you come here! How dare you come here and breeze in to my flat as though everything's sorted. It is most definitely *not* sorted. I could still lose this flat because of you!'

She appeared surprised, as though all she had to do was show up and flash me her smile and everything would be OK between us.

'Jeez, I come all this way to explain and this is what I get? How about a "Gee, Christie, great to see ya. How's the treatment going?" Do I not even get that first?'

I had practised this moment in my head a thousand times.

'No! No you don't. My career is over because of you.' I jabbed my finger at her to emphasise my point. 'Don't you understand that? I could go to prison for this!'

'Don't be so melodramatic. This was never going to go to court. Our stories would never have held up. Your lawyer must've told you that at least.'

'As a matter of fact, he didn't.'

My father had at least agreed to pay for a proper lawyer

so I was spared the indignity of having to rely on the public defence lawyer who had turned up to my first interview at the station and looked at me as though I was guilty even before she'd heard my side of the story. But even my dad's lawyer had studiously avoided any suggestion that I might actually be acquitted.

'Well that's the truth of it. I would never have let it get to that. Not even Suzy wanted to see you in gaol.'

I found that hard to believe. 'So how come I've spent the last five months having my life turned upside down by the police?'

'Well that's why I'm here. I wanted to explain. I thought I owed you that at least. Can I sit down?'

I begrudgingly offered her a seat opposite where I had been sitting on the sofa. She took off her coat and hat and it was all I could do to stop myself gasping in shock. There was nothing there: the shapely woman of my distant imaginings had been reduced to a brittle, skeletal figure in a sagging skin sack. The burning anger that had been coursing through me suddenly began to abate.

'Christie – your treatment?'

'Oh, thanks for asking. Not going well.' She held up a hand to indicate that this was not something she wanted to talk about further.

Despite everything that had happened, I couldn't help but feel horrified, seeing how she looked. She was ill. Seriously ill. Of that there was no doubt. The fury that I had held on to for so long no longer felt so important, or appropriate.

'Like I say, I wanted to come over to offer you an explanation face to face,' she continued, clearly eager to move the conversation on. 'I wanted you to know that the way things happened…it wasn't how things were supposed to be.'

As her explanation unfolded over the following half an hour, it was as though she was slowly pulling back the curtain on the Wizard of Oz. The devilish, fiendishly complex, international plot that could only have been perpetrated with the assistance of everyone who ever knew me, was revealed to be something else entirely.

'To be honest with you, when we started out it was just supposed to be a simple grift. But then things started getting complicated and it all just mushroomed out of our control. Out of everyone's control really.'

'But you and Suzy...? I don't get it. I don't understand how...'

'Yeah, it's kind of a long story.'

'Well, given what the two of you have done to my career, the one thing I've got plenty of at the moment is time.'

She exhaled heavily and set about her explanation.

'When my diagnosis came through, Liga set up a fundraising page to try and help fund my treatment. Well, hardly anyone from the old days can remember me now, and those who can don't seem to care, so the account was looking pretty empty. That was when she found an appreciation page for Erik on Facebook, so she posted the link on there. There were hardly any followers, so it didn't have much of an impact on the fundraising, but it did get seen by Suzy. She made a donation – I think it was twenty bucks; nothing fancy – and then messaged me through the fundraising page explaining that she had always been a bit of a fan of mine and was sorry to hear of my illness. Well, this was the first time for thirty years anyone had described themselves as a fan, so I kept in touch – nothing too heavy, just polite correspondence, y'know? We ended up using email because it was easier, but after a while things started to wind down and I thought no more about her.

'Then your letter comes through asking for an interview. I'm just about to screw it up and throw it in the bin when I notice the surname – Viejo – and see that it's the same as the one in Suzy's email address. Well, that's quite a distinctive name, especially for someone based in London, so I email her and say *Hey, you'll never guess what*. And she comes back with *Actually, I would. It was me who got him into Erik's work in the first place*, and she tells me the story about you and her at the Redfern. Anyway, cutting to the chase, once she knew you'd been in touch she offered me a deal.'

'If you'd help her to screw me over, she'd help you to screw Conny over?'

'Oh no. Not initially, at least. At that point all she wanted me to do was to meet up with you and try and find out about the inheritance money. She figured that because I knew your grandpa, and you were such a fan of Erik's, you'd be more open with me. She suggested that if I take you out for a couple of drinks you might be tempted into an admission. She told me the story about old Jo and the night at the Colony Room just to see if I could try and weave it into the conversation at some point. But that was all she wanted – just to know if her memory was right. The poor woman thought she was going nuts. She said if I'd meet up with you and find out about the money, she'd make another donation to the fund – a bigger one; like a couple of hundred bucks.'

'OK, that all sounds fine and dandy. But it doesn't explain how I ended up being arrested by the police.'

'Well here's the thing. I say, *Sure, I'll meet up with him*. It felt like the least I could do. I mean, it's not enough to keep me alive, but I just thought I should thank her for her donation.

But then she emails me back and says, *Hey, you'll never guess who just checked into the hotel where I'm working.*'

'Conny?'

'Exactly. And that's when my brain starts ticking over. Me and Conny didn't exactly part on the best of terms, but I knew he had plenty of money and an interest in Erik's work, so I thought he might be interested in buying my painting. And I also thought that really *could* help keep me alive.'

'So, your story about the painting was true?'

'Pretty much. I'd always known I couldn't sell it on the open market, because of Mimi, but when I looked up Conny on the internet, the whole story of his extradition was there, and there was a lot of speculation about this money he supposedly had that he needed to get rid of. It seemed like we were an answer to each other's prayers.'

'So, you weren't actually trying to screw Conny over at all?'

'Not at first. All I wanted was to sell him my painting, nothing more. But then I mentioned my plan to Suzy. I asked her whether, if I was prepared to meet with you, she would be prepared to help put me in touch with Conny. That's when things started to get serious.'

'I'm guessing that's when Suzy started to think it might be possible for her to actually get a share of my inheritance money, rather than just find out about it?'

'I guess. She wanted to take things into her own hands rather than paying out for lawyers all the time. That's when the idea of you brokering the sale began to get floated. I wasn't keen – honestly, honey, all I wanted was to see if I could get some money out of Con to pay for my treatment – but I knew that if I was to have any chance of doing that, I needed Suzy's help.'

I felt my heart begin to thaw. I was starting to believe that the whole thing had all been Suzy's doing and that perhaps Christie had just been dragged into a plot she didn't really understand the implications of by her own desperation. There were still things I wanted to understand though.

'But I still can't see why the two of us had to be arrested.'

I had thought that she liked me – not in the way that I liked her, to be sure – but that she at least liked me enough to care about how I was treated. And to differentiate between me and a monster like Conny.

I might have been imagining it, but I thought, for the first time, that I detected a hint of embarrassment in her manner.

'Well, we thought the whole thing through right up to the handover of the money, and it was all perfect. But we couldn't work out how to get away with it. I mean, that's the point at which you're going to realise you're being scammed. Two guys; two defenceless women – I mean, you're just going to grab your money back and go, right? So we needed something to stop you doing that. That was when Suzy suggested we had to call the cops and tip them off.'

Suzy again. I could feel my rage towards her building even as my fury at Christie began to abate.

'And Mimi?'

'Oh God, no. I wouldn't speak to her. I mean, I can't – I don't have her number. But I knew about the will, so we gave the cops that photo and suggested they contact her. That way we had some external corroboration that the painting was stolen. And by the time Mimi had finished with them, you'd have thought they were rescuing the Rembrandt version. Once they'd spoken to her, they were interested in what we were saying. And Mo's an ex-cop apparently, so he called in a favour to make sure they were there when we needed them to be.'

'OK, I get that. But "living off immoral earnings"? What the hell was all that about?'

'None of that was planned, I swear. I mean, I never imagined for a moment that Conny was going to suggest what he did. That wasn't part of the plan at all. Not at all. Suzy was really spooked by it, so she mentioned that to the cops too, just to make absolutely sure they'd turn up.' She looked at me mournfully. 'I didn't really care about seeing him punished up to that point. But after that…well, I was really pissed with him.'

'And I was just collateral damage?'

She leant forward and touched my knee briefly to reassure me. 'No, honey. Not at all.'

Maybe I just wanted to believe her, but I thought I saw something in her face that told me she meant it.

'Like I said,' she continued, 'we were never going to go to court over this. I mean, it would have been too risky. Our stories were never going to hold up. We just wanted to get away with our money, and that was the way to do it. Not even Conny was ever going to gaol. He was just going to end up with a bit less of his money. But it wasn't really his anyway. Just like your money wasn't really yours.'

I decided not to rise to the bait. 'And what about Mandalay? And Daniel?'

'Mandy was nothing to do with me or Suzy. It was as big a surprise to me as it was to you. As for the whole theft thing – well, that was just a last-minute bit of embellishment from Suzy when she worked out that you'd still got twenty-five grand left. I knew nothing about that until she turned up at the Dorchester and told me. She said she'd spent more than that on her useless lawyers, so she thought it was fair – if you hadn't lied to her in the first place, she'd never have had to spend all that money trying to get to the truth. But I never approved that. I just wanted to get the money I needed off Conny. That was Suzy.'

Of course it was Suzy. I could see now, how from Christie's perspective the whole thing had looked like it would work out beautifully with no real victims. She hadn't meant to put me through any of it and I was too shocked at how she looked to want to argue with her now over what I'd gone through. Yet there was one thing that I had not been able to work out, and which she still hadn't explained.

'But you lost the painting, Christie. *Susanna & the Elders*: it's going to end up with Mimi. I thought that was the one thing you definitely didn't want to happen.'

She looked at me coyly. 'Yeah, that was the one bit of the story where I wasn't being completely truthful.'

'What? You don't mind if Mimi gets to keep it?' After everything she'd said about her feelings towards Mimi – and the painting – I found this very hard to believe.

'Why not? It's worthless anyway.'

'Worthless? Christie, that was a bona fide Erik von Holunder original. It was signed. The canvas was stitched on the back. There was even a photo: you showed it to me. That proved it. You said so yourself – it was one hundred per cent genuine.'

'Oh, I don't think I ever said that. Not one hundred per cent.'

'I don't understand.'

'It was probably seventy per cent genuine.'

This made no sense to me. 'How can it be *seventy per cent* genuine?'

'Well, Erik probably painted about seventy per cent of the

painting you saw. I mean, he finished the whole thing – he signed it, stitched the canvas and everything – but I could tell that it wasn't good enough. He just couldn't get the Susanna right. He must have had four or five attempts. I was posing for months. But I always ended up looking like a hooker, and it wasn't what that painting needed. Eventually it was time for the show, and it just wasn't ready. In the end he stuck it at the back of his studio somewhere. He was so depressed. I tried to get him to have another go, but he never touched that painting again. Except when he pulled it out to show Conny.'

'But that makes no sense. The Susanna is there on the canvas. She's perfect. Brilliant. She *makes* the painting.'

'Yeah, but that's not the Susanna Erik painted.'

My mind was reeling. 'I don't understand. If Erik didn't paint her then who did?'

For the first time the old sparkle returned to Christie's eye, and she flashed me a broad smile.

'Well I did, of course!'

# THIRTY-FOUR

In all of the many thousands of scenarios that I had played over in my head during the previous five months, the one possibility that I had not entertained for a moment was the idea that *Susanna & the Elders* had been painted by anyone other than Erik von Holunder. But, if Christie was to be believed, that was exactly the case with about thirty per cent of it. And not just any thirty per cent – not the background or the secondary figures – but the thirty per cent that had captured my heart; the thirty per cent that elevated the painting from being something of interest to Von Holunder aficionados to being a truly great work of art.

This was shocking enough to me: the revelation that, I – supposedly the art world's foremost authority on the work of Erik von Holunder – had not spotted the interpolation of another artist's work in his. Yet, of course, there was a part of me that was prepared to accept that these things happen.

Establishing authenticity was not an exact science and, in the art world, attributions are revised all the time and argued over endlessly. Hell, it had been barely a decade since even the venerable Knoedler & Co. had been duped into selling the work of a Chinese street artist as genuine Rothkos, Pollocks and De Koenings, so I was prepared to forgive myself for this much more understandable error.

But the thing that shocked me to the core – and which something in me just refused to accept – was that the person whose brushwork had so tenderly expressed Erik von Holunder's love for Christie McGraw was not Erik, but Christie herself. This seemed both a logical and a technical impossibility. How could a muse supplant the artist she was modelling for? How could this woman, this brash and raucous arriviste with no formal art training, have produced something of such thrilling emotional depth?

'What did you think I was doing in the apartment for the eight months of the year that Erik wasn't there?' was Christie's response. 'That was part of our deal. I'd leave him alone to be with Mimi if he left me alone to paint in his studio.'

'But you said you hated art.'

'No, honey, I said I hated the art *business*. But I came to New York to paint, and Erik let me do that. I lost my hunger to be a painter, but I never lost my hunger to paint. And Erik would teach me. Until I realised that I didn't need him to teach me. Actually, I could paint pretty damn well myself.'

'But the photo. I mean, you have a photo of Erik and Conny with the painting. There's definitely a Susanna in it.'

'Sure there was. But that photo I showed you – didn't you notice that Susanna was obscured? Here's a photo I took two minutes later.'

She took another photo out of her clutch bag and laid it carefully in front of me. Erik and Conny were standing in the studio at the Dakota just as they had been in the photo Christie had shown me five months previously. But in this photo, instead of being behind them, *Susanna & the Elders* was being held up by Conny, who was laughing and pointing at the representation of him in the painting. Christie was still the centrepiece of the picture, as Susanna, but even allowing for the limitations of analogue photography, it was clearly not the same Susanna that I had seen all those months previously and which had captured my heart. The subtlety and tenderness with which its subject's beguiling beauty had been conveyed was gone.

This Susanna looked like a third-rate porn actress trying to act surprised when the pizza delivery guy walks in on her unannounced. Her breasts and buttocks were almost comically oversized, to the extent that I'm not sure that such a woman could ever have actually stood upright in real life. She was a wholly sexual being, designed solely for the gratification of the watching men. There was no sense that this woman might have any ability, or even desire, to control her own destiny; to stare back at her suitors and take them on.

It was the worst kind of titillation dressed up as art. I hated to acknowledge it, but the MoMA curator's likening of Erik's work to that of Russ Meyer suddenly didn't seem so unfair after all.

The only point in Erik's defence was that at least he had eventually seen sense and abandoned it.

'Actually, he quite liked it,' Christie said when I made this point. 'He'd become obsessed with porn by then, of course, which may have had something to do with it. But he was determined to show it. Thank God I managed to stop him. The *Old Masters* was a big enough disappointment as it was. Can you imagine what a disaster it might have been if Erik had included this too?'

'*You* stopped him showing this?'

'Sure. I hated what he'd done. He'd turned me into a slut, and I wasn't having it. It made me so upset just to look at it. We argued for weeks, but in the end, he could see that I was serious, so he pulled it. His agent was furious, but Erik knew that I could tell better than he could which of his pictures was good.'

This was said as a throwaway remark, but it immediately raised a troubling possibility in my mind. 'So, did you often veto his paintings of you?'

'Absolutely! I mean I didn't have a veto as such, but I would often get him to repaint stuff if I didn't like it. I'd talk to him about how I'd felt when I was posing and how the painting made me feel when I looked at it, and how those two things were different. I'd make suggestions about how he could change things – just subtle changes, to the way I was looking at the viewer, or the parts of my body he chose to emphasise.'

I tried to remain calm, but I found myself immediately leaning forward and fixing Christie with an urgent stare. 'And he'd do it? He'd change things the way you suggested?'

'Usually. And sometimes, if he wouldn't do it, or if I still didn't think that he'd got it right, I'd change it myself when he wasn't looking.'

Christie could obviously see a look of mounting horror spreading across my face because she then sought to offer me some reassurance. 'Just subtle things, honey,' she said, touching my knee for a moment. 'Not the whole painting.

Some of the time he never even noticed. And even when he did, he'd never change it back.'

'Never?'

'Not once,' she said, proudly. 'We'd discuss it for a bit, he'd sometimes get angry, but in the end, he always agreed that I was right. He called me his art director, although I don't think he always meant it as a compliment.'

An edifice that I had spent the last fifteen years carefully constructing was suddenly starting to crumble. I had no desire to accelerate this process, but something within me drove me to ask the obvious follow-up question: 'And how long was this going on for?'

'Oh, I don't know. I think I always offered him suggestions, right from the beginning. But at first, I didn't really pay attention to whether he took them on board or not. That happened gradually, I guess. I became more insistent. I still didn't change anything myself at that point, but I made sure that he did. I can absolutely tell you the first painting I changed myself, though.'

I didn't need her to tell me. '*Within Arm's Reach of Desire*,' I said.

'Yes! How did you guess?'

'That was the one where everything changed. The one where Erik seemed to become a more interesting painter. Or so I thought.'

'I didn't do much,' she said. 'I was too nervous – but I definitely toned it down. I wanted to get away from the "sexy young girl" thing and start focusing on different stuff. He must have painted fifty paintings focusing on my bo-sooms. I was thirty-one by then and wanted to move on. I said to him, "Honey, I know they're great, but don't you think people might be getting a little bored of them by now? There are other interesting things about me, you know. Why don't you try and paint them?" But he refused to even consider the idea that people could ever get bored of pictures of my boobs.' She paused for an eyeroll before adding, 'I also don't think he knew how to capture the other stuff – the *really* interesting stuff about me.'

She offered this observation in her usual matter-of-fact manner, but to me it sounded like the saddest thing she ever said.

I was still reeling from this revelation, when she floored me with another, once again casually dropped into the conversation as though it were nothing at all.

'He didn't spot what I'd done so it stayed in. I got so excited because I knew I'd improved it. Even when people criticised it, you could tell from their comments that they'd have hated it even more if it hadn't been for my changes. And the people who liked it always liked it because of something I'd changed. Even you. So I changed pretty much all his pictures from then on.'

I couldn't stop my eyes from saucering in alarm. 'All of them?'

'All the New York ones. I couldn't do anything with the ones he painted in Paris. Unfortunately for Erik, I think that's where he did nine of the twelve for the *Old Masters* series.'

I slumped back in my chair, the room starting to spin around me. For the past year or more I'd been fighting to write a biography of Erik that would convince the world that he really was a better painter than he was given credit for, yet now it appeared as though this had been a fundamentally flawed enterprise. Indeed, what Christie had just told me suggested that my whole fifteen-year career had been a fundamentally flawed enterprise. Or at least, built on a fundamentally flawed premise.

Suddenly everything that hadn't made sense about Erik fell into place. And everything that had seemed so inexplicable about *Susanna & the Elders* was now explained.

I could see that my biography of Erik was going to need some major revisions. But what Christie had just told me raised another troubling issue in my mind.

'Do you think he ever really loved you? I mean, really?' I thought I'd seen it in his paintings, but now I wasn't sure.

Christie turned her head to look out of the window, and then she did something she'd never done with me before. She fell silent.

A long and generous pause opened up between us, but it never felt uncomfortable and so neither of us felt the need to break it. She stared out of my window in a calm and dignified silence, while I stared at her in a kind of marvelled awe. After a while, a small tear emerged from the corner of her eye and began to amble, slowly and noiselessly, over the creases and lines of her face – the scars of a life that had fought to be lived. They glistened in the milky sunlight in a way that only made them seem more beautiful to me.

Eventually the tear reached the corner of her mouth, and her reverie was broken. She turned back to me, taking a tissue from her sleeve and dabbing her face.

'I think he loved what he could *see*,' she said. 'But he couldn't see the underneath of things. I guess a lot of guys can't – at least when it comes to women. But it always disappointed me about him. Especially as he was an artist.'

'So that's what you tried to put into his paintings? The

underneath of you?'

'I guess so. I wanted to show him the woman he *could* have fallen in love with.'

And my heart broke for her right there.

'Christie, we need to get this story out there. People need to know this. It changes everything. And it also means you might finally get one over on Mimi.'

This interested her. 'Really? How?'

'Because you are the creator – or at least the co-creator – of these artworks. Mimi can't just have them. You're owed something for your part in creating them. Even *Susanna & the Elders*: yours is a materially different painting to the one Erik painted. When did you repaint it? After he walked out?'

She nodded.

'Because if that's the case then you can argue it's yours. It's not covered by the will if it was created after the will was written.

'Mimi will argue about it. It's not clear-cut. Still, if this story gets out it would be very embarrassing for her. So there'd probably be a bit of an argument, but I'm pretty confident she'd offer you a settlement eventually, even if it was just to protect Erik's legacy. This would destroy it in an instant.'

'Eventually?'

'I understand it might be frustrating, but if you're just prepared to be patient—'

'Ah – that's the other reason I wanted to come and see you, honey.'

I had assumed that this was simply about an explanation, and maybe an apology. I couldn't see that there was anything else for us to talk about now.

'I don't understand.'

She paused, took a deep breath, and fixed me with a sombre stare. 'Like I said, my treatment's not been going well. And now this virus has complicated everything.'

This news alarmed me. It appeared obvious that delaying her treatment any further could be seriously prejudicial to her chances of recovery.

'But surely they have to keep things going. You're ill. Anyone can see that.'

'Don't get me started – the whole thing's ridiculous!' She stood up defiantly. 'I can't believe a virus is worse than cancer. It's not like no one's had the flu before.

'Anyway, no one seems to have told my cancer cells – they're all busy multiplying regardless. I shouldn't really have flown. I told them I wouldn't, and I lied on my landing card. But,' she looked up and met my astonished look head-on, 'I guess what you need to know is…"eventually" isn't going to cut it for me, I'm afraid.'

I had invested more emotional energy than was healthy over the previous five months in wishing Christie McGraw dead. Not every day, but plenty. Yet now she had delivered her news I could feel tears burning their way down my cheeks and the whole room seemed to fall apart around me. I tried to grab hold of her hand because it appeared to me to be the only solid thing left in my world. But she pulled it away, as though refusing to be drawn into my sadness.

'Sorry. I'm meant to avoid physical contact,' she explained. 'My immune system's been so shot by the chemo. They're terrified this virus'll finish me off.'

She paused and took a deep breath.

'I'd like to take you to tea to make up for what you've been through, though,' she said. 'What I put you through, I guess.'

I spent five minutes protesting that she didn't owe me anything, but to be honest, I wanted to see her again. Something of her exterior lustre had undoubtedly gone, but the thing that made her such engaging company – her 'underneath', as she'd put it – was still there, and I wanted to drink it in one last time.

# THIRTY-FIVE

When I recount the story now there are people who tell me I was too quick to forgive Christie and I still wonder if they're right. Maybe I always will. All I can say is, her news made my anger seem trivial. Whatever she had taken from me, Christie was going to lose far more than she had gained and far more than I had lost. To hate her now felt, to use a Christie word, ungallant.

I think it's also true that there are some people you can never truly hate because of how they make you feel when you're not being furious with them, and Christie was one of those for me. And, of course, her explanation made it easy for me to transfer all of my rage onto Suzy. I knew how to hate Suzy and found it easy to slip into doing so without feeling an ounce of guilt.

But the thing that truly burst the dam and allowed my heart to flood with forgiveness was understanding what Christie had done. Not what she'd done to me; what she'd done to those paintings. And understanding too, what had been done to her.

In any event, we met for afternoon tea the following day at Claridge's. Christie was staying there, and the staff seemed to know her and be perfectly happy to fuss around her. I had hoped that a good night's rest might have perked her up but, if anything, she appeared even more pallid. She picked at her sandwiches and didn't even touch the cakes, but she ordered champagne for me. If she was sad then she hid it in the shadows of a wide and joyous smile.

Without ever quite saying as much, we made our peace and she seemed to take comfort in that fact. For my part, I didn't want the afternoon to end, but there was a point when the conversation seemed to tire, and Christie called over to one of the waitresses. I assumed she was going to ask for the bill, but instead she said, 'Can you bring it over now?'

'Certainly, madam,' the young woman replied, and she disappeared off.

A couple of moments later she returned carrying what looked like a substantial canvas, but it was underneath a cloth so I couldn't see what was on it. On Christie's instruction the waitress set it up on a chair next to her, but the cloth remained draped over it.

'Young man,' Christie said, looking at me purposefully. 'I owe you an apology. Or at least, an apology of sorts.' I wasn't going to protest this. 'When Suzy explained to me what you'd done, I thought it was only fair to help her get her money. You did wrong hiding that money from her. I know there's a lot of rights and wrongs in this world, but somehow it always seems to be the woman who misses out. I felt for her – because of what happened to me. So I wanted to help her because of that too. But I guess when I met you, I saw that maybe you weren't quite as much of a crook as I'd thought. Anyway, I figure that I owe you for everything we put you through.

'Obviously, I can't give you the money back. Suzy's keeping her share for herself, and I need all my share to see me through to the end, honey – I'm sorry. But I thought I'd give you what I could. It's not much, but it's something to remember me by. And who knows, maybe it'll be worth something one day. Although probably not as much as a Von Holunder original.'

She pulled the cloth off the canvas, and there beneath it was the most extraordinary painting. I recognised it immediately as a representation of Judith beheading Holofernes. All the familiar elements were there – the radiant and bewitching beauty wielding a broadsword; the terrified, ungainly soldier realising his end was upon him; the sly maidservant loitering in the background with a drape, ready to assist her mistress with carrying their trophy home.

Erik had painted a version of the scene for his *Old Masters* series, but I could only assume it had been painted in Paris and had not benefited from any of Christie's input because it had been pretty terrible and largely derided by the critics. This one, however, was altogether different. There was an energy and urgency about the figures that Erik's version had lacked, and an oil lamp in the corner cast dark shadows over the scene, creating a dramatic contrast in the colours and tones of the skin and fabrics that was, perhaps, surpassed only by Caravaggio himself.

The thing that really struck me though, was the Judith. She was supposed to be an astonishing and beguiling beauty who drove any man who saw her wild with lust. At the same time, however, we also had to believe that she was determined and capable enough not just to plot Holofernes' execution, but to actually behead him expeditiously under the most extreme pressure. She had to convince us both as a siren and as a cold-blooded killer. In my experience, artists invariably tended to capture one aspect better than the other. There was no doubting that Gentileschi's Judith, for instance, was furious enough to behead Holofernes, but it was less clear on what basis she would have been invited into his tent in the first place. Klimt's Judith, in contrast, oozed sexual allure from every pore of her body, but, looking at her, I couldn't quite believe that she would have been able to grab Holofernes' sword without worrying about breaking a nail. She might enjoy posing with his head, but she certainly didn't look capable of removing it in just two blows, as the narrative demanded.

But the Judith before me was altogether different. She was almost completely naked, and it was not difficult to see how seductive her generous curves and flowing hair must have appeared to her would-be rapist. Yet her face, with its finely sculpted features, was contorted with rage. Holofernes looked not just surprised, but genuinely alarmed. There was no doubting that his adrenalin-fuelled attacker was about to behead him, and it was far from clear that she would require a second blow to do it, given the ferocity with which she was pictured driving the first into his throat. It was a truly thrilling work.

The framing was very different to most portrayals of the scene, with Judith square on to the viewer, towering over a prostrate Holofernes. And Holofernes himself, rather than being a muscular soldier in his thirties or forties, was portrayed as an ageing and rather paunchy figure with greying hair. Yet something about it looked familiar. I examined the canvas more closely.

'Is that Erik?' I asked, astonished.

'Yes! And did you recognise me too?' Christie replied.

I hadn't, and couldn't quite believe that I had missed her, so I took another look and immediately saw that the Judith was indeed a younger version of Christie. But she looked very different to how she had been portrayed in Erik's paintings. This Christie was not aloof, ironic or knowing, nor did she fix the viewer with a hard but beguiling stare. She didn't implore them to approve of what she looked like, nor did she taunt them with her beauty. Frankly, she didn't seem bothered about the viewer at all. Her attention was focused on the task in hand. What mattered was what she was doing, not what she looked like while she was doing it. Which was just as well because her make-up was smudged with tears, and mucus was dripping from her nostrils. Strands of her hair were glued to her face by sweat, and her cheeks were flushed puce. This was so arresting a sight that your attention was diverted from her breasts, but upon closer inspection it was clear that they were unmistakably Christie's.

'Wow!' I said, sitting back in my chair. 'This is certainly a lot better than the one Erik painted.'

Christie looked pleased. 'Why, thank you, young man!'

I immediately sat forward again. 'What? Wait – *you* painted this?'

Christie's shoulders dropped, she fixed me with a despairing look, and let out a weary sigh. 'What? We have to go through all this *again*? Yes, I painted this. All of it,' she clarified, opening her eyes wide to emphasise the point. 'I painted it after he walked out. I was really pissed with him. Why do you find that so hard to believe?'

'I'm sorry, it's just that... Christie, this is good. Really good.'

She didn't seem impressed. 'Well, *of course* it's really good – I painted it. I'm a really good painter. Haven't we established that already?'

I considered myself admonished. Christie had indeed shown a prodigious aptitude for improving Erik's paintings. But, in my defence, that is an altogether different discipline to conceiving and executing an original composition. I had no difficulty in believing that Christie could paint. What I was struggling with was the idea that she was an artist, just like Erik had been. And maybe even a better one. It just seemed so unlikely. Nothing about her demeanour suggested it.

I offered her this observation and was struck by her reply.

'People want to paint us in certain parts, and we pose for them as though we have no choice. I arrived in New York wanting to be a painter, but no one wanted to paint me in that part. They only saw me as a muse because of how I looked. I became aware of the effect I had on men and what was driving that – and it wasn't the quality of my art. So I played along. And before I knew it, the pose had become the real me. I guess I didn't understand the truth of that until Erik was gone. But by then it was too late. Everyone looked at me, but no one listened. No one was ever gonna take me seriously as an artist.'

It was clear from her voice that this saddened her. However, if the painting before me was in any way indicative of Christie's abilities, I wanted to believe that she was wrong.

'You could have made it, Christie. If you can paint stuff this good, I can't believe you wouldn't have made a decent living.'

There was a pause while she considered this. 'You're wrong. The world just doesn't work that way. But thanks anyway.'

'I mean it. This is really well crafted, and brilliantly

conceived. It's a compelling image that says something very powerful.'

She looked at the painting for a moment. 'I'm not sure what I wanted to say, but then again, if I could say it, I wouldn't have had to paint it, I guess. All I know is, I was angry – with him, yes, but not just with him. With the whole damn thing. And I wanted to capture that anger. I wanted to capture the anger of a beautiful woman – that's a very particular type of anger that affects a woman's face in a very particular way. That's what I'm most pleased with in this picture. I got that look just right. I'd wasted so many years with a man who just wanted me to look beautiful, as though that was some kind of an achievement in itself. He said that he worshipped me and expected me to take it as a compliment. But actually, I didn't want him to worship me – I wanted him to love me. And I'm not sure he knew how to do that... I don't think I ever met a man who did.'

It might just have been the champagne, but I couldn't stop myself blurting out, 'I love you, Christie. I really do.'

She looked at me warmly, but not in any way romantically. 'That's so sweet of you, honey, but I think maybe you loved the painted version of me more. I always tried to paint myself slightly better than I really was.'

That seemed unfair. But Christie cut through all my sentimentality with her usual bluntness. 'Or maybe you just loved the surface of me, like the other guys.'

I wanted to tell her that it wasn't true. But the painting before me, and everything that had passed between us, stopped me in my tracks.

'Fifteen years we were together in one way or another,' I said. 'And I never saw what you were capable of.' It seemed as true of Suzy as of Christie, which made me question whether this was a broader flaw in me. 'What did I miss?'

'You missed what I was telling you. Or maybe you just didn't ask the right questions. Whatever. I suspect you were blinded by what you saw. I've always taken that as a kind of consolation prize, which is wrong of me. I guess I should have held out, but I got tired of waiting.' For once she left a pause, but I didn't know what to say. 'At least I don't have to worry about that any more.'

She seemed rueful, but I wondered if it wasn't a release. People had painted her as a particular part; maybe now she could play a different one.

A thought occurred to me, and I decided to pursue it.

'Christie, have you got any more of these?' I asked.

'Are you kidding? I was on my own for eight months of the year in that apartment with a fully equipped studio. I did nothing *but* paint. I threw a lot of the early stuff away because it wasn't very good, and Erik didn't really like them. But eventually I began to wonder if he didn't like having them around the studio because they showed up how boring his stuff had become.' This seemed to me entirely plausible. 'So I started putting them in storage. He didn't know anything about it, but I must have ended up with about a hundred finished paintings in there.'

'And they're still there?'

'They should be. I've been paying the rental charge every month. I haven't actually ever been down to check, but I've always paid the rent on that crate – even when I was behind on the trailer. I said to them, if you're gonna foreclose on that storage crate, write to me because I will sell a kidney to keep those paintings. I guess I hoped that one day I would find someone who believed in me. Anyway, they've never written to me, so everything should still be there.'

'So, you went and got this one out of storage to bring over to show me?'

'No, not this one. I never got to finish this one before Mimi threw me out of the Dakota. So I took it with me and kept it under my bed – along with the *Susanna* – in the hope that one day I could get myself back on my feet and finish it off.'

'It looks pretty finished to me.'

'Yeah. Once I had the money from you, I could hire some studio space, get myself some oils and brushes, and finally paint the maidservant I'd always wanted to put in. I got Suzy to come over to New York for a couple of weeks and pose for me. Do you like it?'

Although I did think the representation of Suzy was skilfully done, this was not my primary concern. 'Christie, do you mind me asking, is this the best one?'

'Oh, goodness, no! I kind of like the energy of it, but I think maybe I was too angry. It blinded me a bit. I mean, it's great, but even then, I knew that sometimes you've got to temper things for the market. This was never really for the market. This was just for me. And now it's for you. I want you to have this. To remember me by.'

I was touched by her gesture, although also saddened by the implication of this comment. But I wanted to keep my focus elsewhere. Despite everything, I felt as though I'd failed Christie somehow. I had painted her in the same part that everyone else had and I regretted that now. Even as she was shrivelling away in front of me, I realised that there was so much more of her to love than I had ever seen. Maybe that's true of all of us.

Anyway, I wanted to show the world what it had missed. I

felt I owed her that at least.

'Christie: these other paintings. Do you think they're good enough to show?'

'*Of course* they are! The question is whether anyone wants to look. If you want to get people to look you need to get the valuations up, and to do that you need someone inside the industry to help you. Erik never offered, and then, after he broke up with me, he and Mimi made pretty damn sure that the industry was turned against me. No one was prepared to give me a chance.'

'But what if I change my book?' I suggested. 'What if, instead of being a celebration of Erik's centenary, it becomes a revelation of the truth?'

Christie's eyebrow flicked up. 'A celebration of me?'

I chuckled to hear her say it. There was still a heart of blazing colour underneath all that grey, and that fact itself was a joy to me.

'I guess so,' I said. 'I think people deserve to hear that story, and I definitely think you deserve to have your story told. And if I can do that, then I think that it might just prompt people to want to take a look at those paintings you've got in your storage crate.'

The prospect clearly intrigued her. I could see her face change as the played with the idea of herself as an artist in her own right, rather than a muse. Then something dropped and she snapped her head towards me, fixing me with a conspiratorial stare.

'So,' she said, leaning forward and inviting me to wallow once again in the oceans of her eyes. 'Do you think you could help me sell them?'

# EPILOGUE

Judith 'Christie' McGraw finally succumbed to her cancer at the Memorial Sloan Kettering Cancer Center, New York, on 21 April 2020, along with 11,000 other Americans who died that day, 2,683 of Covid-19. There was no obituary in the *New York Times*. Her body was transferred to the Delaware Valley Cremation Centre, Pennsylvania, where she was cremated the following week because New York's four crematoria had been overwhelmed. Because of lockdown restrictions covering New York at that time, and the distance between it and Pennsylvania, Liga Bogdanova was the chief, and indeed only, mourner.

Following the conclusion of the police investigation, Mimi von Holunder was recognised as the rightful owner of *Susanna & the Elders* and the painting was eventually handed over to her. After extended correspondence between Gabriel Viejo and Mimi's solicitors, it was put up for auction at Sotheby's in New York by Mimi in September 2020 with a reserve price of

$650,000. Following further correspondence between Gabriel and Sotheby's it was listed as the joint work of Erik von Holunder and Christie McGraw. No bids were forthcoming. In January 2021 it was sold privately, for $40,000, to a collector in Venezuela who wished to remain anonymous.

Gabriel sought out the other paintings that Christie had indicated were in storage, with the intention of organising a retrospective of her work. However, it transpired that, owing to an administrative error, Christie's crate had been lost at some point, probably when the storage company moved sites in 1996. Its contents have still not been found. The storage company offered to reimburse Christie's estate for $53,000 in rent payments taken since the crate was most likely lost, plus interest on the sums paid. As the value of the crate's contents could not be established (and there was no separate insurance in place) they offered a nominal $10,000 in compensation for the loss of the paintings themselves.

Because of ongoing legal difficulties, Gabriel Viejo's planned biography of Erik von Holunder has still not been published.

In the spring of 2021 he put *Judith Beheads Holofernes* up for auction as 'an original work by Judith McGraw'. It failed to reach the reserve price of £25,000.

# ACKNOWLEDGEMENTS

There is a myth which persists in the popular imagination that the construction of a book is an essentially solitary process; that a hermitical genius locks themselves in a garret, or similar, and only engages with the world once their *meisterwerk* is completed. In this conception, all everyone else has to do is wait for the writer to produce their novel, and then gasp in astonishment at its brilliance. The writer then retires to their boudoir whilst teams of people disseminate the book uncritically to the reading public.

If this was ever true (which I doubt) it is certainly not true now. Today the production of a book is a team process in which the writer is supported, steered, cajoled and sometimes simply bossed about by a great many other people whose job it is to see that the novel which the writer has written is the very best that it can be. These people do not get their names on the front cover, so the reader might suppose that they are unimportant. They are not.

And so the last task of the novelist, once the final draft of their novel is delivered, is to publicly acknowledge the contribution of others towards the finished work, and to thank them for helping to make it better than it would otherwise have been. In my case, this first involves acknowledging the contribution of Kelly A Drake to making sure that there was a finished work at all. Without her encouragement at a critical juncture when I really didn't know what to do with my life, let alone my book, I wouldn't even have got to the end of draft one.

Then Rufus Purdy at the Write Here Academy helped turn that messy first draft into something sharper and more professional. Rufus was the first person who believed in the novel, for which I will always be grateful, and his perceptive editorial advice allowed me to start to believe in it too.

I then rewrote the novel whilst on the Jericho Writer's Ultimate Novel Writing Course and I was also lucky enough to have an incredibly diligent and supportive tutor group around me. This comprised Becky Jones, Kate McDermott, Nicky Downes Anne McMeehan Roberts, Barbara Webb, James Pierson, Harriet Martin, Jackie Kowalczyk, and Alastair Crombie. Each week they would faithfully read an excerpt of my novel and assiduously offer suggestions for improvement. Some of them I even listened to. A special thanks go to Kate and Nicky who, in addition to Rowena Wilding, volunteered to read the whole manuscript, and who provided invaluable feedback as the book neared completion.

My tutor, Helen Francis, gave a frank and honest assessment of the novel's strengths and weaknesses which helped improve it further. And she also gave me the crucial kick I needed to have 'just one more go' at submitting the novel when I'd given up hope of it ever being published.

But the book would not be in your hands now without Dan Hiscocks and the team at Lightning Books. Simon Edge was a fantastic editor to work with whose insights helped to polish the novel so it became more fully what I wanted it to be. And Clio Mitchell was a fastidious and diligent copy editor whose keen eye was just what I needed. I will be forever grateful to all of them.

All of these people have contributed in some way towards improving *The Muse of Hope Falls* as a novel. Responsibility for its shortcomings, however, remains firmly with me.

Finally, I also want to thank Sharon Fraser, who has stood by my side throughout the whole process, and kept me going at all the points when I thought of giving up – and who got me restarted on the couple of occasions when I actually did give up. Living with a writer is a thankless task which she has borne with good grace, for which I am forever in her debt.

A.K.F

If you have enjoyed *The Muse of Hope Falls*, do please help us spread the word – by putting a review online; by posting something on social media; or in the old-fashioned way by simply telling your friends or family about it.

Book publishing is a very competitive business these days, in a saturated market, and small independent publishers such as ourselves are often crowded out by the big houses. Support from readers like you can make all the difference to a book's success.

Many thanks.

Dan Hiscocks
Publisher
Lightning Books

Also from Lightning Books

# The Outsiders

## James Corbett

### Shortlisted for the Portico Prize

Liverpool 1981. As the city burns during inner city riots, Paul meets two people who will change his life: Nadezhda, an elusive poet who has fallen out of fashion; and her daughter Sarah, with whom he shares an instant connection. As the summer reaches its climax his feelings for both are tested amidst secrets, lies and the unravelling of Nadezhda's past. It is an experience that will define the rest of his life.

The Outsiders moves from early-80s Liverpool, via Nadezhda's clandestine background in war-torn Europe, through to the present day, taking in the global and local events that shape all three characters.

In a powerful story of hidden histories, lost loves and painful truths, ambitiously told against the backdrop of Liverpool's fall and rise, James Corbett's enthralling debut novel explores the complexities of human history and how individual perspectives of the past shape everyone's present.

*A gripping debut novel with surprising twists that is part love story, part mystery and part love letter to a city, and also asks profound questions about the very nature of identity*
**Nick Harris, Mail on Sunday**

*A brilliant achievement. I loved it*
**Paul Du Noyer**

*A novel full of intrigue. Liverpool – its history, culture and atmosphere – shines brightly within the pages. This has leapt into my list of favourite reads*
**Buzz Magazine**

# The Prison Minyan

## Jonathan Stone

The scene is Otisville Prison, upstate New York. A crew of fraudsters, tax evaders, trigamists and forgers discuss matters of right and wrong in a Talmudic study and prayer group, or 'minyan', led by a rabbi who's a fellow convict.

As the only prison in the federal system with a kosher deli, Otisville is the penitentiary of choice for white-collar Jewish offenders, many of whom secretly like the place. They've learned to game the system, so when the regime is toughened to punish a newly arrived celebrity convict who has upset the 45th president, they find devious ways to fight back.

Shadowy forces up the ante by trying to 'Epstein' – ie assassinate – the newcomer, and visiting poetry professor Deborah Liston ends up in dire peril when she sees too much. She has helped the minyan look into their souls. Will they now step up to save her?

Jonathan Stone brings the sensibility of Saul Bellow and Philip Roth to the post-truth era in a sharply comic novel that is also wise, profound and deeply moral.

*Erudite, trenchant and touching*
**Michael Arditti**

*There are crimes aplenty within the prison walls...but Stone is after something more diffuse and philosophical.* The Prison Minyan *occupies terrain few others will likely explore*
**New York Times**

*Rare is the book which is so delectable that, once you have finished it, you want immediately to read it all over again, but Jonathan Stone's glorious* The Prison Minyan *is just that... Stone's dry tones surely reach an apogee in this most cherishably Jewish of books*
**Jewish Chronicle**

# Future Fish

## Conor Sneyd

Sacked from his first job in Dublin, Mark McGuire arrives in the dismal town of Ashcross to take up a new role as customer service assistant for Ireland's second-biggest pet food brand, WellCat. From his initial impressions, it's a toss-up whether he'll die of misery or boredom.

He couldn't be more wrong. For starters, the improbably cute receptionist, Kevin, seems willing to audition as the man of Mark's dreams. There's also the launch of a hush-hush new product, Future Fish, on the horizon. Not to mention the ragtag band of exorcists, alien-hunters and animal rights warriors who are all convinced WellCat is up to no good. Why are these crackpots so keen on getting close to Mark? And will their schemes ruin his career prospects?

In a deliciously daft comic caper, Conor Sneyd perfectly captures the powerlessness of low-rung office life as well as the seductive zealotry of our times.

*What I thought was going to be a heartwarming small-town gay love story took off in a completely unexpected direction and carried me joyfully in its wake. Without doubt the pet-food conspiracy anarcho-thriller romcom of the year. With nuns!*
**Adam Macqueen**

*Fast, funny and freaky. A book for everyone who ever hated their job. Soylent Green for the QAnon generation*
**Luke Healy**

*A joyously unlikely yet completely relatable comedy. I was in fits*
**Tim Ewins**

*This endearingly daft and strangely compelling caper*
**Saga Magazine**